THE CHRYSILLIUM TREE

LAKEN HONEYCUTT

THE CHRYSILLIUM TREE BY LAKEN HONEYCUTT

WWW.LAKENHONEYCUTT.COM

COVER DESIGN: LANCE BUCKLEY
EDITING SERVICES: GEORGE ROSETT
ARTWORK: MARK DUFFIN
MAP: DEWI HARGREAVES

PAPERBACK ISBN: 978-0-578-95319-9

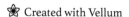 Created with Vellum

For Marcus

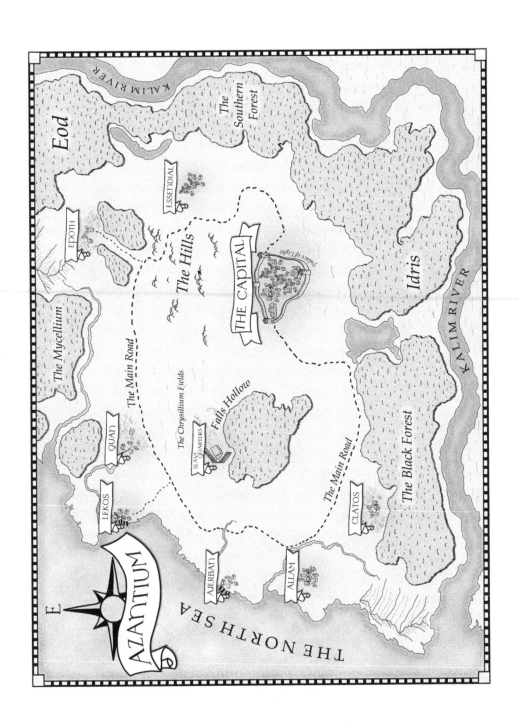

PART I
THE PALACE OF LIGHT

WEAVERS OF OLD
WIZARDS OF LORE
ROSE FROM THE SEA
WALKED ON THE SHORE.

CIRCLE OF POWER
ASH AND BONE
A SEAL THEY WOVE
OF TWISTED STONE.

ZAMA'S LAMENT
THE BIRTH OF THROES
MAGIC WITHERS
AND A KINGDOM ROSE.[1]

---

1. *Source: The Book of Origins: The Binding of the Mycellium Forest.*
   Year: 3765. (Azantium: year 76 of the Light. 274 years prior to current date)
   Current location of text: Kråshain library on the outer rim of Eod

1

Mæve tried to ignore the man in the doorway, gritting her teeth as she worked. He had found her again. She had woken early, and had even taken the long way to get to her destination. Yet there he was, devouring an apple, his eyes upon her.

Crown Prince Lucius was attractive, with eyes the color of a stormy afternoon and sunset hair swept back from his face in windblown waves. His lecherous gaze hinted at someone far fouler than his pleasant looks suggested. As the queen regent's beloved nephew, certain behavior went unchecked.

Mæve ignored him and remained focused on her dusting in the throne room, hoping that he would become bored and leave her alone. She was painfully aware of the low cut of her servant's dress.

Lucius entered the room and fear bloomed in her gut. Seeming to sense her unease, a cruel smile played on his lips. She straightened, lowered her eyes, and dropped an obligatory curtsey.

"Your Highness," she murmured.

"Oh please, please. Be at ease," he said, continuing to chomp his apple, not at all attempting to disguise his wandering eyes.

"You're new here, aren't you?" he asked. Mæve listened carefully to his words. He spoke so fast and she was just learning the Azantium language. A language she had needed to learn quickly in order to survive.

"Yes, sir," she answered his question.

She had only been here for three moons and yet with every opportunity, Mæve had absorbed information about her captors. She wanted to find her parents and to do that, she first needed to understand this foreign land. So when no one was around, she studied maps mounted on the library walls, pretending to clean around them. The Azantium kingdom had no boundaries with other countries. There was the sea to the north, cliffs to the east, and a massive forest around the rest of the kingdom, with a wide, fast-flowing river just beyond the trees. The kingdom's isolation was a good thing and also not a good thing. The chances that her parents were traded after arriving was slim, but it also meant that once she did find them, there was nowhere to run.

She'd thought about escaping to the forest. The other slaves had warned her that there were wild things living in the woods, more terrible than nightmares, and those that ventured into the forest often went missing. Even her Azantium captors avoided the trees.

Mæve didn't believe the stories, certain they were nothing more than fables. She missed the forest of her homeland and would never fear the woods. Still, she remained in the palace looking for her parents, hoping that they were here and not assigned to one of the many other slave positions within the capital.

Lucius finished the apple and tossed aside the broken core without a glance. Mæve couldn't pull her eyes from it. Rumor had it Lucius treated slave women in a similar manner.

"Please, call me Lucius." He stepped closer and put his arm around her shoulders, a sadistic smile on his lips.

Mæve could not resist him. To do so could mean her life. She tried to remain calm as he pulled her close to him, his eyes cold as slate, but she couldn't stop herself from turning her head away.

"Oh, come now. That's not very friendly." The cruel smile deepened.

"Lucius Verres," a shrill voice called out.

Lucius's head snapped up. He released Mæve as Queen Regent Druscilla entered the room, her skirts whisking about her. Her glacial blue eyes stared at the scene before her, contemptuous, and her tight lips puckered.

Grateful for the interruption, Mæve curtseyed. "Your Highness."

Lucius's eyes sparkled. "Auntie."

"You have duties to attend to," she snapped at her nephew.

Disdain twisted the queen's face as she advanced towards Mæve.

"And *you* must not have enough work to occupy you. Trying to seduce royals will get you nowhere in my palace, harlot!" She slapped Mæve hard. "Out with you!"

Mæve fled, confused and afraid.

That night the head of house whipped Mæve on her backside and legs to remind her not to tempt royals again. The whipping was more infuriating than painful, intended to wound the spirit more than the flesh, but Mæve was not wounded. Instead, in that moment, she understood more, and knowledge was a form of power. Not only was she completely defenseless against Lucius' unwanted advances, she would be blamed for them.

———————

Mæve rode quickly through the cool spring night. Despite the risk, she could not stay confined any longer. She had tried to submit. She had tried to obey. But a fire burned within her. She needed to break free; she needed to ride, lest the fire consume her.

Thank the gods for Tráthóna. In her sparse free moments, Mæve often visited the stables. The presence of the horses calmed her and it was there she had befriended the forgotten mare in one of the rear stalls. Another slave had warned her to stay away from the unbroken mare. But Mæve hadn't been afraid of the matted and dirty creature, she felt bad for it.

The next time, Mæve had brought a few pitted dates and the horse had gobbled it up. Afterward the mare had approached Mæve tentatively, nostrils flared, eyes still wild with fear. Mæve stood still as the creature drew closer, until she calmed and rested her soft muzzle in Mæve's hand, looking for more treats. Mæve had named the horse Tráthóna, which meant twilight in Mæve's mother-tongue.

A kinship had grown between them over the past three moons. Tráthóna's stall was the first place Mæve thought to go after her punishment. It had been foolish and reckless to use her magic to lull the guards to sleep. This had involved Mæve traveling through the veils, which had taken up much of her energy. At least the guards along the western wall would be out the rest of the night. Still, it was important that Mæve keep her magical abilities secret from her captors until she found her parents and could escape with them.

She had snuck down to the stables, only intending to pat the horse. But when the urgency to ride overcame her, the horse had allowed her up on its back and off they went into the night.

Following the light of the full moon, Tráthóna sensed her need and ran from the sleeping castle so fast it felt like flying. Hot tears clotted Mæve's vision. Her long hair billowed wildly around her as she rode to the sanctuary of the woods beyond.

It was a golden era in the Azantium kingdom, so they said. A time of peace. The palace walls were only minimally guarded. The stables opened to the west of the palace where there was only forest stretching as far as the eye could see. It reminded her of home.

Home. The rolling, sage-laced shores of Callium. Her woodland village tucked within the forest just beyond those fields.

Memories hit Mæve hard. She pictured the rose-colored eyes of the Witching Woman, and her withered hands as she'd tattooed Mæve's fingers. She'd etched sacred markings from Mæve's fingers to her wrists—Ghealaich, the symbols were called, a record of her aptitude in magic earned on Mæve's sixteenth birthday. For the next seven years Mæve trained with the Witching Woman learning how to travel the veils including the way station, the spirit world, the realm of mirrors, and the veil of dreams. It was a gift becoming rarer in Callium with each passing year, and Mæve feared she would never complete her training in the witching ways now.

She had been riding the day the Azantiums came, nosing their large slave ships into the harbor. Alarm had coursed through her body. Her people used small boats to fish, but these ships were something else entirely. The vast size of them, the odd flags... she knew something was wrong.

She had rushed home to tell her parents, but the soldiers were already there, dressed in their odd clothing and shouting in a language she did not understand. One of them grabbed her and when she tried to fight back another knocked her out.

She had awoken in the dank bowels of a ship. She had looked for her mother and father, but did not see them amongst the unfamiliar faces. The ship had contained only strangers, everyone as scared and confused as she.

She remembered peering through the portholes and gasping at the great many ships sailing beside them. They must have raided other villages too. The thought of her family in one of those ships, so close and yet unreachable, had tortured her.

Three moons later, she continued to worry for her parents. There had been no trace of them since arriving at the Palace of Light.

When she finally reached the forest cover, Mæve exhaled and said a brief prayer. Not that she believed any kind of deity may answer. The Gods were all dead here in Azantium.

Tráthóna slowed to a trot and then a walk. Mæve dismounted and led the horse through the forest. They traveled deeper into the woods and came to a stream that trickled into a pond.

This will do.

Illuminated by the light of the full moon, it was an enchanting spot. Mæve walked over to the edge of the water. The days were just starting to get warmer, yet the mid-spring nights still clung to winter's chill. Mæve wrapped her arms around herself and focused on the gentle flow of the moonlit stream emptying into the pond.

Reaching into her pocket, Mæve wrapped her fingers around her obsidian pendant. Her mother. She had given it to her as part of her rite of passage when she turned sixteen, unbraided her hair, and received her Ghealaich.

Mæve turned the circular pendant, running her tattooed fingers over its smooth surface. It was an ornately carved tree. She kept the pendant close to her every day, treasuring it more for the memory of her mother than for the marriage ritual it was intended for—the ritual she had little chance of fulfilling now.

Something cool and hard touched the side of her neck, startling Mæve out of her thoughts. She gasped and a soft, male voice said, "Don't move."

Her eyes shifted down to the dangerously curved blade pressed against her neck. Runes embossed upon the blade glowed with a blue hue in the darkness.

She looked down the length of the blade, and golden eyes met her gaze. Frightened, she gasped again and slipped off her rock onto the damp ground. A firm hand grasped her arm, hoisting her to her feet.

An unusual-looking man stood before her. His skin was light gray, darker around the edges of his face. He was well-muscled and tall, and there were three crystals—tiny silver circles—between his eyebrows. His long dark hair flowed down his back and he wore a necklace made of black feathers.

He positioned his sword back at her throat. "What are you doing here?" he demanded.

Mæve moved quickly, rolling inward along his sword as her hand came up to grab his forearm, and pull him close. She struck him in the jaw with her elbow, following the first strike with the heel of her fist.

He stumbled back. "Zama's breath!" But he regained his balance immediately, and before she could track his movement the weight of his hands dropped her to the ground, into the muck. She was filthy now, and wet.

"Don't do that again," he said with a measured calm. "Why are you on Lumani land? Perhaps you are an Azantium spy?" His eyes narrowed with suspicion.

"I'm sorry. I didn't know I was trespassing. I'm not a spy, I promise," she said as she rose to her feet, not taking her eyes off him. "I just needed to get out of the palace. I'll be in a great deal of trouble if I'm caught."

Before he could speak, Mæve rushed on, "Yes, my father, the queen's brother, would be most displeased with me." If he thought she was royalty, perhaps he would not kill her. "And should anything happen to me, my aunt, the queen regent, will be very upset."

"I see," he said. "Then you are here by mistake?"

"Yes. And I'm very sorry. But I will go now."

Mæve began to leave, but he interrupted her.

"Not so fast," he said, still staring at her. "How can you be of the Royal house and not know these woods are forbidden to your people? Are you unaware of the Treaty of Falls Hollow?"

Mæve scrambled, looking for an ounce of truth to cover her lies. It was possible this man knew more of her captors than she did.

But then she thought about the women of the Azantium royal court. Lazy and entitled, concerned with gossip, beaus, and fashion. It was plausible they might not be aware of the treaty.

"I'm afraid high society women have no use of politics or history or things of that nature. We busy ourselves with the matters of court. If you please, I would like to be going now before I am missed."

He said nothing as he considered her. Mæve's palms were sweaty, her heart pounding in her ears.

"One more thing," he said

"Yes?" she replied, her voice tight.

"What is your name?"

Mæve exhaled.

"Lana. Lana Acilius." It was one of the names of the terrible women from court.

"I'm Armaiti Avari from the Water Clan of the Lumani."

"Pleased to meet you, Armai—"

"I care nothing for your empty pleasantries."

Mæve recoiled. Damn, she had been doing so well.

"You have trespassed onto our land," he continued. "Are you so impudent to think yourself exempt from violating the treaty?"

Mæve opened her mouth, but couldn't think of a response. Her mouth clicked shut.

Armaiti met her eyes. There was something... yes, something familiar there. How could that be?

The pond rippled and the air tingled.

"The penalty for violating the treaty is steep. But I will forgive your trespass if you give me something in return."

Befuddled, Mæve asked, "What is it you seek?"

"Information," Armaiti replied. "What do you know of the Chrysillium trees at Falls Hollow?"

Mæve swallowed. "I don't know anything about them."

He squinted at her. "Fine. Then to pay for your insolence, you have one moon to gather as much information as you can about the Chrysillium trees. Then we meet back here and you'll tell me everything you learn."

Mæve gaped at him. He had no idea how dangerous that was for her.

"I understand you've led a sheltered life, but don't you recall," Armaiti said with exaggerated politeness, "... that before the treaty, Lumani warriors used to sneak into the palace and murder royals in their sleep? No?" He flashed a ruthless smile, baring two pointed canine teeth. "Yes, a skill we haven't forgotten."

He faded back into the night. Mæve remained, still as death, afraid to move.

Her eyes fell upon Tráthóna. The mare, usually skittish and unruly, was munching contentedly on the grass, unbothered by the dramatic encounter.

"Big help you were," Mæve said as she stroked the horse's forehead. Tráthóna tossed her mane and whinnied. It sounded like a taunting laugh.

Mæve looked back into the woods. There was no trace of him; not a sight, not a sound. He had vanished.

She leapt onto Tráthóna and hugged herself close to the mare as they trotted back to the Palace of Light.

HER MOTHER'S PENDANT. Damn.

In the excitement of her strange encounter, the precious heirloom must have slipped off her lap unnoticed. Later that night, she cursed her foolishness as she lay in her lumpy bed.

Mæve remembered the night her mother had given her the obsidian tree pendant. It had belonged to the women in her family for generations.

When it was time, Mæve would give her tree pendant to a prospective suitor. The suitor would then return the tree pendant to her, fastened on his own family's chain, thus completing the Callium engagement ritual.

As much as it pained her, Mæve decided to wait for the next full moon to retrieve it. She didn't dare go back sooner and risk getting caught. No, she needed to wait until she met with Armaiti again.

The more Mæve thought about it, the more meeting Armaiti excited her. Beyond his frightful demeanor, there was something... kindred, something vaguely reminiscent. He felt a little like home.

She thought about his request for information. She would need to dedicate herself to paying attention to all that happened around her for the next month. Like a spy. And she guessed she was, in a way, and this thrilled her. It added hope to her days. She had a purpose.

2

Isaac knew he was trying far too hard with what was such a simple task. It had become a point of great concentration for him now, trying to get the damn key in the keyhole. The other keys on his ring clinked around, getting in his way. He fumbled and dropped the ring with a resounding clank on the steps.

"Fuck," he mumbled. He bent down to retrieve them, but stumbled and grabbed onto the trim around the front door, steadying himself. A flush of anger coursed through him. He finally, clumsily, got his key into the keyhole.

His eyes adjusted to the light just in time to see Amber Levre storm around the corner. Amber wore her typical Azantium fineries, her tits pushed up to her chin. She smelled of lilac and some other exotic flower from god-knows-where-the-fuck.

"Drunk again?" she asked, arching her delicate eyebrows.

He tried to smile, tossing about his infamous charm.

"Wipe that smirk off your face. I don't have to put up with this."

She had already gathered her things. A coat of fine mink fur made from some poor critter raised on a farm in Ralouq, no doubt. Little fancy purse. Fine silk shawl. As the embers of his anger began to ignite again, Isaac couldn't help himself.

"Yeah, but you will. You'll be back," he slurred. "Like some recurrent purgatory."

"I'm tired of the drinking. I've had enough. I can do better."

He laughed, stumbling a bit more. "Ha! Better? Than me? Oh, I don't think so, but by all means try. And don't come back this-"

She slammed the door before he could finish. A stifling silence remained.

Irritated and hollowed, Isaac walked into his study. Oak bookcases lined the walls, filled with volumes of leather-bound books. He poured himself more caramel-colored liquor and downed it in one gulp, then stared at the empty glass in his hand. *Expensive crystal glass. Expensive liquor.* He yelled in rage and tossed it into the fire.

He sat down hard and grasped his already pounding head. *Shit. How did I get here?* But soon he found himself sinking onto the table as he fell into a drunken slumber.

HE WOKE BEGRUDGINGLY, his back screaming. Early morning light streamed through the window. Bird song filtered through the silence of his home. As he rose from his seat the world spun, his stomach churned, and he vomited across the clean white marble of his writing desk.

His head seared with pain. *Ugh. No more. No more drink.*

But he knew he would be back at it that night.

A brief look in the mirror confirmed what he already suspected. He looked as awful as he felt. Stubble shadowed his chin and jaw. Circles cradled his deep brown, almond-shaped eyes. His tousled hair framed light brown skin. He was handsome and he knew it. And like any adept person of commerce, he played it; in business, in the bedroom, in life.

He headed outside to the stables, pulling the brim of his black top hat low over his sun-sensitive eyes. He mounted his prancing horse and took off for the Chrysillium Fields.

The queen had sent a message two days prior requesting he check on the crop. Despair had risen in him at the prospect of returning to Falls Hollow, and the drinking had been his only reprieve from the memories and the guilt.

Now, his anguish amplified as he journeyed to that once sacred grove of Chrysillium trees. The trees were a sight to behold in the wild. Even after so much time, Isaac remembered their splendor. Silver trunks with a thick, healthy bark, they grew straight and tall with long, spindly branches that birthed thousands of bioluminescent labas beans. They were magical to witness on a quiet starry night; sparkling indigo blue in the dark forest. And there was no item more desired in all of high society, in all the world now, than labas. Thanks to Isaac.

The Azantiums, always proficient at recognizing profitable resources, had turned their eye to the beautiful little bean a hundred and fifty years ago. They had called it labas and picked it from the Chrysillium trees that grew in an area called Falls Hollow, completely irreverent to the fact that the trees were sacred to the Lumani. The Azantiums found a myriad of uses for the beautiful little bean. It was made into a paste then sculpted and hardened into the most stunning azure jewelry. It could also be ground into a powder and ingested to heal anything from digestive issues to chronic pain.

Isaac made decent money selling the beans to other countries. But it was only after the Treaty of Falls Hollow ten years ago, with the acquisition of the large grove of Chrysillium trees from the Lumani that the Azantiums could finally meet the demand for the product. It had been a desperate barter for peace to end a hundred years of war.

Money came pouring in. Isaac was named High Merchant of Azantium and, between his fabulous wealth and the new title, was suddenly not just a part of high society—he dominated it.

Then, five years after the signing of the Treaty of Falls Hollow, the Azantium engineers discovered that when heated, the chemical composition of labas changed and became an acidic poison. To use the poison, the engineers designed the labaton - an incendiary device that launched small projectiles encased in labas. Once the projectile pierced skin, the high heat from its launch released the poison. A terrible new use for labas had been discovered.

He spurred his horse onward. At this pace, it should only take a few hours to reach the Chrysillium Field from his home in the hills.

ISAAC REMEMBERED the idols of the old saints that his mother used to arrange with care upon the sill. She had had a brother who could do odd things; rumors circulated that he could hear thoughts and move objects with his mind. In the slums of Thalis—a country that was a three-day ship journey off the southern coast of the Azantium kingdom—this was not allowed. Thalis's Azantium overlord had executed his uncle.

The people of Isaac's homeland had long been under Azantium subjugation. He had watched his parents struggle to make ends meet, toiling long hours in the Azantium-controlled silk factories that dominated Thalis's economy. As a young man, he knew that the options offered to him were either working in the factory and living in the slums, or being sent to work as a slave in Azantium.

Isaac had accepted neither.

Growing up, Isaac had adored the Azantium kingdom: the wealth, the power, the push for progress. Tired of the dying mysticism in the desert culture of Thalis, Isaac knew that Azantium was the future. Let the old ways be damned. His people had battled pestilence and famine until the Azantiums pulled them out of those dark ages.

Isaac's father was a manager at one of the silk factories and their family often received visits from an Azantium silk merchant to discuss upcoming shipments and production rates. When Cyprian came to visit, his mother pulled out all their finery. Isaac recalled how Cyp flirted with his mother and shook hands with his father, his eyes twinkling.

Young Isaac studied Cyp's square jaw and flaxen blond hair and mimicked his mannerisms. Cyp took a liking to the boy. As Isaac got older, Cyp recognized teenage Isaac's considerable intellect and offered to take him on as an apprentice at his home in the capital.

"It is all a game," Cyp had said once, his face unusually serious. "It is a game, lad. A game of houses and coin, smoke and mirrors. None of this is real. It is but an illusion and we are its weavers; us, the merchants of Azantium. Don't take it so seriously. Simply stoke the image."

When Isaac was younger, his lessons from Cyp were his holy book; his guide star. Only now did he question his teacher. Now that he had done the impossible, what no other merchant of Azantium had done, and brought the elusive, deadly Lumani to the bargaining table with the royals.

The difficult part had been gaining the Lumani's trust. This had taken years, but it was worth it. In the end, the royals had made a great amount of money and Isaac had acquired all the notoriety and wealth he had desired.

As Isaac's horse crested the final hill and Falls Hollow came into view, Isaac no longer felt proud of what he helped create so many years ago. The Chrysillium trees before him now were withered, tortured things, their bark scorched and brittle. A wild Chrysillium tree produced thousands of beans, but these yielded only a few hundred each—and those ones were sickly, their bioluminescence dulled. These were no longer the sacred Chrysillium trees of the Lumani, but something different; something perverse. Isaac's legacy.

Isaac dismounted and tethered his horse. He looked out over the field. The trees were not all that suffered here. Slaves from the far reaches of the empire dotted the fields, engaged in the grueling work of harvesting the beans.

Isaac recognized a figure in a nearby group. "Mohlin," he called, approaching the tall Lumani. Careful to hide the movement from the enforcers of the Red Guard, Isaac handed Mohlin his own water flask and a kerchief wrapped around bread and cheese.

An enforcer strolled by, and Isaac moved to hide the kerchief— but the man caught his eye and nodded. It was Adrian. Good. Still, Isaac guided Mohlin away from the other slaves.

"Are you ready?" Isaac asked, speaking Lumani.

Mohlin swallowed a mouthful of crusty bread and cheese.

"I think so," he replied, a quiver in his voice. Then he gave a nervous chuckle. "I mean, yes. I have been waiting for this day."

Isaac placed a heavy hand of support upon Mohlin's shoulder, masking his own worry.

"The Red Fox assures me everything is in place for your escape, Mohlin," Isaac said. "For your return to Idris, for your return to your family."

The look of gratitude from Mohlin turned Isaac's stomach. He hated it.

Lilya had looked at him like that once too.

Isaac continued through the field. It was spring, and yet the sun blazed down harsh and hot. It was one of their many errors in cultivating the Chrysillium Field. They had cut down the other trees to make room for growing more Chrysillium trees. Without the tree canopy, there was no shade, no protection, no respite from the scorching sun.

But no one consulted the Lumani, or even the scientists, on what was good for the trees. The royals had not even considered it while they bulled onward, rushing to make their fortune.

And what a fortune they had made.

Isaac turned away from the blighted field, away from the slave quarters with spikes on the roof, some of which bore the severed heads of slaves who had attempted to escape.

Sweat dotted his brow as he approached Berit, who was sifting through a vat of labas beans for damaged ones. When she finished, she would pour the vat of beans into barrels and place them on an ox-driven carriage bound for the factories.

Berit was from Lind. She wasn't a slave, but an indentured

servant. Though taxing, this job was far more desirable than being forced to work the salt mines of her homeland.

She smiled at Isaac as he approached, her blond hair tucked into a red bandana and blue eyes sparkling in her leathery face. Slightly stooped with age, she was strong from lifting the barrels.

She was not a person to take any shit from Isaac, even though he was her superior and a shameless flirt. Over the years, this had endeared her to him.

"Berit," he nodded at her. "Aren't you looking lovely on this fine day?" He flashed her one of his melting smiles.

Cold as the ice of her homeland, Berit raised a critical eyebrow. "Yes, it be a fine day but you're a lying bray of an ass, Isaac, and I'm too old to fall for your charms," she said. He leaned in and kissed her cheek, then grabbed one of the beans and examined it.

"How are they looking these days, Berit?"

"They looking alright. I seen better, I seen worse," she replied.

"Humph," was all Isaac replied. "Any more scientists?"

"No, sir. They stopped coming around it seems. Haven't seen one since the fall."

This did not surprise Isaac. When the trees had first begun to wither, he had arranged for scientists to come examine them. The scientists had concluded that the trees were dying; one of them said they only had a few years left before they stopped producing completely. Chrysillium trees lived for thousands of years in the wild. The majority of the trees at Falls Hollow were barely ten years old, having been planted from the seeds of the original Chrysillium trees there.

Rumors about the labas began to spread. The scientists disappeared.

Isaac had a sinking feeling he knew what that meant. They had a year or two before the royals broke the Treaty of Falls Hollow and attacked the Lumani for more resources; for more trees.

Isaac had lied to himself for years and said he had done the Lumani a great service by gaining their trust and coercing them to part with one of their sacred groves; that he had done the entire kingdom a great service by ending decades of war. But it was simply smoke and mirrors. There would be more bloodshed. It was coming.

Isaac tossed the bean back into the vat. "You good, Berit? How's the family?"

"We're all good. Little Erik is about to finish primary school. Can't believe it. Helene is just starting to cook with her father. Anders is planning a grand feast for the harvest holiday this year for friends and family. Why don't you join us?"

Anders, Berit's husband, was one of the best damn cooks Isaac had ever met. He worked in the palace as a chef for the royals. They didn't pay him much, certainly not enough to buy out his wife's contract, but enough that they could afford to raise their family in a humble house just outside the palace walls.

"Oh, I'll be there, Berit," he said. "I wouldn't miss it."

"Bring a date. How about—what's her name again? Andel or...?"

"Amber," he grumbled. "No, it'll just be me."

"She wasn't right for you. Stuck up little thing. You need a woman of substance."

Isaac looked at her, amused.

"You got someone in mind, Berit?"

"You're getting older, you know. Good looks only gonna last you so long. Settle down, think about starting a family. You've done good, Isaac."

Isaac dropped his eyes.

"I need to head out," he said. "Got an important meeting with the royals."

He hugged her before he left because he loved her and the way she cared for him.

Isaac walked back across the field, past the wilting trees and emaciated slaves. Falls Hollow, where everyone came to wither and die. He mounted his horse and headed towards the palace. A far worse place.

3

Mæve strolled the meager slave garden with her friend Betha who chattered away about the most recent palace gossip. Just being in Betha's company was comforting. She was the first and only friend Mæve had made here, and she had helped Mæve understand what was expected of her.

Betha was the only other slave in the palace from Callium, although she was not from Mæve's village. Betha had been enslaved when she was a young child and remembered little of her homeland.

Her friend liked to talk and when they had a spare moment together, this is what she did.

"Poor Malqi," Betha said, her arm entwined with Mæve's. "Some wealthy lord took a fancy to her, and that was it. I didn't even get to say goodbye. Better pray that never happens to you. Being sold to some high society man and expected not only to wait on him for the rest of your life, but service him in the bedroom too. No, thank you. That's why I'm grateful to be a royal servant. At least we can't be bought.

"Oh, then there is Halma..."

Betha went on, and Mæve began to drift off. Her thoughts turned to her parents. She wondered where they were, if they were okay.

Mæve thought she had seen them that day when she first arrived in Azantium and got off the ship, but she couldn't be sure.

She remembered those first awful moments upon Azantium soil, in a cold, dank room in the port-city of Allam. She was stripped of her clothes and given a rough washing by a woman in white robes. Naked, Mæve shivered uncontrollably, hiding her mother's pendant in her hand.

The acrid smell of the room accentuated its sterility. It stung Mæve's nose. Harsh, obtrusive, the scents were so different from Mæve's wooded homeland. A stern-looking woman with a line for a mouth approached Mæve and shoved her onto a stool. She looked as if touching Mæve might sully her despite the cleansing Mæve had just received.

The harsh woman produced a pair of shears and grabbed at Mæve's hair.

"Stop it," Mæve protested in her mother tongue, though she knew the woman neither understood nor cared. In Callium, women grew their hair long. It was a source of pride and identity for any Callium woman.

The harsh woman pushed Mæve's protesting hand away. Cruelty twisted her line of a mouth.

Snip. Snip. Hair fell. Gentle wisps of memory—ocean breezes upon sage-laced shores, her mother's warm embrace, the sweet smell of incense wafting from the Witching Woman's hut—falling. The woman cut Mæve's hair to her shoulders and wrapped it into a bun.

The woman guided Mæve into an adjacent room lined with shelves packed tight with folded clothing.

Outside her fear and confusion, Mæve noted how ordered a process this was. *They've done this many times,* she thought.

The woman placed a pile of clothes upon a small table. She continued to talk in her odd language that Mæve did not understand. She gestured at the clothing—two dresses, a white shift, and a long, hooded cloak.

Mæve fumbled her shivering body into the shift and next came an odd piece of clothing. There were no words for it. It fastened around her waist. The woman showed her how to hold it in place and then pull the ties, cinching them off, before handing Mæve one of the dresses.

Mæve pulled it on, then blushed as she guessed the purpose of the odd contraption. It pushed her breasts up, exposing the tops of them over the low-cut bodice. What a shameful way to dress.

Mæve smoothed the dress out. There was a pocket in the long skirt. This gave her a flush of hope. A noise from the other end of the room distracted the woman, and Mæve snuck her mother's tree pendant into the pocket.

The noise was becoming a situation. Another new slave was pleading hysterically with their captors.

"What do you want with me? Where is my son?" It was one of the other women from the ship, speaking in Callium. She sobbed as she shoved the woman who was dressing her, then recoiled in terror at her own violent outburst.

The scene horrified Mæve. She started toward the crying woman, but the woman in white stopped her.

Two soldiers burst into the room. The slave woman flailed like a bird with clipped wings as they carried her off, only partially clothed.

Mæve gaped. *Just breathe, just breathe.* What would happen to that woman? Where had they taken her?

Divorced from her family, her land, and the magic there, Mæve was powerless to do anything other than go along with what her captors wanted. A stark shiver rolled up her spine.

"Are you all right?" Betha asked. They had stopped walking and her friend looked concerned.

Mæve nodded as the memory faded and attempted a smile as they continued to stroll through the hedges, arms linked. Betha had explained that the slaves and servants needed an outdoor space for their health and hygiene, but the nobles—reluctant to share their own lavish gardens—had requested that the royals give the slaves a separate garden.

Other slaves roamed along the paths. Mæve wondered about their stories, where they were from. All the palace slaves were chosen for their beauty. Betha was no exception, with her dark hair and icy eyes.

"And Lucius? Has he been bothering you again?" Betha asked.

Mæve grimaced.

"Yes. I've been able to dodge him so far. But he's persistent. He follows me, taunts me... I think he's playing with me."

"That's not good, Mæve," Betha switched to their native tongue, which was not allowed, but it would be a lesser punishment than being caught speaking ill of a royal.

"You need to be careful," Betha drew Mæve close, even though there was no need. "We should try to get you bumped up to royal servant status. Lucius impregnated Jaline, and others, too. They take their babies from them and send the mothers off to work the rest of their lives in the Chrysillium Field."

"That's horrible," Mæve responded. Betha had explained the Chrysillium Field to Mæve, that it was a place of great importance to the royals and feared by the slaves. She had asked her friend soon after her meeting with Armaiti.

"I see him again tonight," Mæve said.

"The Lumani?" Betha breathed, still speaking Callium. "Mæve! Why are you meeting him?"

"He told me he'd find me if I didn't," Mæve answered.

"Oh, come on, Mæve. No Lumani would threaten the peace treaty and step foot on Azantium soil. The treaty ended decades of war. They gave up one of their sacred groves to end it. They won't come anywhere near the palace except for migration," Betha said.

"Migration?" Mæve asked.

"Twice a year the Lumani travel between their two homes, Idris in the west and Eod in the east. They used to stop at Falls Hollow, just north of the palace, along the way. But the grove there—what is now known as the Chrysillium Field—belongs to the royals, so instead they march along the southern route, past the capital walls. The treaty protects them from harm during migration.

"Listen Mæve, there's a lot about this place you don't understand. I'm telling you, it's really very dangerous for you to meet him."

"I'm intrigued by him," said Mæve.

"Intrigued?" Betha squinted at Mæve. "You mean Lana is intrigued."

"Yes, well, I had to tell him something. I think he wants to understand more about his enemy."

Betha laughed out loud. "Oh, Gods Mæve. It would be the blind leading the blind! You can't pretend you know things that you don't. You need to tell him who you are."

"You're probably right," Mæve admitted.

"Here," Betha pressed a pointed object into Mæve's hand. "Put it in your pocket. Quickly!"

"What? What is this for?" Mæve asked, as she shoved what she thought might be an ice pick into her pocket.

"In case he does decide to kill you," Betha said. "It's not much, but you jab that into someone's eye and it'll do the trick."

It wasn't a terrible idea.

"Be careful. I still think this is foolish."

They took a seat on one of the stone benches. From behind the hedge at their backs they overheard two slaves talking.

"The red fox will send word when it's time," said one of the women. She sounded young.

"It's so exciting," said another woman's voice.

Mæve's head snapped towards Betha, surprised. Betha raised a single finger to her lips. But then they heard the padding of feet on the other side of the hedge and they knew the women had left.

Betha's face screwed into something sour as she looked out after them.

"Stupid, dangerous talk," Betha said in their mother tongue.

"Who is the Red Fox?"

"He's a vigilante helping slaves escape the Chrysillium Field. They say he's encouraging the palace slaves to revolt. It's only a matter of time before the royals catch him and put his head on a spike—and anyone who talked to him, anyone who dared to hope, will fall with him."

Mæve was about to protest, but the head of house hurried around one of the hedges towards Mæve and Betha.

"Blue, Doe," said Ms. Eda, addressing them with their slave names. "I need you immediately."

Despite her contempt for the Palace of Light and the Azantium royals, Betha was one of the most valued slaves in the palace; a royal servant to the queen regent and her family, which was the highest ranking position a slave could attain.

"The queen has a very important event this evening. And the two I had scheduled to work... well, one is sick, and the other had to be removed from service," Ms. Eda sighed, rolling her eyes. "Regardless, I need you, both of you, to serve the queen's guests tonight. You must be at your very best. I have clean uniforms waiting for you."

"But Doe has no experience serving the royals," Betha reminded her.

"Doe, just mimic what Blue does, keep your damn head down, and don't talk to anyone."

A cool flush of panic washed over Mæve.

"This is an opportunity to re-establish yourself in the queen's graces. You should thank me."

Ms. Eda ushered Betha and Mæve inside the palace, which loomed before them like a magnificent beast with teeth.

HUNDREDS OF CANDLES encased in glass prisms twinkled on large wrought iron contraptions hung from the ceiling. Mæve tried not to stare at the beautiful lights. She needed to stay focused.

She adjusted her new uniform with trembling hands. The gathering had begun, and the royal meeting chamber sparkled. White walls trimmed in gold. Silk upholstered furniture with elegant stitchery. Side tables displaying fancy pastel cakes and delicate sandwiches on porcelain stands. Everything carefully arranged to demonstrate splendor and opulence.

Mæve stood back, just in front of the servants' nook, ready to serve drinks to the guests. The cut of her velvet dress was even lower than her typical uniform. The head of house had made her wear a special corset, too. Mæve could barely breathe.

She wasn't the only one in fancy attire. The queen had on a brilliant navy gown with ruffles upon ruffles spilling down it. She was lovely, her make up done to perfection and her ruby hair shining.

Lucius was there too, dressed in a long silk coat and collared shirt with ruffles at his throat. He never bothered Mæve at official functions. Still, the sight of him made her flush with indignation.

A handful of court ladies glided through the room, looking like little cakes in their fine silk dresses. Their dewy skin glistened as they exchanged pink painted smiles, flashing their white gloves and sparkly gems. They were as breathtaking as the twinkling lights above.

Mæve watched as two of the court ladies' smiles disappeared as soon as one of the other girls turned her back. Their faces contorted with disdain as they murmured to each other. Their loveliness was simply a facade.

A handsome, charismatic man entered the room, dressed in the Azantium style. He had bronze skin and his hair was a mess of thick, black curls—a stark contrast to the pale strangers around him.

He bowed deeply and greeted the queen like an old friend. Mæve watched as he flirted with the court ladies and welcomed the other men in the room. Despite his foreign features, he was clearly someone of great importance and stature. How unusual.

Another group of foreigners appeared, older men wearing odd gray robes, their hair and beards long. These men conducted their conversations amongst themselves, distinguished, their hands clasped.

Mæve watched silently as the oldest of the foreign men left his comrades and approached the queen. His silver-laced dark hair flowed down his back over his long gray robe. His slate eyes were deep-set and shadowed in his pale skin.

They stood close enough to the servants' nook that Mæve could hear their conversation.

"Your Majesty," he said.

"Ezio," the queen regent replied. "Thank you for gracing us with your presence tonight, Your Excellency. May you walk in the light. How was your journey from Arkas?"

"Uneventful. How fares King Regauld, queen regent? Last we heard he had fallen ill." The man flashed a serpentine smile at the queen.

"Ill only in body; his mind remains strong and fit to lead," she replied.

"We should hate to think the wealthiest kingdom in the realm may be run by someone not in their right mind."

"We understand your concern," the queen replied, her voice becoming more pitched. "But as you can see, everything is fine here in the glorious kingdom of Azantium. Enjoy your stay at the Palace of Light."

Ezio's stormy eyes followed the queen as she returned to Lucius's side. Then, unexpectedly, his gaze fell upon Mæve.

She quickly lowered her eyes. A terrible pressure bloomed in her skull, and she reached for her forehead with her free hand.

Ezio approached her.

"What interesting eyes you have, child. Like a wild thing escaped from the Mycellium."

Confused, her head splitting with pain, Mæve could only gaze at the frightful man.

Ezio let out a deep, malicious laugh.

"That fool of a queen has let her doom in through the front door."

The pain in Mæve's head intensified, and Ezio's eyes grew darker still.

"Ezio, my good friend." It was the handsome man. His jovial interruption broke the dread that had come over Mæve, and the vice on her mind released.

The handsome man flashed her a brilliant smile and then turned his attention to Ezio.

"Did I hear you mention the Mycellium?" the handsome man asked.

Ezio's dark eyes narrowed. "We worked hard to bind the Mycellium Forest for *your* people. You greedy Azantiums would be wise to stay away from there. Forget it even exists."

The handsome man's mouth ticked up into the hint of a smirk.

"Oh trust me, the royals have no interest there. No, it's more of a personal thing, a fascination of mine."

"What interest could a merchant have in such things?" Ezio's scowl deepened. "Stay away from the Mycellium." Then he turned to rejoin his companions.

The handsome man took one last look at Mæve, widening his eyes in feigned awe of what Ezio had just said, and Mæve suppressed a giggle.

Betha joined her side. "You okay?"

"Yes, I think so," Mæve said. "Who are they?"

"They're wizards of an ancient order, from an island in the North Sea. They have a lot of power here. Even the queen is nervous around them."

"Betha, what is the Mycellium?" Mæve asked.

"The Mycellium? Who's been telling you stories?" Betha said with a faint chuckle. "It's an ancient forest east of the palace. I don't know much about it, just that magical things are said to live there; terrifying things. The creatures of the Mycellium wrought havoc upon the early Azantiums, almost destroying them until the wizards of Arkas came to their aid. In fact, their leader, the man just talking to you, was amongst the original circle to bind the Mycellium. Some say the seal is weakening, that some creatures have slipped out. It's one of the reasons people don't go into the forest."

Betha placed a steadying hand on Mæve's arm. "It's time. Ready?"

Ezio had returned to his companions and the queen to her court ladies. Mæve tried to quell the jitters in her stomach. She balanced a silver tray laden with sparkly pink drinks in one hand and followed Betha.

Betha approached the court ladies with a slight curtsey, keeping her eyes downcast as the ladies plucked the delicate crystal glasses from it, their smallest fingers raised. Betha waited until the last glass was gone before she returned to the servants' nook.

Mæve mimicked Betha as she headed towards the gathering from Arkas and bobbed a curtsy. The wizards from Arkas didn't seem to notice she was there, and they did not take the drinks. The minutes stretched on uncomfortably. Mæve waited, uncertain.

One of the men from Arkas gestured towards the handsome man, who had just left their gathering.

"I think he's losing his touch," he said, with contempt.

Another one chuckled. "He's just a playboy. This kingdom *is* falling to hell." More malicious chuckling.

"It's an act, you fools. Trust me, he's the man we need to talk to. If we underestimate him, he will walk all over us," Ezio said.

Mæve risked a quick glance up, looking for Betha, and saw her motioning from the servants' nook. Relieved, Mæve hurried toward her.

Inside the nook was a raucous melody of clinking dishes, hustling feet, and muted demands. Mæve turned to Betha. "They didn't take the drinks!"

"It's okay," Betha assured her as she arranged her tray with more drinks. "That happens. We'll make another round in a few moments and they may take them then."

The second round of serving drinks went smoothly. Mæve was adept at mimicking Betha's movements. When it was time for dinner, everyone took their seats at the enormous marble table and the slaves brought out the plates.

Mæve tried not to tremble when she set Ezio's plate in front of him. Engrossed in conversation with the handsome man, he did not seem to notice her.

"Is there any truth to the rumors I hear that your product is deteriorating?"

Mæve paused only a second before placing the handsome man's dinner plate in front of him. He appeared unruffled by Ezio's question, instead looking up at Mæve. "Thank you."

She tried not to show her surprise, but her eyebrows arched anyway.

"Sir," and she gave a slight curtsy, hurrying to the next plate.

He turned back to the wizard.

"Oh, come now. As if I'd waste my time, or your time, with anything that wasn't top notch. I have my reputation to defend." There was laughter from the others at the table.

"A merchant's coin is only as good as his word," chimed in one of the court ladies.

Mæve continued to serve the dinner plates. She noted how, as the dinner guests laughed, a darkness settled into the handsome man's eyes. He judged the visitors; he weighed their mood.

"The scientists in Shí Lou have created something similar to labas." Ezio silenced the banter at the table with his words. "Every bit as potent as the poison from labaton, and half the price. So, of course, we are considering this option."

The merchant's smile faded slowly, and he took a swig from his drink.

"We all know labas is far superior to the shit they're slinging in Shí Lou. Not to mention the disease and pestilence that any form of trade with that god forsaken place would bring." This produced a few more rumbles of laughter from the table.

The handsome man looked up over his drink. His hawk-eyed stare honed in on the old wizard.

"I was at the fields this very morning. The beans are as healthy as ever. And we continue to produce at our peak rate. I am aware of the rumors you speak of, sir, but I assure you they are not true."

The queen chimed in, with her high-pitched voice; eyes darting about.

"Yes, our stock is the best. We have an abundance of the precious labas beans; even more than the Lumani themselves." Mæve's ears perked up at the mention of the Lumani. She filled water glasses, tidied the table with the little delicacies, did whatever she could to keep herself near the table. "Our labas is hand-picked and then processed here inside the capital's gates. It is the finest and purest, far better than anything engineered in a laboratory. And you should know, Ezio, we are in the development stages of a new weapon; one even more powerful than the labaton."

The merchant's head snapped towards the queen as Ezio said, "A new weapon would interest us."

"Yes, our engineers are constantly researching new uses for the potent fruits of the Chrysillium tree. Please put your worried mind at ease. It is as Isaac said, our stock thrives and is well worth your investment." The queen sipped her drink.

"Yes," said Isaac. If the knowledge of a new weapon had unsettled him, he did not let it show. "In fact, you might invest more than you did last year. Demand for labas is increasing and this new weapon, once the word gets out, will only exacerbate that. Just yesterday I met with representatives from Jalin who were interested in upping their purchases and a few weeks before we had new buyers from Maz. So, my friends, it is not a question of if prices will go up this year, but when."

There was nothing else for Mæve to busy herself with. She returned to the nook, despite the tug of curiosity to know more of secret weapons and wilting trees. She had gathered enough information that Armaiti might find it useful tonight.

The dinner was drawing to a close. Betha and Mæve prepped the beautiful desserts the cooks had brought up and opened fresh bottles of wine.

But there was no need for another round of drinks, or desserts, for that matter. When Betha and Mæve returned from the servants' nook, the visitors were standing, exchanging handshakes and smiles. Isaac seemed to be at the center of it. It was obvious they had struck a good deal. Even the queen wore a smile.

Soon, the group began to disperse, the squawking court ladies following them out. Mæve and Betha busied themselves with the cleaning.

"Why don't you take care of things in here and I'll finish emptying the servants' nook," Betha suggested, and then she whispered in Callium. "Get you out of here with plenty of time to sneak out."

Betha giggled and left with her first cart of dishes for the kitchens.

As she returned to the dining room, Mæve was surprised to find herself looking forward to meeting Armaiti again.

"I like the new dress."

Mæve froze at the sound of that dreaded voice, then turned to face Lucius' haughty smile.

She managed a slight curtsy. "Sir."

That cruel smirk of his played on his lips as he sauntered towards her.

"Nice to see you amongst us royals tonight. You're a good little serving girl," he said.

But before he could advance any further, Betha entered the room.

"Doe!" Betha shouted at Mæve. "Stop slacking off! Get over here."

She paused, feigning surprise. "Oh, apologies, Your Highness. I didn't see you there. This one likes to dillydally." Betha rolled her eyes, grabbing at Mæve's arm and hauling her back to the nook.

"Get the hell out of here," she whispered to Mæve. "I got the rest of this. Get up to your quarters and away from him."

"Are you sure?" Mæve asked. "What about you?"

"Nope. I'm a royal servant, he wouldn't dare. Now go."

Mæve exited into the main hallway, looking around for any nobles. None in sight. She stepped out onto one of the open verandas and stared up at the starry night sky, breathing in the fresh air.

"Good evening."

Mæve gasped. Behind her, leaning against the wall smoking, was Isaac. A small grin lit his face as he straightened himself.

"I'm sorry, sir. I didn't see you. I'll be leaving now," she stammered, cheeks flushed.

"Please don't," he said, leaning towards her. "Your hands; the writing. It's very interesting. What is it?"

"Sir?" She was sure she should not be talking with him.

"Please look at me. What is your name?"

Mæve tentatively looked up at him, unsure if this was some kind of twisted trick. But as her violet eyes met his dark brown ones, there was only sincerity there.

"Doe," Mæve responded. "I mean Mæve. My name is Mæve."

"Mæve?" he repeated. "What a lovely name, and your accent... I am well-traveled, but I'm unfamiliar with it."

"I'm from Callium, sir," she responded.

"Oh, Callium. That is very far away. Please, call me Isaac."

Mæve bobbed her head and dared a question.

"Why are you interested in the Mycellium?"

His brows arched in surprise and he finished a drag of whatever he was smoking.

"It may hold some answers for me." He gave an awkward chuckle, clearly uncomfortable discussing it further, and Mæve didn't push.

"I should go," she said. She paused a moment. This was the first Azantium she had met who treated her like a person.

"Thank you." And she hurried through the door.

As she rushed up to the slave quarters, Mæve turned her attention away from the merchant. Something more intriguing was on her mind now. The full moon was rising. In just a few hours it would be time to sneak out to meet Armaiti.

4

The moon illuminated the Chrysillium Field. It was a wolf moon, an omen of fecundity and good luck in Isaac's home country. Isaac hoped at least some of the old superstitions were true. He would need some luck tonight.

He waited in the shadows, his red scarf tied around his nose and mouth to obscure his face. He wasn't sure if he should put an end to this business. He knew the rebellion was far bigger than him, that it had infiltrated the enforcers and even high society inside the palace. Isaac was but a cog in the wheel, though his mounting notoriety as the Red Fox was making his job harder. It had been far easier, far safer to do this work when nobody knew about it.

The moonlight outlined the silhouettes of the tortured Chrysillium trees and Isaac remembered Lilya's eyes searching for him in the night as the enforcer's blade rose.

A movement around the corner of the slave quarters caught Isaac's eye. It was Mohlin, crouched down low, creeping towards the tree line.

Isaac stepped from the shadows and grabbed Mohlin's arm. "I'll show you the way."

Adrian, an enforcer of the Red Guard and friend of the rebellion, had assured Isaac there would be no enforcers guarding the building for exactly ten minutes; he had devised a distraction during the changing of the guards. Adrian couldn't always be the enforcer on duty when these escapes happened or he would be caught, so they were getting creative with their plans.

Isaac glanced around once more, checking for guards, then led Mohlin to the path through the forest that would lead him to the Main Road. Once he crossed it, Mohlin should be able to reach Idris with ease through the Black Forest.

"Let's go," he whispered. The Lumani man was fast and Isaac struggled to keep up. The moon lit their way, but it also did little to obscure them. They sprinted toward the forest line, and kept going as they entered the trees. Isaac had always been in good shape, but these jaunts through the forest challenged him every time.

He knew the way well and as they approached the Main Road he placed a hand on Mohlin's arm, stopping him. Isaac motioned for him to be quiet and stay where he was, then crept silently to the road. At this hour, it should be empty. He listened, but only the sound of crickets greeted him. He stepped out onto the road and motioned for Mohlin to cross. They sprinted to the other side, ran a few paces into the woods, and then dropped behind a mound of earth and tree roots. Both men were panting.

Isaac handed Mohlin a bundle of food and a flask of water.

"We part ways now," he whispered, obscuring his voice.

"Thank you," Mohlin said, squinting in the moonlight. "Isaac, is that you?"

But Isaac only gave a wave of his hand as he disappeared into the night.

THE INDIGO NIGHT embraced the luminescent wolf moon. The early summer air was pleasant even at this late hour and Mæve smiled at the soft twinkle of dancing fireflies. Magic lived here in this secret meeting place.

Mæve looked for Armaiti as she dismounted Tráthóna and adjusted her long white shift. She wished it had been possible to change into her dress, but with so many women crammed into the narrow sleeping quarters, changing was too risky. At least she had remembered to slip Betha's little weapon into her shift pocket before bed.

The woods were quiet. He had not yet arrived.

Mæve stepped across the glade to the spot where she had stood a month ago. She lowered to the earth and sifted through the leaves and grass, but there was no sign of her obsidian tree pendant.

"You returned." His deep voice cut through the night and Mæve stood abruptly. He was so quiet. Twice now he had caught her off guard.

Mæve schooled her face to be calm, betraying none of her inner jitters. Admitting her lies now seemed daunting.

Armaiti regarded her with a slight smirk. His feet did not make any discernible sound as he walked towards her. The gray of his skin blended in and out of the moonlight and shadows.

"It's good that you came back. Spares me the effort of having to kill you."

She could not tell whether he was joking.

"I need to... clarify something." Mæve cleared her throat, trying not to sound awkward and failing. "You see, last we met I was... afraid. And I'm very sorry, but I lied to you. I'm not royalty and my name is not Lana, it's Mæve. I'm not even from Azantium."

There. It was done. Mæve released a breath she had not realized she was holding.

"I know," he said.

"Yes, well... wait. What?"

A mischievous smile played on his lips. Her confusion transformed into irritation.

"Yes, you're not a very good liar." His smile deepened.

"Oh, really?" she asked sharply.

A gentleness crept into his voice, "Your accent. I've never met an Azantium with an accent like yours. And the markings on your hands, your unusual eyes... It's obvious you are not Azantium. The way they bring in slaves, well, I figured it out."

"Oh," Mæve said. "If you knew I was lying, why did you ask me to come back?"

He fiddled with a piece of grass while he answered.

"Slaves hear things. They know more of the comings and goings in the palace than anyone else."

That made sense. Maybe they both had been afraid during that first encounter. Just as her heart began to warm towards him, he continued speaking.

"And... I wanted to see how long you would continue to lie to me. It was... amusing, watching you fumble about."

Mæve rolled her eyes and turned away from him. How insufferable. But she remembered the meeting in the Palace of Light earlier that evening and the ensuing conversation with the wizards from Arkas. *He's right*, she thought. Intrigued, despite her annoyance, she glanced back at Armaiti and considered the mysterious man.

He knelt by the pond and scooped a handful of water into his mouth. The way he moved, coiled strength and elegant grace, Mæve wondered if he was one of the dangerous Lumani warriors Betha had told her about. Despite the two large curved blades strapped to his back, he didn't seem dangerous to Mæve. He certainly had a powerful presence, but it was a calm, resolute strength, not a dangerous one.

"You're right," Mæve said. "We do hear things. There was an important meeting today in the palace. They talked about the Chrysillium Field and beans. What did they call them? The labas beans?"

He stood, wiping drops of water from his chin. She had his full attention, and the intensity of his stare threatened to drive her back a few steps. But she held her ground.

"Yes," he said. "The Chrysillium Field is our sacred grove. We gave them to the Azantium royals as part of the treaty. Labas is what they call the beans of the Chrysillium trees. We never pick the beans. We leave them on the trees. Where they belong."

Mæve swallowed. He appeared... full of dread. *He suspects*, she thought. She had not realized the trees were sacred to his people.

"There is a rumor that the Chrysillium trees are dying."

"They said this?" Concern graced Armaiti's face, but he did not seem surprised.

"Yes," Mæve said. "That was the claim, but according to Isaac and the queen, the rumor is not true."

"Yes, but those two, they lie through their teeth," he hissed. "Especially Isaac."

The merchant's name rolled off Armaiti's tongue like poison syrup. Mæve recalled her own unease around the merchant. Perhaps there was something more concerning about Isaac.

"The missing—"

"The missing?" Mæve interrupted.

"Every so often Lumani go missing. They enter the woods and do not return. A few moons ago one returned, Malwa. He had been forced into slavery at the Chrysillium Field and he brought back harrowing tales of what was happening there. Then on the next moon, another returned. Both said the trees did not look well, but this is the first I have heard of them dying. Chrysillium trees are as old as Zama herself. They do not simply die and now that there are no more Shalik, we cannot create more trees."

Even though Mæve did not know Armaiti well, she understood his pain and she reached out to place a hand on his arm.

But before she could lay her hand upon him a howl cut through the night—bestial, cruel, and close. She froze and they both snapped their heads to the nearby woods.

Something entered the glade, freed from the shadows of the forest.

Its body was black and lithe, with two spiraling horns extending from its forehead. It moved fast, staying low to the ground, its pointed muzzle pulled back to expose rows of serrated teeth. Its long, curved talons ripped through the grass of the clearing and as it approached Mæve it rose on its hind legs as if to slice at her. Mæve clutched her ice pick, which was ridiculous, but it was all she had.

The air sizzled, and the creature turned, letting loose a terrible screech. A slice of blue cut through the night. A blade hidden amongst light.

Armaiti stood with both swords drawn. The runes on his swords glowed a phosphorescent blue. The silver markings upon his chest shone in the night.

He moved as if dancing. Fluid, circular, he maneuvered his blades with a blinding quickness and Mæve thought he would strike out at the creature again. But he did not. He leapt into the air, swords raised, and then slammed them down into the earth.

The ground shook. From Armaiti's blade, an azure light coursed across the earth. It struck the creature, and the beast screeched. Armaiti advanced, but his foe recovered and slashed at him with one of its forward talons.

It grazed his shoulder, but Armaiti didn't hesitate as he spun his swords around, then drew them together close to his body. The creature was advancing fast, hissing a steaming drool.

Mæve gathered her courage. Letting loose her most fervent battle cry, armed with only her ice pick, she ran towards the beast.

She wasn't sure what she would do when she reached the creature. But before she got there Armaiti swung open his swords in an arc. A concussive force rippled through the night, knocking the creature to the earth.

Mæve caught the end of the air wave, and it blew her to the ground, where she nicked her cheek on a branch. She sat up in time to see Armaiti leap into the air again and swing one sword down in a killing strike.

Silence.

The quiet after a kill. Armaiti wiped his blade clean. It was only then, with the threat gone, that he looked shaken.

He approached Mæve and helped her to her feet.

"Are you all right?" Concern laced his deep voice. She stared over his shoulder at the creature. Black blood oozed from its neck.

"I'm okay," she answered.

With an unexpected gentleness, Armaiti cupped her chin in his hand and wiped the blood from her cheek. A chill coursed through her body.

"Are you sure?" he asked.

"Yes," Mæve said. She gestured at the gash on Armaiti's shoulder. "You're hurt."

"It's nothing serious. I'll be fine."

His playful smirk returned.

"What exactly were you going to do with that?" He nodded towards her ice pick as he sheathed his swords.

Mæve felt defensive over her little weapon. "It's all I had."

Armaiti's face sobered. "You were going to attack that wretched beast with just a... a needle... to help me?"

"Yes, well, the Azantiums made me check *my* fancy magic swords at the palace gates when they enslaved me, so." She put the ice pick back in her pocket.

"What was that thing?" she asked.

"I'm not sure." Armaiti breathed, looking out at the surrounding forest. "It looked like a glyphium. But that's impossible."

"A glyphium?" Mæve also peered around, hoping the creature, whatever it was, didn't have any friends out there.

"I have only heard of them in myth, stories told to frighten children. They are creatures from the Mycellium, far to the east of here, guardians of the gods and the ancient forest. They are typically peaceful unless there is a threat. A child's tale. Or so I thought, until tonight."

The creature certainly hadn't seemed peaceful.

"Thank the Gods you were here. I've not seen anyone fight in that manner before."

"I channel the element of water. Wherever there is water, even in the air or the earth, I can manipulate the energy there. Water permeates and therefore much of my magic travels through things. Each clan has an element we are born with the ability to channel."

"Are all of you magical?"

He looked at her, puzzled. "But of course."

"It is rare for a person to be born with magical ability in Callium.

My great grandmother said there used to be more. Now, it is perhaps one person in a decade."

"Interesting. We have noticed some abnormalities in our magic lately," Armaiti said. "A problem that seems to be getting worse."

"Oh?" Mæve asked, her curiosity piqued.

"Yes, sometimes we have difficulty finding the threads of our element, or weaving them to do our bidding. We have no idea why this is happening."

His gaze dropped to her hands. "I've been wondering, what does it mean?"

Mæve shared with Armaiti the meaning of her Ghealaich and her ability to travel the veils.

"One of the old gods could take a person to the different realms," Armaiti said. "Malrain was his name. He was said to carry an elder wood walking stick and wear a long cloak that obscured his face save for his vermilion eyes. And there was Phela, goddess of healing. She would slumber as an earthen mound and rise to bless the growing things each night. Malrain and Phela weren't much worshipped by the Lumani, but they were important to our neighbors and allies, the Allanians."

"The Allanians?" Mæve asked.

"Yes, a people who lived on the plains of Ulli—the same land that our enemies now call Azantium. I don't know much about them other than what is written in our people's records. The Azantiums annihilated the Allanians 200 years ago. They would have done the same to us, but we learned how to fight back."

A pause, and then with a gentle voice he asked, "How long ago did they abduct you from your home?"

"Four moons ago," Mæve said. "We'd never seen ships like that. We had no ability to understand what we were seeing. It was all so foreign: the ships, the weapons, this idea of taking people."

Armaiti's brows knit. His eyes focused on the ground in front of her, his anger apparent. "We should have rid the world of these people. And now I am expected to keep peace with them."

"Why, if they are causing such harm?"

"They developed a weapon five years after we signed the Treaty of Falls Hollow. We cannot defend against it. So we must maintain the treaty, we must keep this peace with the Azantiums, or die. The Lumani are tired of warfare. We became warriors as we needed to, to survive, but we do not enjoy it. We lived in peace with the Allanians before the Azantiums came."

"Can't you just slay the royals in their sleep?" she asked.

He laughed out loud at this. "Yes, we tried that for a time. It's not as easy as one might believe. Though I do like the way you think." He smiled at her. "I am glad to have met you, Mæve. I would like to consider you my friend."

"Yes, I would like that," Mæve said.

She held up her open right hand. It was a greeting or agreement between two people in her homeland. Armaiti looked a little confused at first, but he figured out the appropriate response and raised his left hand to meet hers. A current coursed between them. Her violet eyes met his golden ones.

What was that?

Armaiti broke their gaze, reaching for his pocket.

"I found this after our last meeting. I thought you may be missing it."

He held up her obsidian tree pendant. "I hope you don't mind. I fastened it to a cord, so you can wear it and not lose it again."

Armaiti stepped behind her and fastened the necklace around her neck.

He could not have known of her people's engagement tradition. Still, Mæve turned, looking at him, her hand over the pendant. Too surprised to say much.

"Thank you," she managed. Tears filled her eyes. "It's very meaningful."

Mæve paused, still getting over her surprise, when she remembered. "Armaiti, there is something else I should tell you. The queen mentioned a new weapon tonight, made from labas. She didn't say much about it, just that it was worse than labaton."

Armaiti frowned. "This is reason for concern." His nervous eyes met hers. "You have risked much for this information. You must not put yourself at such risk again."

"I will be careful, I promise. But I want to help you. The Azantiums have caused us both irrevocable harm." Mæve moved towards Tráthóna and he followed.

"The next full moon, then?" Armaiti asked.

"The next full moon," Mæve responded. "And thank you for this." She fingered the tree pendant.

Mæve mounted Tráthóna and Armaiti placed his hand on her forearm.

"And one more thing. Stay away from the royals, and Isaac, as much as possible."

Those eyes that had terrified her only a month ago were gentle now. It stirred a part of her that had been dormant since her abduction. She felt safe in his presence.

"I will. I promise."

As she spurred Tráthóna onward, Mæve looked back. He stood looking after her with his hand over his heart.

5

Armaiti raced through the forest, the cool breeze blowing through his long hair. His footing was solid and sure. He leapt over a large boulder as he channeled threads of water in the misty night air to elevate him, before landing and continuing to run. He was going to win this time.

No sooner had the thought crossed his mind, than Iraji sped past him, her ki shining a bright blue as she channeled threads of air for speed. She turned, looking back at him with a smile of self-satisfaction.

"Still faster," Armaiti conceded, trying to hide his smile.

"And you're getting older," she replied, jabbing him in the ribs. "You have little hope of ever beating me now."

Iraji had been besting him at racing since they were children. She could also beat him in a grappling match, although Armaiti was twice her size.

"That's right," he said as he walked away, smirking. "Let your guard down, underestimate me. It's all part of my plan."

She laughed out loud over this.

"Oh, I know better, Armaiti Avari," she said.

"Why don't we move over to the eastern patrol site," Armaiti suggested. "Everything is quiet here."

She nodded and joined his side as they walked the perimeter of Idris.

"We should celebrate," Iraji said. "This may be your last time doing patrols. Soon you'll be King Armaiti and too good for patrolling the grounds."

"You may find yourself in a similar situation, if the elders have their way." Iraji's face fell and Armaiti wished he could take his words back.

Their friendship was an unusual one. The Water and Air Clans had frequent disagreements. With only about 20,000 Lumani left after decades of war with the Azantiums, it was important that they all - Æther, Water, Fire, Earth, and Air Clans—live in harmony.

Each clan had their tasks to support the larger community. The Water Clan hunted; the Fire Clan lit the orbs and fire pits of Eod and Idris; the Earth Clan were scholars; and the Air Clan were mind manipulators. The Water and Fire Clans also served as warriors, protecting their home and people.

The Æther Clan—six elders who acted as the spiritual rulers of the Lumani—were tasked with determining the next king. Often, they would also designate a queen, although the previous ruler— King Babak—had been allowed to choose his own wife. However, Armaiti was assuming the throne in a very different political environment.

He and Iraji spoke at the same time.

"I'm sorry," he said. "I shouldn't have—"

"Neither of us want this and yet—"

They broke off, giving each other pained smiles.

"We'll talk to them," Armaiti said. He put a hand on her shoulder. "We'll talk to Jaleh and propose our idea."

Iraji shook her head. "Jaleh is so stubborn. She might not even hear us out."

"They'll see the harm of forcing us together."

Iraji still looked doubtful. "But that harm is small, compared to the rift between our clans that a marriage would heal."

It was true. The strife between the Air and Water Clans had deepened in recent years. They needed a strong show of leadership to smooth it over.

Still, Armaiti was hopeful they could find another way. "The Air Clan will see that your role as my advisor would be more powerful than a queen."

"I hope you're right," Iraji said.

"And if we fail, I mean, marrying me cannot be so bad," Armaiti meant to jest, to lighten the mood, but Iraji looked up at him with watery eyes.

"No, of course not. And you will make a magnificent king," Iraji said.

"But your heart belongs to another," Armaiti said. "I know. And you should be with Ariol."

She smiled at Armaiti as she said, "And whoever I marry needs to be able to beat me in a race, sometimes."

Armaiti laughed and swiped at her, but she took off into the forest. He followed.

They stopped in a clearing along the western edge of Idris. As they caught their breath, Armaiti's raven cawed above them. He extended his arm and the raven landed there, a note tied to his left foot.

Armaiti opened the note.

"Another missing has returned," Armaiti said, anticipation in his voice that dropped as he read on. "A man. Mohlin. Jaleh wants me present in the morning to talk with him."

Iraji put a supportive hand on his shoulder. "I'm sorry."

He knew whom she meant. Lilya. He shook his head.

Armaiti wondered to this day if that smooth-talking Azantium merchant had something to do with his cousin's disappearance. He could only hope Lilya had run off to be with Isaac. The other possibility, that Lilya was enslaved at the Chrysillium Field, weighed upon Armaiti.

In the early days of their conflicts with the Azantium, the Lumani had forbidden foreigners into Idris and Eod. They had been wary of Isaac Houghton when he had approached them, asking to learn more about the Lumani, hoping that together they might find a way to bring about peace.

The merchant's interests had seemed genuine. He lived with them for three years, learning the language and befriending some of the Lumani, though others were distrustful.

Isaac's offer had enamored him to King Babak. Never had an Azantium shown interest in Lumani ways. It lit a spark of hope. Maybe if the Azantiums could learn more about their ways, there could be peace between them.

Lilya, Armaiti's cousin, had fallen for the merchant—his witty sense of humor and crooked smile—but Armaiti and the rest of the clan had not approved. He had warned his cousin to stay away from the merchant and she had listened.

But then she had gone missing. And Armaiti continued to wonder.

Armaiti looked back at the note. "If this man has the same stories as the others, we must treat it as truth. The trees are dying, and soon the royals will come looking for more."

Iraji lowered her eyes. It echoed the sadness he felt in his own heart.

"I can't believe they damaged the grove so quickly. There was always a part of me that believed we'd get it back somehow."

"I don't think that's likely, Iraji." Armaiti continued, "And there's more. The Azantium appear to be working on a new weapon. Something fouler than labaton."

"What?" Then her eyes narrowed. "How do you know this?"

"I have a... friend... an insider. She's a slave—"

"It's not like you to trip on your tongue, Armaiti. 'She's' a slave, you say..." Iraji's eyebrows arched in mock innocence.

"Yes," Armaiti grumbled. "I caught her on Lumani land during one of my patrols two-and-a-half moons ago. As payment, I had her spy for me."

"What is the matter with you? That could have gotten her killed," Iraji said.

Armaiti blushed.

"It's true, but the information she brought back—the trees dying and the new weapon—it could save lives. I asked her to stop, to not endanger herself any further, but she wanted to continue."

"She sounds very brave." Iraji's mouth ticked up in a slight smile. "Is this why your cheeks are red?"

"My cheeks are fine—"

Iraji laughed. "Formidable Armaiti, always so focused on his duty, never had time or interest for any girl, has finally turned his eye on someone?"

Now he was blushing.

If there was anyone he could trust with his burgeoning feelings for Mæve, it was Iraji.

"I like her smile and her sense of humor. And yes, she is very brave..."

He trailed off, and Iraji flashed him a conciliatory smile.

"We can't help who we fall in love with, Armaiti." Iraji's voice was gentle. She slid her hand into his as they continued to walk. "Though it would be easier, maybe, if we could. Does anyone else know you are meeting her?" Armaiti shook his head no. "I do not think this is information you should sit on, Armaiti."

"I know. I will tell Jaleh."

"You look worried," she said. "Let me help you."

Iraji, and other Air Clan Lumani, could soothe ailments of the mind. It wasn't permanent, but it did provide some relief. Iraji had done this many times for him in the past.

He nodded and she lay her slender hands on his temples. But nothing happened.

Armaiti opened his eyes to see his friend's distressed face.

"I can't reach the air... I can't reach the air threads," Iraji said.

"Don't worry about it," he said. "You're tired. I'm sure that's all it is."

"No, it's never... that's never happened, Armaiti."

"Get some sleep, my friend. You can try to heal my tortured mind tomorrow." Again he had meant to be funny, but his words fell flat. Iraji nodded and turned back toward Idris.

Armaiti continued to walk through the forest. He wasn't ready for sleep yet.

The sweet sound of lalos lifted his mood. Their tiny azure wings created a hushed lullaby in the nighttime forest as they feasted on the sweet nectar of the makrial blooms. The bioluminescent flowers came alive at night, illuminating the forest floor with a rusty saffron glow.

The smell of home filled Armaiti's nostrils—moss, wood, and smoke. He could hear the gentle lapping of the sacred Kalim River in the near distance. The beauty of Idris always brought him such joy, even during times like this.

A whisper on the breeze. Armaiti stopped and listened. It was Oyela, oldest of the Chrysillium trees in Idris. The trees were the place where two energy sources of Ulli converged: the æther, a webbing stretching across all things above ground, and the mycelia, a similar energy existing below ground. It was said the ancestors and the old gods used to speak through the mycelia, though no one had heard from the gods in centuries. The Lumani connected with the webbing to talk with their ancestors. So when the trees spoke, they listened.

Armaiti placed his hand on Oyela's trunk, but the only message he received was *Lost. She is lost.*

Who? Armaiti placed his hand back on Oyela's trunk and asked, *Mæve?*

But Oyela kept repeating the same message.

Armaiti sank to the earth under the tree's branches and considered the information Mæve had given him. An Azantium attack would happen, and it would happen soon. The Azantiums had greater numbers, more advanced weapons. No doubt the royals meant to annihilate his people this time.

It made sense. King Babak was dead. What better time to strike than during a power transfer?

Armaiti remembered well the night the Azantium had come and his family, the very basis of his world, was ripped apart. He had only been nine years old.

They had come with the dark sky of a new moon, catching his family unawares. Within hours, they were in dungeons in the capital. The soldiers took great pride in breaching the home of such an important family in the Water Clan. Armaiti still remembered the smile that had split the weather-worn face of one of the soldiers as he had come into the cell for Armaiti's aunt, his dull eyes smug.

"Aunt Mallon!" Young Armaiti had reached for her as she put on a stoic face.

His mother pulled him back, into the safety of her arms.

"What are they going to do to Auntie? Where are they taking her?"

He got his answer soon enough, as her screams tore through the dungeon. Nine-year-old Armaiti recoiled. Surely that wasn't his aunt. Aunt Mallon did not scream.

Mallon had been one of the Water Clan's fiercest warriors. Armaiti had learned all he knew of combat and magic from her.

His mother, Humana, had held him close as he trembled in that putrid cell in the dungeons of the Palace of Light. The screaming would stop, and his family would fear for the worst, and then it would start up again. It went on for days and towards the end young Armaiti had wanted his beloved aunt to die, to put an end to her suffering.

The day she died, Armaiti remembered the pleased looks on the Azantium soldiers' faces. They had wanted her family to hear those screams because they were next.

Humana held Armaiti close to her as the guard approached. He was staring right at Armaiti and Humana held him tighter as she growled, "No."

But as the guard reached for his keys, he burst into flames. Armaiti stared at him as he screamed in agony.

The Fire Clan had arrived to free the Lumani prisoners.

The memory had stayed with Armaiti. It was with him the day, ten years later, when King Babak announced his signing of the Treaty of Falls Hollow, Isaac Houghton smiling beside him.

Now, once again, an attack was coming. They were not ready. Armaiti could only hope that the onset of winter might deter the Azantiums from attacking, giving the Lumani more time to prepare in their winter home at Eod. Eod was much further away from the capital—a two-day journey, instead of only a few hours.

So many worries. He supposed he should get used to it if he were to be king. He and Iraji would talk to Jaleh tomorrow about the trees, the weapons, and the alternative to their marriage. Then he would bring Mæve to Oyela. He wasn't sure how Mæve fit into this or if it was just a dream of his heart, but he hoped Oyela might provide some answers.

6

Cornflower blue skies and a soft summer breeze greeted Mæve as she made her way to the stables. It had been a week since she snuck out to see Armaiti, and the fresh air invigorated her. Mæve had a rare free morning and went to see Tráthóna. She entered the barn to the familiar scents of straw, urine, and horse musk.

Tráthóna's stall was a mess, and Mæve grabbed a pitchfork to muck it out. None of the other slaves would go near the unruly mare.

Mæve was rubbing Tráthóna's muzzle, offering soothing words, when a guard entered the stables.

"You, put that horse back inside the stall! Are you mad?"

"I'm cleaning it, sir," Mæve responded.

"I don't care. She's a senile nag and should never be taken out."

Tráthóna reared up, kicking out at the guard. Mæve gasped, hurrying out of the way.

"I said put that cursed beast back in its stall!" the man yelled, and Mæve obliged.

"You're up for auction, you wretched creature," he called after them. "Now, slave girl, I've got a task for you."

A flush of anger was coursing through Mæve's body. Tráthóna, up for auction?

"I need you to bring the High Merchant his horse," the guard said. "He waits by the front gate. Make haste."

The High Merchant. Isaac.

The guard gestured at a magnificent black horse and left. Mæve saddled the horse and led it toward the front gates.

Isaac waited there, a red scarf wrapped about his throat. As he turned, Mæve's stomach did a nervous flip.

"Sir." Mæve bobbed a curtsey as she handed him the lead to the horse.

"Oh, what a pleasant surprise. Mæve, was it?" he asked. The brim of his top hat hovered above bloodshot eyes.

"Yes, sir," she replied.

He flashed one of his charming smiles. "Call me Isaac, please."

She nodded. She wanted to run back to the stables and finish taking care of Tráthóna.

"It's a beautiful day. Care to go for a ride?" he asked.

"No," Mæve practically shouted. He raised his eyebrows in surprise. "I mean, I couldn't possibly. I have work to do and I'm pretty sure palace slaves are not supposed to leave the capital—"

"You can leave with me," he replied. "I'm the High Merchant."

She would be alone with him. He could take her anywhere. Thoughts of Lucius flashed through her mind.

As if he could read her thoughts, the merchant said, "I promise, a quick ride and we'll come right back. No funny business."

That sounded nice, and she did still have Betha's ice pick in her pocket.

"Okay," she replied.

He smiled and walked towards one of the guards by the front gate, taking out a small leather-bound notebook from his satchel and scribbling something in it. Then he opened a circular ring on his finger and stamped the page with it. He tore the paper free and handed it to the guard.

"See that the head of house receives this. Tell her I'm borrowing this slave for the afternoon."

"Sir," the guard replied, and took the paper as he made his way to the palace.

Isaac leapt upon his horse and extended a smooth hand down to her.

"Shall we?" he asked. She hesitated to take his hand with her calloused, dirty one, but he didn't seem to notice or care. He pulled her up onto the saddle in front of him and settled her in place, one arm around her waist.

They passed through the front gate. Before them was the expanse of the kingdom's countryside. Rolling hills as far as the eye could see, and the forest on the near horizon. Most of it was farmland, fields that slaves and indentured servants worked to feed the kingdom.

Mæve relished in the fresh air as she held the pommel of Isaac's saddle. Eventually Isaac stopped under a large tree a good distance from the palace, and they dismounted.

"Take some time for yourself. I'm sure it's a luxury not afforded to you in the palace," Isaac said, walking away from her.

"Thank you," Mæve replied, unsure of why he was being so gracious to her. It made her nervous, but she seized the opportunity all the same.

She looked toward the palace. She had never seen the palace from this vantage point before. She imagined the slaves working the fields, looking at the great looming castle, taunting them with all they would never have. It was a beautiful structure, light gray stone stretching above the capital walls. The Azantium flag, red with a gold sun upon it, flapped atop the slate black spires.

She walked to the other side of the tree, away from the palace. Isaac was there, smoking and she sat down beside him. The smoke made her cough, and he put it out on the sole of his boot.

What a foreign feeling, to just sit and be.

"Over there is the Southern Forest," Isaac said, pointing. "And that large town you see in the distance is Essential. Outside of the capital and Allam, it is the largest town in the kingdom. It's full of religious zealots. They worship the Azantium God and are not at all welcoming to foreigners. Terrible place."

"What is that large building with the pointed middle?" Mæve asked, gesturing to the structure in the middle of Essendial.

"The Church of Light. The largest house of worship to the one God. Even bigger than the one located inside the Palace of Light."

"Is the Azantium one God the same as the gods from the Mycellium Forest?"

"Oh, goodness no," Isaac chuckled. "Couldn't be more different. The one God is the only god in the Church of Light. The old gods of the Lumani and Allanians were a pantheon of different gods and they regulated the magic of this world, or so it is said. Followers of the Azantium one God do not practice magic. So you see, they are quite different."

Mæve thought about her conversation with Armaiti about the gods of the Mycellium. She wondered if they were real; if they'd really been locked inside the Mycellium for all this time.

"And over there," Isaac said, pointing slightly more to the east, "are the hills. That is where I live."

"You don't live in the capital?" This surprised Mæve. Isaac certainly seemed important enough.

He laughed and replied, "No, I get out of the capital as often as I can."

"You don't like it there?"

"I did when I first came here. I wanted nothing more than to be like them. When you come from a poor family in a place with no options, coming here is a dream. But the dream has faded, over time."

He took off his hat, fiddling with it in his lap.

"Enough about me. I don't need to cry my woes to a slave. How long have you been here?"

"Five moons now," she replied.

Isaac handed her something from his satchel, wrapped in brown paper.

"What's this?" Mæve asked.

"Honey cake. A delicacy from Shí Lou."

He took one out for himself as Mæve opened the wrapping. It was a little rice ball. She bit into it and sweetness exploded in her mouth.

It was warm and chewy. Mæve couldn't remember the last time she'd had good or sweet food, and as she chewed, her heart warmed and tears fell from her eyes. She couldn't stop them.

He looked at her with warm sympathy and said, "Hey, it's okay."

He wrapped an arm around her, and the sobs came rushing forth as she buried her head in the crook of his arm.

Isaac remained steady as she cried, and when exhaustion replaced her grief, she sat up, wiping her nose and eyes.

"I'm sorry," she said.

"It's okay. Perfectly understandable."

"I worry every day about my parents. I'd very much like to find them."

Isaac turned to look at her.

"Maybe I can help you with that."

Her heart hitched again in warning. She barely knew this man. She shouldn't have cried.

"The conversations, the ride today, this offer, it is all very nice, but you are an Azantium High Merchant. Why are you helping me?"

"I have made it my mission these past few years to help slaves however I can. Of course, the royals can know nothing of this."

"Aren't you worried they'll find out?"

"Yes, and no. I used to worry in the beginning. I find I care less these days. I'd like to help you; help find your parents. I listen to my instincts and they're drawing me to you. I hope that's okay to say. I expect nothing in return."

She blushed at his straightforwardness, but appreciated it. Still, the unsettling in Mæve's core grew, and she remembered Armaiti's words to be careful around Isaac.

"To start, it would be helpful to know their names."

Mæve hesitated, but she couldn't see any harm from sharing her parents' names.

"Isa and Jal Faolái," she said.

Isaac took out the notebook again and jotted down the names.

"Okay. I'll start there." He took off his riding jacket and laid it on the ground. "Why don't you take some rest and then I'll ride you back to the palace."

She looked at him, nervous, but he smiled, "I promise I will not bother you."

Exhausted from her emotional outburst, the merchant's words were enough for her to sink down upon the warmth of his jacket, where she fell asleep to the sweet smell of cinnamon and clove.

When she woke, the sun had begun its descent and tall shadows stretched along the countryside.

"You're awake," came his voice from above her.

Mæve looked up at him, still sleepy, but amazed at how much better she felt. She got to her feet and handed him his jacket. He stood close to a foot taller than her, so she had to look up at him to say, "Thank you. I'm really so grateful for today."

He put his jacket back on. "We'll find your parents. Maybe even get you out of the palace."

"How?" she asked.

"I'm not sure yet, but I'll find you once I have answers. Until then, let's keep it quiet."

She nodded.

She had so many questions, but she wouldn't burden the merchant with them now. She was grateful for the simple peace this day had brought her.

7

Mæve's soft footsteps were the only sounds in the wide, still hallway. Rays of early morning light streamed through the tall windows.

The hallways were adorned with paintings, vases, candelabras, and more; there were bowls, weapons, and clothing from other countries set up for display. None of it appeared to have a use. Nothing moved here. Nothing flowed. Stagnant. Sterile. Muted.

Three weeks had passed since her ride with Isaac, and the peace that day had brought her had long since diminished. She'd been woken that morning by Ms. Eda, who informed Mæve she would now serve the queen as a royal servant. As Mæve made her way to the queen's chambers, her dread mounted.

To calm her nerves, she focused on a happier thought. Two weeks ago, while mucking out the stalls, a raven had visited Mæve and dropped a small leather wrapping by her feet. Mæve picked it up and saw a single black feather fastened to the rawhide. Armaiti. It was one of the feathers from his necklace.

She had looked around to make sure no one was watching, then woven the tip of Armaiti's feather into her tree pendant before unwrapping the little gift, unsure of what she might find. Inside was a black rawhide bracelet with three crystalline gems affixed to it. They were small and reminded Mæve of the tiny circular crystals on Armaiti's forehead. She had held it close to her heart, admiring it one last time, and then put the precious gift in her pocket before anyone could see it.

She held onto the pleasant memory as she approached a set of enormous doors, where a pair of Royal Guards stood at attention. One nodded to her and entered the chamber, closing the large door behind him. Mæve smoothed her skirt and stood tall. The remaining guard looked straight ahead, as if she did not exist. There was a faint murmur of conversation behind the doors, and then the guard returned.

"You may enter," he proclaimed. Once again, his eyes found their place above her head. She dropped a quick curtsey, her eyes on his impassive face, then hurried past him.

Queen Regent Druscilla sat in an immense red chair by the windows, peering out at the courtyard below, haloed by the gray of the cloudy sky. Despite all her finery and all her power, she looked... small. A hollowed woman with teeth.

"Look at them. Milling about down there. Plotting, scheming," the queen regent said as she brought a cup of tea to her pursed lips.

Mæve was silent.

Queen Druscilla placed her delicate cup on its saucer with a clink and turned her sharp blue eyes to Mæve. It was difficult to believe that this was the same woman from the dinner two months ago. She was duller and smaller, and even though she could not have been much older than Mæve's own mother the queen seemed brittle, like cracked earth desperate for water.

"But come now," the queen said as she rose from her seat. Mæve dropped an obligatory curtsey. "What could a simple slave girl know or care for such musings?" She walked away from the window.

"Your Highness," Mæve replied.

The queen walked to the hearth and lit a stick of incense. With her back still to Mæve, she continued, "You are to be my new personal servant. It is so tedious, finding someone capable of handling the responsibilities and decorum of a royal servant. I do hope you are up to the task."

"It is an honor, Your Highness."

The queen turned again to face Mæve, and her features softened.

"What do they call you? Doe?"

It surprised Mæve that the queen knew her name, but she did not let this show.

"Yes, Your Highness."

"A pretty name. It suits you," the queen said with a glassy sheen in her eyes. "I used to be like you; young, lovely, full of hope. I was sixteen when King Regauld's eye turned to me. Thirty years my senior." She paused, drawing her cups to her lips again. She cleared her throat before she continued, "Men do like their pretty little things, don't they?" Those icy blue eyes darted back to Mæve again. Tendrils of fear bloomed in Mæve's heart.

"Yes, I suppose they do, Your Highness," Mæve answered.

The queen let out a high-pitched laugh, and Mæve jumped at the jarring sound.

"Oh, yes, isn't it true?" The queen wiped her eyes, still chuckling. "But then again, it makes it easy for us to lay a pretty trap."

"It must be difficult to be a woman in such an environment, Your Highness," Mæve dared.

The queen looked at her, the slightest of smiles forming on her lips.

"Yes, I suppose it is. Exhausting too. I will need your help to restore this face each morning, helping me look my best."

"That should be no trouble, Your Grace," Mæve responded.

"As you have probably heard, the king is quite ill. He's not long for this world."

Mæve looked for sadness and found none in the queen.

"He is still ruling from his bedchamber while I'm in the public eye like a puppet with his hand up my ass," she said.

"That must be quite stifling for you, Your Highness."

"Twisted old coot. Still supports that asinine treaty we signed with the Lumani," the queen scoffed. "Once he passes and Lucius ascends the throne, our kingdom will flourish beyond our wildest dreams."

"Yes, Your Highness. For the greatness of Azantium," Mæve said.

The queen regent straightened and smoothed her skirts.

"Being appointed a royal servant is a serious position, Doe, but not without its privileges. You will bring me my morning tea each day. I enjoy pleasant conversation and expect your full attention. Then, you will help me prepare for the day. Is this clear?"

"Yes, Your Highness. It is a pleasure to serve, my queen," Mæve responded.

"You start tomorrow. You may go now." She returned to her tea and her window.

"Thank you, Your Highness." Mæve curtseyed and backed out of the room.

As Armaiti walked toward the glade, butterflies danced in his stomach. He would see her again tonight. He had been looking forward to this, but now he wasn't so sure. His palms were sweaty.

He took a deep breath. Two weeks ago, the elders had denied the idea to make Iraji his personal advisor.

"That idea is preposterous," Jaleh had said. "The Air Clan will accept nothing less than a member of their clan as Lumani royalty. For you to back out of this marriage would be a major affront and a grievous, selfish error on your part."

"But Iraji would wield just as much power as an advisor. To force us to be together, it's archaic. And it's cruel."

Jaleh had laughed and said there were far worse things.

Two weeks later, the elder had pulled him aside again tonight. "The time has come, Armaiti. The Air Clan grows restless, now that you are king."

Armaiti shook his head at the memory. He would take Mæve to Oyela tonight, seeking answers. Iraji had agreed to stand guard, which he appreciated—though he knew it was merely her curiosity about Mæve that had spurred her to make the offer.

Mæve wasn't in the clearing yet. He stood and waited, watching the stream trickle into the pond, creating ripples. He heard the horse first, long before it appeared through the trees, Mæve on its back.

His breath hitched at the smile that spread across her face as she saw him. Then his eyes found her tree necklace. Woven into the finely worked obsidian branches was the feather from his own necklace.

He stood and placed a hand over his heart, not really aware of what he was doing, and they greeted each other.

"I got your lovely gift," she said as she dismounted. She held up her left arm, displaying his bracelet on her wrist. The smile on her face was genuine.

He gestured to her necklace. "They go well together, the feather and the tree."

"They do, don't they?" she said.

A pause between them as Mæve's hand covered the necklace. Armaiti found himself nervous again.

"I have something I would like to show you, tonight," he said.

"Oh?" Mæve asked.

"It's not far. You'll be back with plenty of time to return to the palace, if it is okay with you?"

He held out his open hand. An invitation. Mæve's eyes traced his hand up, past his muscled arm, up to his eyes.

"Okay," she said, and fit her hand into his.

ARMAITI'S HAND was rough like hers, although she imagined his calluses were from training with his swords, rather than hard labor. Still, his hand was large and warm. He smelled of rain and earth.

They left Tráthóna in the glade, munching grass and looking quite content.

Armaiti led her into the forest, away from the palace. Where in the gods could he be taking her?

She tried to let go of her curiosity and keep her heart steady.

Still holding her hand, he picked up his pace and broke into a run. Her booted feet fell on the soft earth, following his lead.

It was as if she were back home in her own woods. She half-expected to glimpse the other huntresses through the trees, to hear their laughing voices as they ran. Oh, to run through the woods again, a cooling mist upon her face!

Her smile widened. She looked at Armaiti and found her joy mirrored in his eyes. Gods, he was beautiful.

The surrounding trees were getting bigger. Their trunks widened, stretching up higher into the sky. Saffron-colored blooms came alive under the moonlight, dotting the path they ran on. Little winged creatures danced amongst them in a frenzy that made her laugh.

"The lalos. They are my favorite," Armaiti said with a smile.

He led her off the trail. She leapt over a small fallen log. He caught her mid-air and gently set her down on the other side.

They ran hand-in-hand through the folds of the deepening night, silver moonlight illuminating the ebony forest around them. Soon, Mæve detected a faint hum. Though she was unsure of what it was, it struck a chord within her.

And then they emerged into a clearing, and Mæve stumbled to a stop.

"Oh, Armaiti," she said. Before her was a Chrysillium tree; small, with thin, flexible branches that swayed elegantly in the breeze. They were dotted with crystalline beans that clinked gently against each other.

Armaiti guided her, their hands still clasped.

"This is Oyela," Armaiti said. "Oldest of the Chrysillium trees. His mate Ayin has spoken to my family for generations."

As they neared the tree, warmth coursed through the ground. Mæve noticed tiny mushrooms amongst the moss that let loose spores as she passed them.

Armaiti looked up at the tree as he spoke. "They say two lovers born of stars danced in the night sky, until the day Shadowlair gave birth to Zama and called down the stars. One lover fell in the west, the other in the east; Ayin of the autumn and Oyela of the spring. Though far apart, the lovers rooted deep into the earth and through their roots they connected once again. Now, when one sleeps, the other is awake. Only on the equinoxes do the two lovers meet. Equilan and Equilīum."

He turned to her and smiled. "Zama is the earth, a gift from the stars that fell. Its energy courses through the trees and settles in their fruit. See?"

Armaiti pointed to the glowing beans. "The beans amplify that energy as it is released back into the æther and into elemental threads that we channel. It is through the branches of the Chrysillium trees that we access our magic."

Still holding her hand, Armaiti placed his hand upon the tree's trunk and closed his eyes. The silver markings along his arms and chest grew brighter, and the darker markings appeared to deepen.

He stepped back from the tree, a surprised look on his face, and looked at her, a question upon his lips.

"What is it?" she asked.

"I saw a chrysalis. It was so clear and yet I have no idea what it means."

An odd bird call cut through the night. Armaiti looked up.

"Come, we need to leave," he said.

"What's wrong?" She was getting nervous now.

"That was my scout. Someone's coming."

Mæve took one last glance at Oyela, drew her hands to her heart, and gave the tree a respectful nod. Then off they ran, back into the forest, heading away from Oyela and towards the glade.

When they arrived, the moon was just past its apex. They still had some time.

"You do well, running through the woods," Armaiti said.

"It's nice to do it again. I was a huntress in Callium."

"Oh?" Armaiti reached for her hand again and guided her to a large rock by the pond, where Mæve was grateful to take a seat. She nodded as he unstrapped a water bag from his belt and handed it to her.

"Yes, I started running with them when I was thirteen, and learned the basics of hunting. Then I picked up my first weapon when I was sixteen." She took a generous swallow and handed the water back to him.

"What is your weapon of choice?"

"A bow or a set of shinal," Mæve said.

"What are shinal?" Armaiti asked.

"They are two small crescent blades with a handle intersecting the larger one. So the main blade curves at your knuckles here." She gestured to the front of her knuckles. She looked at Armaiti, his swords still strapped across his back. "Are the swords your weapon of choice?"

"Yes, and like you my mother taught me how to use them."

"Oh?" Mæve leaned closer, interested.

"My mother is one of the fiercest warriors of the Water Clan. I remember the first time I picked up one of her swords. I was a small child, maybe eight years at the time. She scolded me for handling a weapon I didn't understand, then spent years teaching me the techniques and forms before she allowed me to hold a sword again."

"She sounds amazing," Mæve said.

"She is," Armaiti said. "I think you would like her." His eyes darted away as soon as he said it, an awkward silence engulfing them both.

"And how have you been faring at the palace?" Armaiti asked.

"Better," Mæve said. "They have assigned me to serve the queen. I'll get to work alongside my best friend, Betha, and the crown prince will no longer bother me."

Armaiti's jaw tightened. "He... bothers you?"

"Just little things. But he won't anymore."

"I wish I could get you out of there." Armaiti looked to the earth, as if the ground held the solution to his worries.

"Even if you could, I can't leave my parents behind."

Silence again.

"I learned more information from the queen," Mæve said. "The queen said the king is still ruling from his bed, and as he still supports the Treaty of Falls Hollow it remains unbroken. But she believes his days are numbered. It would seem that once the king passes, she will waste no time breaking it and attacking your people."

"How sick is he?"

"I don't think he has long. I'll try to find out more, now that I'm her personal servant."

"Be careful, especially now..." Armaiti paused, looking suddenly uncertain. Mæve raised a questioning eyebrow.

"I... I ascended two weeks ago. I should have told you sooner—"

"Ascended? What does that mean?"

"I am the new Lumani king."

"You're a king?" She hadn't expected that. "Why didn't you tell me? It would have been nice to know I was gathering information for a king."

"I understand your point and I wish I had told you, but I did not know you then and my first responsibility is to keep my people safe. It is why I wanted to know more about the treaty and why your news about the weapons is so important. I can better decide what to do, to safeguard my people and I..." He trailed off, and Mæve could sense the gravity of his responsibilities upon him.

"And... there's more."

His voice had changed. Mæve looked away, trying to keep her face neutral.

"I am betrothed to a woman I do not love. The elders expect us to marry. It is not right, especially when my heart has been full of someone else."

His eyes left no question as to whom he meant. Mæve's breath caught in her throat.

"That would be quite foolish," she breathed.

"It would indeed."

Her hand still rested on his arm. He was so close.

"I have thought of little else this past month than seeing you again, Mæve."

He leaned in closer to her. Mæve stood abruptly, letting her hand fall from his arm, feeling his warmth replaced with the solitary coolness of the air.

"I should go," she said, her voice trembling, and she turned toward Tráthóna, but Armaiti reached for her hand. "Please... the next full moon. Meet me."

"Okay," Mæve whispered.

She leapt upon Tráthóna's back and rode off towards the palace. From a safe distance, she gave one final look back at Armaiti. He stood with one hand over his heart again.

Mæve spurred Tráthóna into a quick gallop, her necklace tapping against her chest as she rode.

8

A cool late-summer breeze graced Valentina Ceionius' face and lifted the perfumed folds of her silk skirts as she reached for her crystal goblet, bringing it to her pink painted lips for a sip.

Valentina sat with the other court ladies in one of the Palace of Light's many outdoor terraces, enjoying the summer sunshine. They ignored the delectable pastel cakes that adorned the table. Lovely, but meant for no more than decoration. Fattening delicacies could ruin a girl.

There was the familiar sound of clinking glasses, the twinkle of gems in the sunlight as Valentina and the other ladies gossiped.

"That's a beautiful piece, Valentina," Amelia gestured at the large yellow diamond on the middle finger of Valentina's right hand. Valentina drew her hand to her chest, turning her head slightly with feigned modesty.

"A gift from the baron," she replied. "If only he didn't have the propensity to snore like a pig, there might have been some hope for us."

"And that he was old enough to be your father," Sabina snickered.

Valentina pretended to laugh. The truth was Baron Cato had a penchant for very young slave girls, but she couldn't exactly say that without losing face. So snoring like a pig did the trick. He was indeed a pig.

"I'm not sure where he picked it up from," Valentina said, drawing attention back to the diamond. She lifted her hand to let it sparkle in the sunlight. "But does it matter?"

The eyes around the table followed her every movement. Oh how she loved to play the game. She returned her hand to the table and continued, "My estate in the hills is under remodel, again." An elaborate eye roll. "But once it's complete, you all need to come out for a visit. We'll have a roast. Raid the wine cellar. It will be divine."

She floated her expensive hand to her mouth for another sip of her drink.

"And now you're free for a better engagement, dear," said Loelia, one of Valentina's best friends, with a wink.

"I hear a certain wealthy, handsome merchant has become available," Sabina's face lit up, long lashes batting, as she conspicuously ignored the court lady sitting on her right—Amber, the merchant's recent ex. "He'd be perfect for you."

"Why would you waste your time on a merchant when you could be courted by a royal?" scoffed Amelia.

"Because this merchant is as rich as any royal and far more handsome," Sabina answered, and the table erupted into laughter. Except Amber, who remained silent.

"Not to mention that what Isaac lacks in stature, he makes up for in influence," Loelia added. "You see the way the other high society members act around him at court."

"But he's not even Azantium. He's from Thalis, of all places," Amelia said, screwing up her face, still unconvinced.

"And a drunk," Amber added sourly, reaching for her own drink.

"Sometimes a man just needs a little light in his life, a little spark, to cure him of such indecencies," Valentina said, a coy smirk upon her lips. Amber's cheeks grew red. Loelia and Sabina smiled maliciously, hooding their eyes in mock consideration.

Amber spoke up, attempting to change the subject. Valentina let her. She sat back in her chair, not bothering to listen as Amber droned on about something insignificant. Some people just did not play the game well.

Her day would consist of this late morning tea with the girls and then court with the royals in the afternoon.

It was a tiring schedule, always having to be on display: her hair perfect, her outfit stunning, her makeup flawless. But Valentina did not mind. She had worked hard to get to this position, and she intended to keep it. Bedding Isaac would help with that and unlike that idiot Amber, she would not lose him.

The bells chimed. It was time for court. Valentina's heart fluttered.

Valentina smiled at Sabina and Loelia as they all stood and hooked arms. Loelia's blond hair hung in loose ringlets, framing her stunning blue eyes. Her family were wealthy landowners of crop fields and slaves. As high society members, her family lived inside the capital walls while Loelia, a court lady, lived inside the palace. Sabina's blond hair, so light it looked nearly white, was done up in a fancy twist. She was the only child of a duke and had grown up with her father in the palace.

Valentina loved having them on either side of her, two perfect porcelain dolls.

The girls laughed together, arms around each other's waists as they made their way to the Royal Court Chamber. The game was on. Let the hunt begin.

Valentina looked without appearing to look. It was a skill she had mastered. There was Isaac, talking to Lord Stefor. Stefor was Baron Cato's son. Her face puckered at the thought of the foul Baron.

Isaac, though, was finely dressed—handsome and well-built. She imagined it would thrill him to be involved with a high-class woman like her. She could improve his status far more than Amber ever could. He had probably never bedded a woman as high-ranking as she. The thought thrilled her. When he finished talking to the lord, she would get his attention.

In the meantime, she approached the Countess Birgette.

"Don't you look delightful today, Valentina," the countess said.

"Why thank you. But I pale in comparison to your radiance, my lady," Valentina said, with a curtsy and a smile.

The countess's best years were behind her, but if a girl wanted to succeed, she needed to befriend the woman. Her connections were impeccable and she had all the latest dish on fashion.

They talked of the new fabrics and colors of the season. But Valentina could not focus. She continued to look, without looking, for Isaac.

Finally Isaac stood alone, checking his watch. Valentina excused herself and sauntered over to him.

"Pleasant day, sir," she began.

Isaac looked up at her and raised an eyebrow. Then—could it possibly be?—he rolled his eyes. It stunned her. Surely she had imagined it.

One of the servant girls approached them with a tray of drinks. She had tattoos on her hands, the poor, hideous little beast. Valentina helped herself to a drink and selected one to offer Isaac, but when she glanced up she almost choked to see the way he was looking at the girl. Valentina snapped her head back to her, but the girl had already curtsied and walked away.

Maybe Isaac enjoyed giving it to lesser women. That explained Amber, and that would not suit. Valentina could not afford to foul herself with that kind of man. She had just spurned the baron for the same reason.

But Isaac had quite a reputation too. The High Merchant, the wealthiest man in Azantium. He worked closely with the queen herself. Surely that was worth something.

"Excuse me," Isaac said, with a cold indifference.

Valentina looked Isaac up and down. How dare he. She dropped a stunted curtsy and walked away from him.

By the time the court adjourned Valentina was fuming. The sparkle of the day was gone, and she was left with a foul mood.

The ladies left the Royal Court Chamber. As they started down the hallway, Valentina realized she had left her gloves on the table.

She hurried back to look for them, and had just spotted them on the table when the sound of muffled voices from the servants' nook caught her attention.

"There's a party tonight. Come with me!"

Valentina paused. Slaves sneaking out?

"I don't know. I'm meeting Armaiti tomorrow night."

"Oh, come on! Live a little. It will be fun."

"Okay, but just for a bit. A quick visit and right back."

Valentina scurried away before she was seen and went straight to the head of house's chamber. She hated going to the slaves' quarters. She would have to take a thorough bath afterwards.

"Yes?" snapped the head of house as she opened the door. She was wearing a hideous white bonnet. "Oh, excuse me, my lady. I'm not used to such fine visitors." She gave a deep curtsy.

Valentina put on her most disapproving pout.

"I will have you know I heard two of the slaves plotting to sneak out tonight for some party. It will not suit to have such disobedience in the Royal Court."

"I'm deeply sorry. Which two servants did you hear?"

Rolling her eyes, Valentina answered, "They served the Royal Court this afternoon. One had tattoos on her hands and purple eyes. And the other one had black hair."

"Doe and Blue. That is unfortunate; they're two of our best."

"I hope you take care of it, or I will voice my concerns to the queen herself," said Valentina, imperious, and she turned on her heel and walked away, smiling to herself.

9

It was market day in the capital. Mæve had never seen the markets, and she would have been excited by them if she wasn't so nervous about their plan.

Betha's friend, Anders, was a chef in the palace and had written Betha a note explaining the girls were to go to the market to buy supplies for the kitchens. The note would provide cover for them to sneak away to Anders' house, where the party was being held.

Now Betha stood before the guard at the front gate, handing him the little crumpled paper. Mæve's heart thudded so loudly she was certain he could hear it. He scrutinized the paper, squinting, then motioned Betha and Mæve through the gate.

Once they were through, Mæve let out a wavering breath.

"Were you worried?" Betha asked with a smile.

"Yes," Mæve admitted.

"I told you, I've been doing this for years."

Her friend threw her arm around Mæve's shoulders.

"Don't worry. We'll be back in a few hours, and in our beds before they do the nightly head count. Now try to enjoy yourself."

Betha was right. It wasn't worth sneaking out to a party if she just worried the whole time.

"Hold on," Betha said. "We're meeting a friend on the way."

Maeve's eyebrows arched. Betha had never mentioned a friend.

They walked south, in the direction Isaac had taken her on their ride last month. The market tents peppered the grassy knoll just outside the capital walls.

They stopped at a woodworker's tent.

"Betha!" A stunning woman approached, removing an apron. She had tawny skin and long coffee-colored hair, woven with wooden and jade beads. Her eyes were the color of sandstone.

The two women embraced, and Betha said, "This is my friend, Maeve. She's also a slave in the palace. Maeve, this is Giselle. She's a woodworker from Epoth."

"Selling my wares, raising money for the tax collector," Giselle said with a good-natured smile. She disappeared into the rear of the tent, then returned, with a basket draped over one arm.

"What did you bring this year?" Betha asked, peeking into the basket.

"Black current pie," responded Giselle.

Maeve noticed the way Giselle looked at Betha. She suspected this was the real reason Betha snuck out to the party each year.

"Ah, amazing!" Betha said with a warm smile as she laced one hand through Giselle's arm and the other through Maeve's. "Berit's cottage is right over there." Betha nodded to a small cluster of homes outside the capital walls in front of them, where many indentured servants and low-wage workers lived.

"I'm glad you could join us this year, Maeve," Giselle said. "Berit's party is always a lot of fun. Plus, it's the one time of year I get some time with this one," she said, giving Betha a playful squeeze.

Maeve smiled at her friend, pleased to see her so happy, but feeling oddly lonely.

"I'm glad you're here, too," Betha said, "It'll be good for you to get out, and you never know who you might meet."

"It's how I got connected with the rebellion," Giselle added, smiling.

Maeve's head snapped towards her.

"And I wish you wouldn't," Betha replied. "It's foolish and dangerous."

"Well, you best keep those thoughts to yourself, Betha Ceallaigh," Giselle said. "Because there will be a lot of us at this party."

Mæve's heart fluttered, and her palms grew sweaty again. She thought about turning around, but Betha squeezed her arm tighter.

"Well we're not here to talk politics," Betha said. "We're going to the party to have fun."

"And here we are," Giselle added.

They'd reached a humble cottage, with laughing children scampering through the yard. Small, circular lights hung across the trees and shrubs, casting a soft glow. It was so charming, Mæve almost forgot her trepidation at being there.

The front door stood open, allowing the smell of baking bread to waft out as the three women approached. Once inside, Betha ran up to a tiny blonde woman with twinkling blue eyes and hugged her.

"Berit! It's so great to see you," Betha said.

"Betha! How long has it been, dear? Oh, no matter, no matter. It's great to see you," she said, and gave Betha a wink. But Betha missed it, distracted by the table of food.

"You remember Giselle?" she responded, "And this is my friend, Mæve. She's new here."

"Oh, yes. Welcome, welcome. Help yourselves to drinks and food." Berit approached Mæve, lightly clasping her arms as she smiled up at her. "Mæve. Wow, you're a looker, aren't you? My, my, but far too thin. Need to eat up while you here. Give you some good food to take back with you, stuff in your pockets," and Berit wrapped her arm around Mæve's waist. "Come with me, honey. I've got someone I want you to meet."

As they entered the adjacent room, Mæve's jaw dropped in surprise. Isaac, High Merchant of Azantium, sat in a chair, drink in hand, dressed more modestly than his typical palace attire. His hair was an impossible mess, as if he had been running his fingers through it all day.

When he spotted Mæve, a look of surprise danced across his face.

"Isaac, meet Mæve. Mæve, Isaac," Berit announced, a triumphant look on her face.

"What a pleasant surprise," Isaac said with a wide smile.

She curtsied and replied, "Sir."

Isaac laughed out loud. The sound jolted Mæve. What was funny?

"You know each other?" Berit asked.

"We do indeed," he said, raising his glass towards them, his drink sloshing over the side. "Nice to see you out in the world, though I'm a little worried as to how you're here." Was he slurring?

"No need to worry, Isaac. She came with a friend. Anders wrote them a note. They'll be just fine."

"And what are *you* doing here?" Mæve asked. "This doesn't seem like your crowd."

"Oh, no dear, Isaac is a good friend of our family," Berit answered. "A little rough around the edges. Could use some work." And Berit nudged Mæve, flashing her a smile. "Needs a girl that won't take any of his shit, that's for true, but he's a very good man here, you mark my words. Now I need to get back to those biscuits." And Berit waddled off.

"Please, have a seat," Isaac said as he took a sip of his drink. His eyes were glassy.

"You're drunk," Mæve said.

"I am."

"I should find Betha—"

Isaac interrupted. "I've been looking for your parents." Mæve drew in a breath and Isaac continued, "A few friends of mine are scouring the Hall of Records. If they were logged, we'll find them."

"Thank you," she said. She felt bad about wanting to leave now, and then she wondered if that was what he had intended, but as she looked at him sitting alone she recalled the pain she'd seen in his eyes the night she had met him.

"Why do you work for the royals?"

"That is a long and complicated story," Isaac responded.

"You're not from here, are you?" Mæve asked.

"That's right. I'm from Thalis." A deep swig of his drink. "I gathered all my intellect, all my passion, and I battled my way up a giant mountain of shit, from the slums of Thalis to the high society of Azantium. Now, I sit up here on my liar's throne, surrounded by more fineries and wealth than any man could need."

"Give me that." Mæve took his drink and dumped it in a nearby plant.

Isaac looked at her, incredulous. "Did you just dump my drink in that plant?"

Mæve raised an eyebrow. Isaac chuckled.

"That's something I've probably needed for the past ten years."

Betha and Giselle entered the room, sharing a plate of food and laughing together.

Betha glanced at Mæve and mouthed *you okay*?

Mæve nodded.

"How are you doing? Life in the palace cannot be pleasant for you." Isaac said.

Mæve hesitated, looking at him. He met her eyes calmly.

"It's terrible."

"Well, we have that in common then," Isaac said. He appeared to be considering something. "There is a way out."

The merchant smiled mischievously, and Mæve's skin tingled.

"If you can trust me," Isaac said.

"Trust you? A man who lies for a living?"

Isaac laughed. "I lie to people I don't respect. And if lying is the worst I do after a decade of working for those royal fucks, then that's not too bad."

"What is my way out that you have in mind? If I trust you. Which I don't."

"At first, I thought I could buy you. But it turns out there are these arcane Azantium by-laws that state royal servants cannot be bought. Probably has to do with sensitivities around working with the royals."

Mæve narrowed her eyes. Buy her?

"So then, I thought, well, if I can't buy you," the merchant continued, ignoring her glare. "I could ask the queen if I can marry you—"

"Marry me!" Mæve stared at him. "You're out of your mind, merchant."

He placed a gentle hand on her arm. "Please hear me out.

Come to my estate in the hills. You'll have as much space as you desire; you need never see me if that's what you prefer. You'll never have to see another royal again, either. We can bring your friend too, if you like."

"I can't leave the palace," Mæve said. "I can't leave my parents behind."

"We can look for them once you're out," Isaac said.

She paused. It was so tempting. She hesitated, thinking of Betha's friend Malqi, and Isaac laughed.

"You mean to tell me you'd rather remain a slave than be free?"

Mæve thought she might slap him, but she paused, trying not to shake with the anger over his arrogance.

"You are asking me to exchange one cage for another."

"No, no," Isaac responded without hesitation. "You would have your freedom. Stay married to me for a year or two. I promise I won't touch you. And then you can leave me—I'll even give you money, if that's what you need. We'll find your parents together..."

Mæve shook her head. Her thoughts were muddy.

"Why?" Mæve asked him. "Why are you helping me?"

Isaac blushed and faltered for a moment.

"I told you, I help slaves however I can."

"Why?"

Isaac ran a hand through his hair, further tousling his dark curls.

"Look, I've done... things in life that I'm not proud of. Made some poor decisions."

He paused for a long moment, lost in thought.

"I guess I'm working on changing that."

She could appreciate that, and it made her very uneasy.

"I appreciate your offer, Isaac. I'm touched, actually. But don't you want to marry someone you love?" Mæve asked.

"I loved someone once, but... it didn't end well."

"I'm sorry to hear that."

Isaac shook his head as if shaking away her apology. A darkness had settled into his eyes.

"She was Lumani. It was ill-fated." How surprising to learn Isaac had also cared for a Lumani.

"Can't you talk to her, try to make it better?" Mæve suggested.

Isaac kept his eyes down. There was a slight tick at the corner of his mouth.

"Not possible, I'm afraid." Isaac seemed desperate to change the subject. "And you? Have you ever been in love?"

Mæve would not tell him about Armaiti but had an ambiguous answer ready when Betha chimed in from the other side of the small room, a bottle of wine in hand, obviously listening in on their conversation.

"Mæve's falling for a Lumani," she said to Isaac, rolling her eyes in exasperation.

"Betha!" Mæve couldn't believe her friend.

"What Mæve? I told you it wasn't a good idea. Maybe you'll listen to Isaac," Betha said.

Mæve was fuming, and thankfully Giselle took the bottle of wine from Betha and led her back towards the kitchen.

"Come on," Giselle said. "I think you've had enough to drink. Let's get you some water. You two need to be leaving soon." Giselle tossed Mæve a wink, and led Betha out of the room.

"A Lumani?" Isaac asked. "Well, you certainly are full of surprises, Mæve. And how did you meet him? They don't allow Lumani slaves in the palace."

"I could ask the same of you."

"I lived amongst the Lumani for a time and something sparked between us but it's forbidden you know."

"I'm aware," Mæve said.

"So I left, and that was that. Then I saw her at the Chrysillium Field years later. She tried to escape, they caught her, and killed her."

"Oh Isaac." She wanted to reach out to the merchant but he continued speaking.

"Mæve, you are in danger at the Palace of Light. I want to help you. You don't need to give me an answer about my proposal tonight. Maybe think about it."

She nodded. "I will. I need to go now."

"I'll walk you out," Isaac replied.

They said their goodbyes to Berit. As they stepped outside, Mæve turned to Isaac.

"I appreciate all you're doing for me and the other slaves." A pause, then: "You're a good person."

She touched his arm, then she turned and joined Betha's side.

As soon as they were out of sight of Berit's cozy home, Betha started bouncing.

"So what was going on between you and Isaac?"

Mæve gave Betha a truncated version of Isaac's proposal and his offer to help.

"Are you fucking kidding me? Isaac Houghton? Gods Mæve, please tell me you said yes?"

"I didn't give him an answer," Mæve replied. "I don't know, Betha. It sounds nice, but there's something not right about him. He's trying to be a good person, but I think he's looking for something from me. Some kind of pardon for being who he is, and I can't give him that. And besides, I don't love him."

Betha laughed. "Listen, love is nothing more than false promises from men to control stupid women. Soulmates don't exist. There is money and there is power and that's all. Isaac has both. All Armaiti has offered you are the reasons he can't be with you, while Isaac is practically begging at your feet. Isaac promises you a future; your freedom. A way to make money. You're a fool to turn him down."

"I don't feel completely comfortable accepting help from someone who lies, drinks, and works for the royals. What's keeping me from ending up like your friend and that wealthy lord who bought her?" Mæve retorted. Betha quickened her walk, getting ahead of Mæve.

"You're being so selfish," Betha responded. "This is about your Lumani friend. Did you even consider that maybe I would like to get out of the palace? Away from life as a slave with no hope for escape? But no, you've turned away our freedom for some blasted guy in the woods feeding you nonsense!"

Mæve gasped and stopped walking. "That's just not true. None of it, Betha." Betha stormed ahead.

Mæve and Betha approached the front gate. The guards took Betha's note and waved them through. They walked to the entrance of the slave quarters located just outside the stables.

They approached the stairs that led up to their sleeping quarters, and waiting for them at the foot of the stairs, was the head of house— arms crossed, a guard at her side. "Blue, Doe, come with me," she said.

They obeyed. Mæve tried to remain calm. They followed her into an empty room and she locked the door.

"It was brought to my attention that you two snuck out for a party tonight."

Betha stepped forward.

"It's my fault, Mistress, really. Doe had nothing to do with this."

"No, Betha," Mæve interrupted.

"I care not," the head of house said. "The punishment for such behavior is twenty lashes."

They blanched, and the head of house continued. "You will be stripped of your titles as royal servants and you will return to your old duties in the palace. Also, I was told that one of you, and I'm not sure who, has been sneaking out to meet a lover. As a result, you will sleep together in the same room with an armed guard outside your door. Clearly, you two cannot be trusted."

Betha cried out as the guard tied her hands to a hook suspended from the ceiling. Mæve trembled as the guard did the same to her. Her back was to Betha, but she heard everything. The crack of the whip, the tearing flesh. Betha's horrible screams filled the room.

Tears rolled down Mæve's cheeks.

When Betha's screams became whimpers, Mæve felt Ms. Eda's

hands on her, pulling the top of Mæve's dress open. The impact of the first stroke would have knocked her to the ground if her hands hadn't been bound. The flesh being torn from her skin was unlike anything she had ever felt. She almost yelled out. Almost. But she stayed silent even as her legs buckled at her seventh lash. Even after the whipping was over and she lay on the ground in a pool of her own blood.

She would give them nothing.

10

Crisp golden corn stalks reached high into a cool gray sky. Farm hands toiled in the fields. Signs of harvest time in the Azantium kingdom. Isaac pulled the lapels of his jacket tighter around his neck and drew a rolled cigarette from his pocket. *Let us hope it's not another Bloody Harvest.*

Berit had been kind enough to let him crash at her place last night. Now the late morning walk suited him. The crisp air was invigorating as he made his way into the city.

He remembered bits and pieces of his conversation with Mæve. She was considering his proposal. He supposed that was a good thing, but he hoped he hadn't made a complete ass of himself last night. He really needed to stop drinking. And that wasn't the only reason.

It had happened again last night. He had moved something just by thinking about it, which was ludicrous and impossible. Until now, he'd thought he must be imagining it. It seemed to only happen when he was drunk and alone. But last night he had bumped into the shelf in Berit's kitchen and, out of the corner of his eye, he'd seen a little porcelain sheep fall from the ledge. Isaac had reached for the object and it had stopped midair. He hadn't even touched it.

Berit had gaped at him. Isaac walked up to the sheep and plucked it out of the air, placing it back on the shelf.

He turned to look at Berit. She was even whiter than normal, her eyes wide in disbelief.

"I think I may have had myself too much wine tonight," she said, as if in a daze. "Good night, Isaac."

Isaac had wished her a good night. So she was blaming it on drinking, too. But Isaac could no longer deny what he had done, even if it was completely unfathomable. He had stopped that sheep from falling. His mother's stories about his uncle came back to him.

Maybe he should take some time off. If he had done that in front of the wrong people, it could get him killed. Ten years working for the royals and he had never once taken a break. He would journey to the eastern edge of the kingdom, where the Mycellium Forest was. He thought there might be answers there.

He had been reading about the Mycellium for some time now, collecting as many books on the magical forest as he could find. It was thought to be the abode of the gods and was forbidden even before the binding. Terrifying creatures were said to dwell there— glyphium protectors, the falstorm. Said to be the personal guardian of queen goddess Shålan, falstorm were giant harpy-like birds that could conjure storms and tear a person apart with their sharp- hooked beaks. But worst were their humanoid eyes, said to be able to lull a person into a trance state even as the falstorm ate them alive.

Well, he could use a good adventure. But first, he needed to make this trip into the capital. It was something that had been bothering him for a month now, and he finally had some time this morning to address it.

Isaac walked through the capital gates, nodding to the guards. They knew him well. Azantium's finest strolled the streets of the capital this afternoon. The clicking of their heels on cobblestone added to the late afternoon cacophony of conversations, laughter, and occasional boisterous greetings between friends. They were the usual sounds, typical sounds, and Isaac exhaled in relief. If another

Bloody Harvest was looming, these folks would not be here. The royals would draw high society members inside the Palace of Light. Like last time.

The deaths had been terrible. Five years ago, for reasons unknown, the royals had pulled the harvest inside the palace—months and months' worth of food, disappearing into the vast royal storerooms while the villagers were left with nothing. They had gathered the high society members within the sanctity of the Palace of Light and put it in lockdown. The guards tripled, and they brought the army inside the castle walls. Starvation wiped out entire families and villages, and many more were executed for stealing money or food.

The royals had kept Isaac safe within the palace walls throughout Bloody Harvest. He was curious about why they were being locked inside, but the only answer he received was that it wasn't safe to go out. At that point Isaac was still enjoying his newfound wealth and notoriety. He hadn't known of the starvation and the killings until the following spring, when the palace opened up again and he saw the hollowed, tortured eyes of the common folk.

For a people to kill their own, so ruthlessly, for such petty things... it disturbed Isaac. Even more distressing was that he seemed to be alone in these sentiments amongst his high society comrades. Isaac had felt powerless, but his eyes were opened. Bloody Harvest was the first sign of many that all was not as it appeared in the capital.

From the fear and terror of Bloody Harvest, the rebellion was born. Isaac learned of it the following year at one of Berit's parties. With the utmost discretion, he had begun funding it. His first move had been to buy three large printing presses to help the rebellion spread news and recruit new members.

Then, the following year, Isaac had helped Malwa escape. It had taken months—Isaac had first needed to get his close friend Adrian established as an enforcer in the Red Guard. What a harrowing experience that first slave escape had been. So much so, Isaac didn't do it again for another year.

Then they helped Ji escape. Another Lumani slave, who had made it successfully out. And then there had been Lilya. Ripped apart by grief, doubt, and self-loathing, Isaac had promised himself he'd never do it again. But one day he'd noticed how quickly Mohlin was deteriorating. He knew the Lumani man would die if he didn't help him.

He hoped Mohlin had made it to Idris.

Isaac pulled deep from his cigarette as he sauntered down the cobblestone street lined with neat townhouses. These were the preferred dwellings of high society, providing a sheltered life for them to carry on business in the palace and live their lives free from the peasantry.

He nodded at a small gathering of fellow merchants mingling with a few high society gentlemen. The wealthy men nodded back with respect and appreciation, but the merchants sneered as Isaac walked past. They eyed Isaac's rolled cigarette and scoffed as they puffed from their more stylish long-stemmed pipes. He loved how he befuddled their narrow scope of existence while they stood puffy faced and bloated, squeezed uncomfortably into their fancy clothes. They could have their decorum. Isaac smiled a wolfish grin as he continued on his way, tall, lithe, and charming.

The Palace of Light loomed above the neat rows of townhouses. Isaac was not going to the palace today, but he wondered what Mæve might be doing in there right now.

Getting lost with thoughts of Mæve was easy lately. She had captured his mind. This was uncharted territory for Isaac, and he wasn't sure he liked it. Everything in his past had centered on his career. He had even designed his romantic relationships on what was best for his image, what was best for business. This was how Isaac's teacher had taught him to be in the world.

But somehow this mysterious, captivating slave woman cut through all of that. Maybe because she was a foreigner and deep down Isaac was still a foreigner too, even after all these years. Maybe because he was ready for something else, needed something else if he were to survive. Mæve demanded Isaac be himself, something no one had demanded of him in some time. Furthermore, she seemed impervious to his charms. Even more surprising was that Isaac was ready for that. Someone who could see him for who he was and still care enough to sit beside him and toss his drink in a plant.

A cool breeze stirred the red scarf at Isaac's throat. He took another drag of his cigarette and then tossed the stub away. He needed to focus. Letting down his guard, even for a moment, could be dangerous today.

For three months, Isaac had been trying to break away from his duties, to venture outside the palace into the capital center. A place he despised and avoided, but today's trip was necessary. He needed to pay a visit to an old acquaintance, someone from Isaac's first years in the capital. Back before he knew better.

He was headed for Darkstar Bookery, owned by Ravial Elvinus.

Rav made Isaac's skin crawl. Tall, skeletal, and alabaster pale, with ebony hair—unusual, in Azantium—the man looked more dead than alive.

Rav had some of the best connections in the kingdom. If anyone knew about the new weapon the queen had spoken about, it would be Rav.

Darkstar was a small but exquisite shop that specialized in rare book sales. Isaac pushed open the door and the musty scents of paper and myrrh infiltrated his nose. Rav pilfered works of literature from countries under Azantium subjugation for a pittance. Then he sold them for an augmented fee here in the capital, safely tucked away behind the castle walls, by pegging them as rare exotic items that the foolish pride-bent Azantium elite could show off on their coffee tables and bookshelves.

A large wrought iron chandelier hung in the middle of the bookstore. Isaac wiped his feet as a tall, impossibly pale figure came striding around the corner to greet him.

"Isaac." Rav's voice sounded like crunching leaves.

"Ravial," Isaac greeted the dank merchant with exaggerated

exuberance, opening his arms wide. The horror that twisted Rav's face was hilarious, and Isaac had to swallow a laugh, though he could not contain his smile. The weasel-like book merchant was *not* a hugger. Rav instead turned and pretended to tidy up a few stray books.

"And to what do I owe this pleasant, quite unexpected surprise? Care to place another order?"

Isaac had bought many books from Rav—and unlike most of Rav's clients, Isaac actually read them. He looked at Rav as he slowly sauntered about the shop.

"I'm looking for something about a weapon. A weapon being kept under wraps by a ruling party. Got anything like that?"

"Ah, yes," Rav croaked. "I think I have something for you, but it's going to cost you, my friend."

"You know me, Rav. Money is no object when it comes to good knowledge."

"Here, it is in my... rare book collection. You'll have to come with me into the back room."

Isaac did a quick look around the shop. Empty. Then he followed Rav into his office. Rav shut the door and Isaac took a seat in the familiar room. Rav grabbed a bottle of wine and two glasses. As he opened the wine bottle, he said, "The information you seek is very secretive and being held tightly by the royals."

Rav poured the blood-red liquid into Isaac's glass and then his own, his hawk-like eyes honed in on Isaac.

"But of course," Isaac replied casually, raising his wineglass to Rav's to clink it. The liquid was warm and hinted of vanilla and clove. Rav really knew his wine. "Will a thousand marks cover it?"

"Make it two," Rav said, without missing a beat.

Isaac almost spit out his wine.

"I risk my neck to tell you this information, Isaac Houghton, and my neck is worth a lot more than two thousand marks."

Isaac ran his fingers through his hair.

"Fine Rav, but this better be good."

"It is," Rav said. He got up and moved around his large desk to sit behind it, across from Isaac.

Isaac took out two coin purses, added a handful of coins to one and handed it to Rav. Satisfied with its weight, Rav began.

"They are calling it the labaldis. It's similar to the labaton—labas is heated through an incendiary device and creates poisonous toxins. But rather than a small projectile like the labaton, it is much larger and capable of creating an explosion that can kill many people at once. Of course it's not nearly as mobile as labaton, but it doesn't need to be. It can rip through an entire chunk of an army in one shot, killing ten, maybe even twenty people at once. I'm told it's so powerful that it can even fell large trees."

Isaac felt as if the air had been knocked out of him. He asked the question he already knew the answer to.

"What do the royals intend to do with such a weapon?"

Rav took a long swig from his wineglass, savoring the taste for a moment before returning his piercing stare to Isaac.

"To annihilate the Lumani, of course."

"King Regauld would never allow it," Isaac said. The king was a fervent supporter of the Treaty of Falls Hollow. He didn't want war. Nobody wanted war.

Rav cackled. "As if the king has much to say about it these days. He is oblivious to the weapon's development as he wastes away in his bedchamber. How much longer do you think he has before death takes him?"

It made sense. The dying trees, the dying king. Isaac thought he might be sick.

He left the bookstore in a haze, finding himself with a stack of books he did not need and his coin purse significantly lighter.

There was another piece of this bothering him. He was the High Merchant of Azantium. His product was labas. Why had the queen kept this information from him?

Isaac needed time, time to think, but he didn't have time. He could not sit idly by while the royals destroyed his beloved Lumani like they had so many other cultures; so many other divergent ways of being in the world snuffed out for the homogeneity of control.

Isaac stepped out into the cool early evening air. The cornstalks reflected the red hue from the setting sun. It looked like blood; it looked like violence, this fire red sun on the horizon and the shadows that followed.

11

A cool mist dotted Mæve's face and chilled her bare chest. The dampness kept her alert in the indigo hours just before dawn. The hunt had begun. Mæve was sixteen, and this was her first time running with the huntresses. They wove through the thickest part of the forest, east of their small village.

Her mother ran beside her, skin shimmering with dew and sweat in the moonlight. Isa had taught Mæve all she knew: how to wield a bow and arrow, how to track, how to fell an animal. Mæve was honored to run beside her; Isa would be leading the hunt that day.

The nine women paused atop a hill. Below them, through a break in the trees, Mæve could see their village. It perched at the edge of the forest, where the trees gave way to rolling fields. The fields ran down toward the harbor, where they abruptly ended with a steep drop to the sea below. Small, dark objects on the waves indicated the boats where Mæve's father and the other men fished in the harbor.

The women took off again. They ran in formation: two in front, two on each side, and two in back. Gale, their tracker, ran ahead of the formation, searching for tracks and scat from the stag they pursued.

The dense canopy of the woods kept the forest floor cool and dark. After years of training, the huntresses knew the woods well. Mæve, however, was still learning and determined to do well.

Like her mother, Mæve wore a flat leather quiver strapped to her back, leather bracers on her wrists, and deer-skin pants tucked into her boots.

"Isa, Gale has spotted the stag over that hill," Quinn reported, slinging her large staff over her broad shoulders.

Isa smiled at her daughter. "Ready?"

Mæve nodded and drew an arrow. Her mother ran to one side of the hill as she ran to the other. It was her first hunt, and she would prove her worth. Nocking an arrow as she ran, she crested the hill and leapt into the air, fully expecting to see the stag on the other side. But it wasn't there.

Mæve's surprise knocked her off balance, and she fumbled her landing. She knew how to fall and did not injure herself, but just before she hit the ground she caught movement in her peripheral vision. The stag stood obscured behind a large boulder.

Stags were fierce creatures, and made even more dangerous by their antlers and powerful necks. As Mæve scrambled to her feet, this one put his head down and charged. He was too close for her to draw an arrow. She dodged, but its antler clipped her shoulder, sending her spiraling to the ground. The pain in her shoulder was excruciating but there was no time. With her good arm, Mæve pulled a shinal from her boot.

The stag charged.

She moved to the creature's oblique and swiped at the tendons behind his forward right knee. The stag stumbled. Mæve looped around the beast and sliced again just behind its ear, dragging the blade down the middle of his neck. The beast fell with a thud. Its legs twitched and then stopped.

The cheers from her fellow huntresses surrounded her. She had done it. The thrill of the hunt still coursed through her veins as the women gathered around the dal-stag to honor him before stringing him up to carry home. Mæve looked anxiously to her mother, expecting approval.

"That was foolish, daughter," Isa said. "We huntresses work as a team. Today you were lucky, but luck will not keep you alive."

Isa turned and walked away, the forest consuming her as it blurred and faded... *No, wait! Please, not yet!*

Mæve woke to a cruel boot jabbing into her side. She groaned in protest and opened her eyes to the red-faced head of house.

"Wake up, you. There is work to be done."

Mæve tried to push herself up from her bed, but searing pain engulfed her body. Her muscles would not obey her command. She attempted to push herself up, but her limbs buckled and she crashed back upon the bed.

"I can't," she stammered. "I can't get up."

Ms. Eda grabbed her under her shoulders and hoisted her up, and Mæve screamed. The abrupt movement ripped open the newly-formed scabs on her back. It hurt worse than the lashing from the night before. The other women sharing Mæve's room backed away from the unfolding scene.

The head of house moved on to her friend. Betha screamed too as the woman lifted her up with a similar callousness.

"Downstairs in five minutes," Ms. Eda shouted, and she left.

Mæve reached for Betha's hand. "Are you all right?" she whispered.

Betha pulled away, eyes cast down.

"Let me help you with that," Mæve offered, and assisted Betha with her corset, tying it loosely before helping her friend into her dress. Betha helped Mæve in return, but her face remained sullen. Mæve's torn and seeping skin burned as she moved. She thought she might vomit, but swallowed it. Slaves that could not work were useless, and useless slaves disappeared.

They shuffled out the door and struggled down the stairs where the head of house stood waiting, tapping her foot. She assigned Mæve to clean tapestries in the west hallway. An impossible task considering her injuries, but she did her best without complaint.

By the end of the day, her back hurt so much she couldn't lift her arms anymore. Her wounds were not healing properly. Her skin was clammy, and a low fever was setting in. Exhausted, she was ready to return to her room. Her body would only mend if she could rest.

As she started back towards the slave quarters, she ran square into Lucius and he smiled like a wolf.

"No more work in the royal chambers?" he asked.

"Your Highness," Mæve said with a grimace and a curtsy.

He stepped in close to her. She kept her eyes down, her stomach doing flips, pain temporarily forgotten. Lucius put one of his hands against the wall behind her and leaned in close. Mæve had to turn her head, or their noses would have touched. His breath smelled like curdled milk.

"I was so sorry to hear of your demotion, but you know there is a silver lining." He flashed her another smile and she seethed.

"I need to get back to my quarters now, sir." She maneuvered her body away from his obtrusive arm and scurried down the hall.

"I look forward to seeing you again," he called out after her.

Mæve kept moving and hoped he wouldn't follow. When she got to her room, she changed into her shift with great care so as not to further tear her back. She climbed into bed and sank into her pillow, grateful for rest.

Later, she woke when Betha curled up next to her in bed. The sun had set. Mæve rolled over and looked at her friend. She regretted not immediately saying yes to Isaac. If she had, maybe none of this would have happened. Maybe they'd already be free.

She knew she could not see Armaiti tonight, and it weighed on her. She hoped he would not worry. Their meeting would have to wait for the next full moon and she could explain then why she had missed their meeting tonight. She closed her eyes and saw the dancing indigo branches of Oyela. She imagined the warmth of his arms around her, and she slipped again into an exhausted slumber.

Armaiti waited by the pond. It was late. He focused on the stillness of the water and the way the late-summer breeze kissed the tips of his ears, flowing through his long hair. He closed his eyes and breathed in the memory of her.

But his tender thoughts were bittersweet. Not only had the elders denied him and Iraji another meeting to further discuss their proposal for alternatives to marriage, things were worsening with the Air Clan. Jaleh told him he needed to marry Iraji now and Armaiti believed she was right. The Lumani needed to be at their strongest. They could not wait any longer.

Iraji did not know yet, but Armaiti planned to talk with her tomorrow. She would not be pleased, but she needed to know.

Armaiti paced as he waited for Mæve to arrive. Her departure on the last moon still sat uneasily with him. She had said his feelings for her were foolish, and she was right. He hoped she would understand, then, about his decision to go ahead with the wedding. She might even have some insight into his situation, something he had not yet thought of.

He waited, and the night stretched on. Still, Mæve did not arrive. Armaiti's worry grew. Was she okay? Had they caught her sneaking out to see him? The moon continued with its descent, and still Mæve did not arrive. Armaiti's conviction grew: something must be wrong.

He ran fast through the night, skirting the perimeter of Idris. Iraji was on patrol; Iraji would understand.

He found her quickly.

"Armaiti! I thought you were meeting Mæve tonight. I was keeping away from the eastern border to give you two some privacy."

"She didn't show up," Armaiti said.

"What?"

"Something must be wrong." Armaiti struggled to keep his voice even. "I'm worried about her."

"Maybe she forgot," Iraji suggested, with a little shrug.

"She would never. I think she's in trouble."

"What can I do?"

Armaiti sighed and arched his eyebrows. "Can you go check on her?" He tried to keep his tone light, to undercut the gravity of the request. He failed.

"Zama's breathe, tell me you're joking," Iraji snapped back at him.

"If you don't go, I will. I need to know she's okay."

"Have you lost your mind? The new Lumani king cannot be peeping in the windows of the Palace of Light."

"That's why I need you to do it. No one will see you. You are the quickest, stealthiest person I know."

"Oh, funny how you admit that now, when you want something."

Armaiti gave her an exasperated frown.

"Okay, Okay," Iraji said. "What do I need to do?"

———

Two hours had passed. If Iraji did not return soon, Armaiti would have to go after her. But at the dark sky's first hint of light, he saw her coming through the trees.

Armaiti ran to her side. "Are you okay?"

"Yes," Iraji gasped, attempting to catch her breath. "I found her."

"You're sure it was her?" Armaiti asked.

"I recognized her through the window, and she had the tattoos on her hands."

"And?"

"She was sleeping," Iraji said gently, her face showing her compassion for her friend. Armaiti's worry melted into relief.

"Just... sleeping?"

"Yes, peacefully," Iraji continued. "She was in a room with many other women, on the third floor of the slave quarters. I could not go in and wake her with so many others in the room, but she looked to be okay."

"Thank you, Iraji," Armaiti said, embracing his friend. "What a relief to know she is okay." But why had she not come to tell him she did not want to meet with him anymore?

Armaiti tried to tell himself that this was better for her. She wouldn't have to put herself in danger anymore to ride out and meet him. But he suspected she had done it for him, so he could do what he needed to. Her actions made sense, and yet some part of him still believed, still screamed, that they could have found a way.

Iraji placed a hand on his arm. "I'm so sorry, my friend."

The two walked back to the center of Idris. Armaiti was laden with grief and yet his mind was clear on what he needed to do next.

12

Mæve tried to keep her hands from shaking. She could not, would not, cry.

The head of house had requested Mæve's help with an intimate gathering in the queen's chambers this afternoon. The queen might even reinstate her as a Royal Servant, which meant Lucius would stop preying on her again.

Yet this hope did little to tame the anxiety tumbling in her gut. Mæve had learned they had not sold Tráthóna at auction, and they now planned to kill the mare.

She bit back her tears as she arrived at the queen's chambers and the guard announced her.

Mæve entered.

"What do they call you again?" the queen asked, without looking at her.

"Doe, Your Highness," Mæve answered.

"Yes, Doe. We have a busy afternoon. A few members of the royal family will meet here today to discuss some important business. The cooks will deliver drinks and food momentarily. You can wait for them there."

"Yes, ma'am," Mæve replied, and she turned towards the antechamber.

She almost didn't see the man hidden in the shadows. As soon as her eyes fell upon him he turned and disappeared altogether in the dark chamber beyond the queen's receiving room.

Mæve gasped, and grabbed a nearby candlestick for a weapon. She hadn't seen much. Pale skin, a black cloth obscuring his nose and mouth, inky-black hair above blue eyes.

"What is it, girl?" the queen snapped, not looking up from her papers.

"A man, Your Highness, there is a man in the shadows," Mæve replied, ready to follow him into the adjoining room with her candlestick, but the queen laughed.

"Sují," the queen said. "Don't worry, you wouldn't have seen him if he didn't want you to. It's his way of saying hello."

The queen looked up from her papers with a wide smile.

"He's my personal protection. A little extra beyond the royal guards that follow me around. He likes to keep to the shadows." The queen removed the candlestick from Mæve's hands, setting it back on the mantel. "Now go, the guests will be here soon."

The queen's guests arrived, nobles and a few merchants who all lounged in her sitting room, sipping drinks and nibbling on the fine delicacies Mæve served them.

The group was discussing the scheduling of a new shipment of silk coming into the capital from Thalis. Mæve ignored them as she replaced drinks and brought new treats for the guests, until something snagged her attention.

"We can't schedule the shipment then," a duke was saying, exasperated. "That's migration day."

Mæve paused. Migration day for the Lumani.

"We can't be making deliveries of such magnitude while that nonsense is going on," his duchess added.

"There will be a new *king* this year," said the duke, mocking. "We won't want to miss that."

Mæve fumed over the way he said king, full of disdain and scorn, and how the others laughed.

"Yes." A duchess's face lit up. "With his new queen, I hear. Just married on this past harvest moon."

Mæve fumbled her tray. Heads turned her way as she steadied herself and then, with all her might, schooled the shock and hurt from her face.

"There is only one king and queen of Azantium," Mæve heard the queen proclaim, but she was already closing the door to the antechamber where bottles of wine and the prepped food were waiting for her.

Mæve's breathing came out in rasps. She wiped the tears from her face as fast as they fell.

It couldn't be. Armaiti had said he was betrothed to someone, but that he didn't love her and he was working to get out of it. Could he have married her, anyway? How could he... why would he... had what they had meant so little to him?

She had heard nothing from him since she missed their last meeting. There had been no way to get word to him. Why hadn't he sent a message with his raven?

Mæve knew she needed to get back out to the gathering of royals. She gave her face one final wipe, smoothed her features, and with a deep breath she rejoined them with a full tray.

THE NEXT MORNING, Mæve went through the motions of getting ready for her day. She hadn't slept, but all of the pain and grief had left her numb.

She was sent to clean a lord's suite. When she entered his study, she realized he was a collector of exotic items from other countries—books and weapons especially, all of them displayed ostentatiously. As she dusted the bookshelves, one volume caught her attention. It was from Callium, and written in her language. It discussed the islanders' early origins as explorers and the intricate system of celestial navigation the tribes used. This was true. Mæve's father had taught her to navigate by the stars, a tradition that he told her had been passed down through the ages.

"Slacking on the job, are we?"

She gasped and slammed the book shut. Lucius.

"Your Highness," she said, curtsying. "Please forgive me."

He smirked and moved closer. "Maybe you can make it up to me."

Mæve edged away from him, busily dusting the top of a large wooden desk in the center of the room.

"I'm sorry sir, really, I am quite busy." But Lucius came up behind her, pinning her to the desk. She turned, ready to hit him, but he grabbed her hand and laughed.

"Now that will get you killed, striking a Royal," and he wrapped an arm around her waist. Mæve groped at the desk with her free hand, desperately searching for anything that might help her. She turned her head, eyes squeezed shut, to avoid the kiss he was forcing on her.

Pain bloomed where the edge of the desk dug into her back. His sour breath fell hot upon her face as he fumbled with his trousers. She knew what was coming. She continued to search with her free hand. Nothing. And then she felt something. The handle of a silver letter opener that tapered into a point.

A rush of life flooded her. She gripped the letter opener and swung her arm, hard, jamming the point into Lucius' neck. He reeled with shock and disbelief, his blood splattering across her face. Glorious.

He made an awful gurgling sound, more blood spilling out of his mouth, and reached for her. She tried to squirm away. The gurgling stopped. Lucius slumped forward, crushing her onto the desk. The blood from his neck gushed onto her shoulder, soaking her dress. She wiggled out from underneath him, giving his body one last heave that sent him to the floor, motionless.

Then Mæve remembered the weapons on the wall. Her eyes fell upon a bow and a quiver of arrows. Although meant for decoration, they looked as if they could be in good working condition. She removed them from the wall, slinging the quiver onto her back and threading the bow across her body.

She needed to act fast. She needed to find Betha and get to the stables before anyone else spotted her and her blood-soaked dress. Her friend was working in the conservatory this week, which was just past the stairs that led to the slave quarters and the stables. The hard part would be getting there from the study. It was still early in the morning. Maybe she would get lucky.

She peeked into the hallway. Empty. Light on her feet, she sprinted down it. She passed a statue dressed in an odd, foreign armor and paused. It had a large golden staff in its hand. She wrestled it free. It was heavy, far heavier than the wooden staffs she used back home in Callium, but it would have to do.

Mæve continued her silent sprint, staff in hand. The conservatory was close, and just beyond it were the stairs leading to the slave quarters and the stables.

And then one of those awful women from the court entered the hallway.

Mæve advanced before the woman could process what was happening. Red-haired ringlets swished with the quick turn of her head, her blue eyes wide. Mæve swung her staff. Gems twinkled in the woman's ears and her pretty painted face froze in disbelief.

The staff connected with the side of her head. A sickening crack echoed through the expansive hallway, and then she dropped, her honeydew silk skirts spilling across the white tile.

Mæve continued. Only a short distance later, a slave emerged from a door as she passed; an older man with white hair and ebony skin. His eyes grew wide upon seeing Mæve, but she put a finger over her mouth, motioning for him to be silent. He obliged and Mæve passed him.

She was so close. She could see the stairs.

The conservatory doors were open and the room appeared to be empty. Curses. Mæve entered the room, keeping her back to the wall, just as her friend appeared from a linen closet. Betha saw Mæve and let loose a scream. Mæve rushed to her and placed a hand over her mouth. Betha's eyes widened, but she nodded and Mæve dropped her hand.

"Holy fuck," Betha said.

"No time, Betha. You need to come with me."

Mæve grabbed her friend's hand and drew her towards the door.

"Mæve, what in the gods is going on?"

"Please, we need to be quiet," Mæve said. She grabbed Betha's hand and pulled her into the hallway, just as two gentlemen entered the hallway ahead of them.

"Stay here," Mæve whispered to Betha.

The first man was mid-sentence, still smiling at his friend, when Mæve's staff connected with his head. His friend scrambled backwards in surprise and fell to the ground. Mæve swung the staff in a downward arc, but the man wiggled out of the way and up to his feet. He screamed as he ran down the hallway. There was no time to catch him. Mæve grabbed a wide-eyed Betha and they sprinted down the stairs and out into the stables.

Thank the gods Tráthóna was still there and Mæve rushed her friend into the mare's stall.

"Mæve, what's going on?" Betha regarded Tráthóna with apprehension.

"Lucius is dead."

Mæve dropped her staff to help Betha up on Tráthóna's back.

"I don't know how to ride," Betha said, looking terrified.

"Here, hang on to her mane. Squeeze with your legs and lean in close. I'll be right behind you."

Mæve prepared to leap up behind her friend, but two soldiers rushed through the stable door. "There she is! Stop right there, by order of the Royal Gu-"

One of Mæve's arrows found its home in his neck. Before the other soldier could react, a second arrow sprouted from his eye. Mæve smiled, put her arm through her bow, securing it on her back, and leapt up on Tráthóna behind a pale-looking Betha.

"Hang on, Betha. Tráthóna's fast." The horse sensed their urgency and took off out of the stables. Betha screamed and hung on for dear life. Mæve helped steady her friend. She turned her head slightly, checking behind them. Soldiers flooded out of the castle gates. They took aim with something—a dark-colored cylinder. Mæve hadn't seen a weapon like it before.

A blast nearly knocked Mæve from Tráthóna's back. It sent a terrifying vibration through the air. "What was that?" Betha screamed. Tráthóna did not break her stride.

Another blast and something whizzed past Mæve. She took another look. An ethereal blue light curled around the dark cylinders the soldiers held. It resembled the light that had come from Armaiti's blades the night the wild beast had attacked them.

"Keep your head down. Hold on." Mæve spurred Tráthóna on. Another blast. Some more projectiles. And then it stopped. Whatever those foul weapons were, they were out of range. Another glance over her shoulder. The soldiers were mounting horses.

They rode towards the Southern Forest. It wouldn't take them long to reach the trees, and once there she could easily lose the guards.

She glanced behind them again. The guards, about eight of them, were still far behind them. She smiled. They were going to make it.

They entered the forest cover. Tráthóna slowed her gait, but she continued to navigate the terrain at a canter. Deeper and deeper into the forest they rode. When the vegetation became too thick for a canter, Tráthóna slowed to a trot, and eventually, a brisk walk.

Mæve eased her grasp on Betha, who leaned back into her, trembling.

"We need to make a plan," Mæve said. They were far into the forest now, surrounded by full trees. The pine-laden ground dampened Tráthóna's hoof-falls. Mæve continued to scan their surroundings, looking, listening, but there was no trace of the soldiers.

"A plan?" Betha said. "You just murdered the future king of Azantium."

"Lucius tried to rape me," Mæve said. The bloodlust of her escape had settled, and the reality of what she had just done dawned on her.

"I couldn't leave you, Betha. If I had, they would have killed you for your association with me. Everyone knows we are friends."

Betha rubbed her eyes. "Gods be cursed. Gods be cursed!"

"I had no choice but to kill him."

"Gods, Mæve, I'm so sorry. Okay, don't worry. We'll figure this out." Betha placed her hand on Mæve's and Mæve nodded, tears streaming down her face.

"We need to find a safe place," Betha continued. "What about Isaac's?"

"We can't go there," Mæve said. "He's too close to the royals. We would be spotted and put him in danger. And I don't think we can trust anyone associated with the royals now. Not even Isaac."

They rode in silence. Mæve remained on edge, vigilant.

"What were those things?" Betha asked.

"What things?"

"The... weapons. I don't know, the blasts. It was so loud and it... was it sending something, like an arrow, but not an arrow, through the air. Was that the labaton?"

"I don't know," Mæve replied. Whatever they were, they were terrifying.

"I'm surprised this ratty old horse got us away from them."

Tráthóna snorted, and Mæve came to the mare's defense. "'I don't think Tráthóna enjoyed being captive in the palace any more than we did."

Mæve patted the side of the horse's neck, grateful Tráthóna was still with them.

"What about Armaiti and the Lumani? Surely he'll take us in," Betha suggested. But Mæve scoffed at the idea.

"We would only put him and his people in danger, Betha. Besides, he's married now. We should leave him in peace."

"I heard about that," Betha said. "Are you okay?"

If Betha had heard about it too, it most likely was no mistake. Armaiti had married.

"We have bigger things to worry about now," Mæve replied, biting back more tears.

"Wait, what about Giselle? She's part of the resistance. Maybe she could help us," Betha suggested.

"That sounds promising," Mæve said.

"She lives on the eastern outskirts of the kingdom. In a tiny village called Epoth."

"Can you get us there?"

"It would take us a few days, and I don't know which direction is east."

Mæve looked up. The sun was just past its halfway point in the sky.

"We are heading east now."

"How do you know?" Betha asked.

"The sun."

"Okay. Sounds like a good plan." A pause. "Mæve?"

"Yes?"

"How did you do it?"

"I jammed a letter opener in his neck."

And Betha laughed. "Good girl."

13

Dawn broke, blood orange seeping into an azure sky as Isaac left his home in the hills. Azantium's hushed countryside had just risen from slumber. The scent of cook fires hung in the crisp morning air. The sound of his horse's hooves cut through the tranquil morning as they pushed on faster. Isaac was anxious to get to his appointment with the queen. He would ask to marry Mæve, and was prepared to offer a generous amount for both the girls.

Isaac had made the appointment a couple of days prior. He had a relentless foreboding that Mæve was in danger. He needed to get her out of there. He needed to know she was safe.

Isaac had directed his housekeepers to set up two bedrooms for the girls on the other side of the house from him. Fresh-cut flowers decorated their rooms, along with bottles of wine, fruit baskets, and clothing he'd ordered in what he thought their sizes might be. There would be time for proper fittings after they had settled in.

Isaac tethered his horse and made his way into the Palace of Light. The palace halls were empty of royals—the only living beings he passed were silent slaves, up early to clean. The high society of Azantium were a late-rising bunch, which suited Isaac just fine.

Isaac's black boots echoed on the polished tile, his red scarf billowing behind him. He adjusted the lapels of his long black jacket before he rounded the last corner.

He nodded to the royal guards, and one left to notify the queen.

Isaac waited. And waited. He paced back and forth. It was torturous. It must have been at least an hour before one of the queen's servants announced the queen would receive him now.

"Isaac!" Her voice cut through the silence like a blade scraping ice.

Queen Druscilla sat in her chair by the window, sipping tea, dressed in folds of fine green silk. Her face was glossily painted. A smaller chair sat beside her, and she gestured at it with a pleasant smile upon her face.

"Your Highness." Isaac gave a deep bow, flashing his infectious smile and planting a kiss on her hand.

She blushed. "What brings the High Merchant to request an audience with me?"

"I'd like to inquire about a slave," he said. "Doe, I think they called her."

"Oh, yes," the queen said. "A favorite of mine."

Isaac's heart stopped. Dammit.

"I wasn't aware she is a favorite of yours, Your Highness," Isaac began. "Perhaps I should reconsider what I had planned to discuss with you."

The queen leaned forward, her interest piqued. Just as her face contorted into a question, a guard burst into the room looking frantic.

"Good heavens," the queen exclaimed. "Do you mind?"

"Your Highness," the soldier looked ill, "The prince, your nephew, there's been an incident."

The color drained from the queen's face. "What do you mean, incident?"

"He's in Lord Aulus' study, Your Highness," the guard gulped. "He's been murdered."

At first the queen only stared, looking quite dumb, her mouth agape and eyes wide. Then her cold eyes turned liquid. She stood slowly. "Show me."

Isaac followed as they hurried down the hallway to the lord's study. Sure enough, Lucius' body lay on the ground, eyes wide and staring, a letter opener jammed into his neck.

The sound that ripped from the queen's throat was terrifying, the tortured howl of some wild thing. She rushed to her nephew's side and knelt, oblivious to the blood soaking into her skirts. Her face broken, she wailed and leaned over his body, placing her head on his back as she wept.

Isaac addressed the guard. "What happened?"

"I believe two slave women murdered him. They then stole a horse and fled the palace. We lost them in the forest. A slave saw one of them as she left this room."

"Bring him at once!" the queen wailed. She rose to her feet, wiping her nose on her sleeve.

The guard left and quickly returned with an older servant. The soldier shoved him into the study.

"Tell us what you saw," ordered the queen.

"I saw a... a woman run from this room. She grabbed a staff from the statue outside the door. She was covered in blood."

"What did she look like?" the queen snapped.

"She had the most unusual eyes," the man said, and a pit of dread formed in Isaac's stomach. "They were purple and... bright. Um, she had brown hair and tattoos on her hands..." His voice quivered as it trailed off.

The queen was shaking. "That treacherous monster, that..."

Isaac put his hand on the servant man's trembling shoulder. "You've done well telling us this. I'm sure you have to return to your duties. You are dismissed." The man nodded, his eyes wide with fear.

Isaac turned to the soldier next. "Please gather the other soldiers who were with you. Bring them here so we may question them."

Tattoos. The eyes.

Isaac looked at the desk next to Lucius' body. It was strewn with papers and spilled bottles of writing ink. A struggle had taken place.

He'd been so close to freeing her.

He ran his hand through his hair as the queen rounded on him.

"You!" She pointed at Isaac, her eyes ablaze. "What were you going to ask me about that servant girl this morning?"

Isaac faltered for only a second before the lie rolled off his tongue. "I came to warn you. I thought something was amiss. I'm so sorry, Your Highness, I was too late..."

The queen broke into more sobs. "Oh, Isaac, he was like a son to me."

The guard returned with the other soldiers. The queen wiped her face.

"I want her fucking head brought to me," the queen shouted.

Isaac's heart sank.

The queen turned her attention back to her nephew. "Oh, Lucius, my beautiful Lucius." And she wept.

"Come, let us look after him," Isaac said. He needed to find Mæve, but first he needed to warn the Lumani. Wanting to leave, but knowing he needed to finish this game, he gently guided the queen away from the ruined body of her favorite nephew.

FREE FROM THE palace at last, Isaac rode west toward the Black Forest, pushing his horse to a reckless speed. The sun had just set and an indigo twilight blanketed the forest. He planned to ride into Idris as an unannounced foreigner. Definitely not one of the smarter things he'd done in his life, but he couldn't sit on his information any longer. The new weapon, the death of the crown prince, the queen's plans... the Lumani needed to know.

Isaac would not rest until he found Mæve. But first he needed to warn the Lumani.

He leaned forward in his saddle. In the near distance, the faint blue hue of the Chrysillium trees peeked through the darkening forest. Above the beautiful little trees, fiery orbs encased in hardened æther floated about like unbreakable bubbles, illuminating the village. Isaac remembered how the elders would harden the æther and the Fire Clan would light small flames in the middle of the orbs. They were an enchanting sight to behold once again.

Isaac readied himself.

He was passing the outer rim of Idris when something struck his chest. The force of it sent him catapulting from his horse, and he hit the ground hard. The air left his lungs and his head cracked on the ground, sending his world into a speckled blackness. Isaac curled onto his side, biting back a slew of curses.

Voices. Lumani voices.

Isaac did not hesitate. He struggled to his knees and yelled into the night, "I carry an important message for the king!"

Two Lumani men and a woman stood before him. They all bore the red kishaye on their foreheads. Fire Clan.

"Balán," Isaac said, and the warriors halted, confused and suspicious that he had spoken the Lumani evening salutation.

"I am an old friend of the Lumani. Please, it is with great urgency that I speak to your king."

The woman stepped towards him, revealing the long obsidian staff she had concealed behind her arm. If she decided to kill him, there was very little he could do. Isaac was no fighter.

"Your people are in grave danger. Tell the king it is Isaac Houghton. Please."

She stepped back, shooting a glance at her companions. One of them took off towards the village center. The other two turned their gaze back to Isaac, weapons drawn, murder in their eyes. He exhaled. Murder eyes he could handle. Armaiti was clever and reasonable. He would listen.

A few moments later Armaiti approached through the trees, walking quickly but not without grace. The young warrior Isaac had known was now grown up into a king, tall and muscular, his kishaye shining a bright, iridescent silver. His gaze intensified when it fell upon the merchant.

A small entourage followed the Lumani king. By the graces— Isaac thanked his good fortune—Malwa, the slave he had helped escape the Chrysillium Field, was amongst them.

"Isaac Houghton," the Lumani king snarled. "I could barely believe my ears. You must have a death wish."

"I risk my life to bring you pertinent news, King Armaiti," Isaac said with a bow.

"I'm sure you do. Care to swindle more trees from us? I hear yours are dying."

Isaac raised an eyebrow but Malwa interrupted. "He helped me escape. He's the one who connected me with the Red Fox and got me out of the Chrysillium Field, King Armaiti."

Visibly surprised, Armaiti said, "This man? You're sure?"

"I am. Ji can corroborate my story. Isaac helped him, too."

Armaiti considered Isaac. "A very odd thing for an Azantium merchant to do."

"Things didn't turn out the way I thought they would with the Treaty of Falls Hollow, Your Highness. I wanted there to be peace, and I brokered the treaty because I truly thought this was possible. But I know the Azantiums better now. I'm trying to make amends for what I've done."

"What do you want, merchant?" Armaiti said.

"A word with you. The crown prince is dead and I believe your people are in danger."

"Come, walk with me. It would be a pity if my new wife or any of her clan should see you and kill you before you can tell me your news."

Isaac swallowed. The Air Clan had never liked him, even before the treaty.

"Thank you, Malwa," Armaiti said as he walked away from his entourage.

Isaac nodded to Malwa, then grabbed the reins of his horse and caught up to Armaiti, who had already started walking away from the village's center.

"Yes, I had heard you were recently married. Congratulations," Isaac said.

But an odd look passed over the king's face. Grief.

"Tell me why I should care about the crown prince dying," Armaiti said.

"He was murdered," Isaac said. "The queen is in a rage. Armaiti, she is developing a new weapon. Something far worse than labaton. She means to destroy the Lumani."

"So why hasn't she attacked?"

"My source told me King Regauld still supports the treaty. The Azantium king is very ill but apparently still ruling from his bedchamber. She can't mobilize the army on her own without his approval."

"But once he dies..." Armaiti said, his face darkening.

"Which could be any day. And there's more."

"Zama's breath, what else?" Armaiti said.

They stopped walking just outside the final rim of Idris, and Isaac turned to the king.

"A slave murdered Lucius. I know her and was trying to help her escape. It looks like the prince attacked her and she killed him in self-defense, then escaped into the woods."

"Again, merchant, I am at a loss as to why I should care. No foreigner will be allowed here."

"You should care because she was sneaking off in the night and meeting someone from Idris. A Lumani man, though I don't know who."

Isaac thought he saw Armaiti's face grow pale.

"You are worried she may come here and contact the person she was seeing?"

"Yes, and if the queen can tie the prince's murder to the Lumani, the treaty will no longer protect you. King Regauld will have no choice but to declare war."

"She has not come here," Armaiti said softly.

"You are certain? She—"

"I am certain, merchant." Armaiti said. "You will look for her?"

Curses, no.

Isaac stared at Armaiti.

"It's you," Isaac whispered.

Armaiti ignored him. "I can tell you in certainty, she will not come here." A pause, and then: "Why are you helping her?"

"I am part of a growing rebellion against the royals. I've been funding it, as well as helping Lumani slaves to escape. They say fighters are organizing in Epoth and Quan. What if the Lumani joined us?"

Armaiti's eyes lit up with this possibility. "I admit it is an intriguing thought, merchant. But one I cannot fathom with migration in just a few days."

"No, of course not. Moving your people to the other side of the kingdom is no small task. I remember."

"Come and see me after migration, once we are settled in Eod. I would like to talk more about this."

"I will," Isaac said. A pause, uncertain if he should continue, but he did. "I won't give up on her. I will find her and make sure she is safe. Maybe I will have news for you on that matter too by that time."

"Yes, merchant, I would very much appreciate that," Armaiti whispered. "I wish my circumstances were different. I might have even joined you."

"Of course," Isaac said. It seemed that whatever had happened between Mæve and Armaiti, the Lumani king still cared for her. "I will see you in Eod, then. Safe journey."

"Isaac," Armaiti said, his eyes deep gold shining in the night. It was as if the Lumani king was looking at him anew. "Thank you."

Part II
Epoth

Ancient

is the lineage of matriarchs

a tree of life

extending to the beginning.

It is carried through the blood, they say

the Shalik

those who create.

And yet the heavy hand of kings

weighed down upon them.

And the old ways were forgotten.[1]

---

1. *Source: The Book of Allan: The Lost Tribe*
   Year: 3917 (Azantium: year 228 of the Light. 122 years prior to current date)
   Current location of text: Kråshain library on the outer rim of Eod

14

Mæve struggled to stay awake. Tráthóna's rhythmic gait pulled her towards the sleep she desperately needed after riding through the night. Just as she thought she might succumb, a wooden sign came into view. Pyrographed into the wood was the word "Epoth".

They had arrived.

Mæve sank further into the deep cowl of the cloak Betha had given to her on their second day traveling through the Southern Forest.

"Here, you need it more than I do. You look terrible," Betha had said, after Mæve finished bathing in a forest stream. Although her face and hands had cleaned up easily, her hair remained a matted, bloody mess without the proper time and soap to wash it out, and her dress would be forever stained.

Betha now slept, leaning against Mæve as they rode, both of them wrapped in the folds of the cloak. Dawn had just crested the horizon and the sleepy village of Epoth stood before them in the early morning light. A series of small cottages dotted a single wide road, smoke billowing out of their chimneys.

After two days of riding with nothing to eat, hunger gnawed at

Mæve's stomach. Neither of them knew how to forage vegetation in the Azantium countryside, and they had decided that hunting would take too much time and risk drawing unwanted attention.

To distract herself from her hunger pains, Mæve had focused upon the memory of her father teaching her celestial navigation. The stars were positioned differently in Azantium. This mattered little, though. All Mæve needed was the Dark Star, Ellindrium, to orient herself.

Mæve was worried about her parents. She hoped they were at least together. As fierce and independent as Isa was, she could not go long without the companionship of Mæve's father, Jal.

Mæve remembered the way her mother would light up when her father returned from one of his fishing expeditions. He and the other men would be gone for days and return smelling of sea brine, his basket full of fish, his blue eyes shining. No sooner would he cross the threshold of their home than Isa would rush to him, laughing, running her fingers through his dark wavy hair. Nothing gave Mæve more comfort than being in the presence of her parents' undying love for each other.

Oh, how she longed for their company, or even just the knowledge they were okay.

They approached the humble entrance to the town. Mæve nudged Betha awake.

"We're here."

Betha stirred and rubbed her eyes. The smell of wood smoke was comforting in the crisp fall morning air. Two men huddled near a small bonfire, clutching mugs of something steamy. One was tall and barrel-chested, with dark hair and piercing eyes, and the other was tall and willowy, with long white hair. They regarded the girls with suspicion and a hint of alarm.

How odd they must look, two bedraggled young women wandering into town on the back of a white horse. Betha's exposed servant's dress was not helping; its fancy cut marked them as being from the capital.

"You might want to ask for Giselle," Mæve whispered.

"Right." Betha shook off the last of her sleepiness and slid off Tráthóna's back, stumbling as she hit the ground. She approached the two men. "Hi... um... I'm looking for a friend of mine..."

"Betha?"

"Oh, Giselle!" Betha ran over and threw her arms around her friend who was walking up the road behind them.

"It's all right," Giselle called out to the two glowering men. "She's an old friend of mine."

Giselle grabbed Betha's arm, leading her away.

"Are you all right? What... how are you here?" Then Giselle's gaze fell on Mæve, and her mouth dropped open.

"Are you in some kind of trouble, Betha? This... this is a bit odd."

"I can explain—" Betha began.

"Wait. Let's get inside first."

Mæve and Betha followed Giselle away from the bonfire, back towards the town entrance, and stopped outside a humble wooden cabin.

"You can leave your horse here for now."

Giselle gestured toward a tree, and Mæve obliged.

Once inside the cabin, Giselle started a fire and put some food on the stove. Then she guided Mæve to the washroom.

"I had just boiled some water for a bath and was letting it cool while I visited Ardra's apothecary when I saw you two." She handed Mæve a towel.

"Thank you," Mæve said, touched that Giselle would give up her bath for her.

"You need it more than I do, to be honest," Giselle said. The warmth in her voice was comforting. "Take your time. I'll have some food ready when you're done."

Mæve thanked her again. She hung Betha's cloak on the door and stripped off her blood-stained shift. Lucius' blood. She kicked it in a corner and vowed to toss it in the fire just as soon as her bath was complete.

She sank into the blissful, lavender-scented water and became acutely aware of her muscles. After her escape from the palace and the subsequent two-day ride, they had tightened into taut, hardened cords that now melted and relaxed.

As her body unwound, her emotions also softened. It began with a few small sniffles. She bit back the sobs so that Giselle and Betha would not worry. Even so, grief—heavy and thick—crashed over her, piece by jagged piece. Soon she could no longer hold back the tears, and let them flow. Against her control, the sobs became elated, bubbly laughter. Good Gods, was she losing her mind? Giselle and Betha must think her mad. But she didn't care.

She had done it: escaped the Palace of Light. Betha, Tráthóna— they were all free.

Mæve remained in the tub until the water cooled. As she dried off with a towel, she noticed the clothes Giselle had left for her. They fit well. Brown leather pants, a gray wool sweater, and a set of tall leather boots. They suited her. It was nice to be free from the corset and skirts they made her wear in the palace.

Outside the small washroom, in the cabin's common room, Betha and Giselle were seated at a wooden table, smiling and talking over steaming mugs.

"Mæve, join us for some breakfast," Betha said with a smile.

Mæve didn't hesitate. She grabbed what appeared to be a corn cake with syrup drizzled over it. It was delicious.

"You're looking much better," Giselle said. "Betha told me what happened in the palace. I'm so sorry. I want you to know Epoth is a safe place for you. No one here supports the royals. Quite the contrary." A chuckle from Giselle and then, "We seldom see any Capital folk way out here. Magistrates venture out here every month to collect our taxes, but we have a lookout to warn us when they're approaching."

"Warn you?"

"The rebellion is based here in Epoth. That scowly man at the bonfire is Chalen, our leader."

"The rebellion," Mæve said, looking at Betha, but her friend's face betrayed none of her feelings about the rebellion.

"You're welcome to stay here with me until you get your feet on the ground," Giselle continued. "I'm sure you can make yourself useful. Try to make friends, though you may find people resistant to newcomers at first."

Giselle took a moment to think, tapping her fingers on the table. Pursing her lips, she said, "Your story may be a bit much, even for us Epoth folks. I will circulate a different story. Something like you were attacked on the road here. Hence all the blood... Why don't you both eat some food, get some rest. You must be exhausted. I have some errands to run and some gossip to spread."

Giselle stood with a wink. "I'll be back late in the afternoon. We hold communal dinners. I can introduce you tonight, if you think you'd be ready for that."

Giselle kissed Betha on top of her head, grabbed her basket, and headed out the door.

"How are you doing?" Betha asked, once she was gone.

"I'm starving," Mæve said, stuffing another corn cake into her mouth.

"She's great, isn't she?" Betha said dreamily. A pause. "We made it." Betha ran her fingers through her hair and laughed, a bit manically. "Holy shit, Mæve. We did it. We escaped the Palace of Light..." Betha shook her head as if to say she still didn't quite believe it.

Mæve reached for Betha and embraced her friend.

"Gods, it's ridiculous, but I scarcely know what to do with myself." Betha's bottom lip trembled and her hand shook as she lifted her tea mug to her lips.

Mæve understood Betha's trepidation. Mæve felt it, too. Their days in the Palace of Light were so regimented. What was freedom? How would they live? Mæve imagined this must be tenfold for Betha. She had only ever known life as a slave.

"We'll find our way. Don't worry. Let's just take it one day at a time, ok?"

"Yes, I like that," Betha said. "One day at a time."

Mæve tried to stay alert, but her eyes drooped against her will. It had been two days without sleep. She didn't think she could stay awake a moment longer.

"Here Mæve. Giselle made a bed for you while you were bathing." It was tucked into a corner of the common room. Mæve curled up and sank into a deep sleep.

Mæve and Armaiti ran together through a beautiful forest at night. Armaiti held her hand and before them a Chrysillium tree sparkled in the moonlight. Still holding hands, they stepped towards the tree, and as they did, the ground lit up under each of their footfalls. A white effervescence, it looked like tiny webbing weaving its way through the earth.

"Our magic," Armaiti said, but she was lost in his eyes, pulled into his orbit. He was so close, and leaning towards her...

And then she woke up. Her heartbeat was fast. Armaiti. Oh gods, it was just a dream. Mæve rubbed her eyes and looked around. Where was she? Then she remembered. Epoth. In Giselle's common room, on a makeshift bed.

The sound of peepers serenaded the sleepy cabin. Mæve sighed and got out of bed. It was late. She guessed she had slept through dinner.

She wasn't ready to return to her bed, though. She didn't think she could handle another visit from the Armaiti ghost haunting her dreams. Instead, she looked out the side window. The moon was full and cast a faint silvery glow over Epoth. She saw Tráthóna through the barn door. Mæve smiled as she watched the horse sleep peacefully, noticing for the first time how Tráthóna's coat shimmered with traces of gold and silver.

Mæve left the sill and stepped through the front door. She perched on the front porch, tucking her knees up to her chest, intending to enjoy the night.

But across the street was a strange sight. A stooped old woman was working in her garden by the light of the moon. Mæve knew nothing of horticulture, but the middle of the night seemed a strange time to be gardening.

Mæve put on her boots and crossed the street.

The woman's hair was long, straight, and silver, and she wore a dark blue kerchief fastened around her head. Her brown skin was cracked with age, especially around her smiling dark eyes. They angled ever so slightly upward, like a hawk. Like Mæve's eyes.

"Good evening," Mæve said.

"Yes, it is," the old woman replied. She smelled of sage.

"Would you like some help?" Mæve asked.

"I'd love help, dear. Thank you." The woman handed her a small shovel.

"I'm Mæve."

"Yes, you're one of the new girls in town. Hello, Mæve. I'm Ardra. Have you done much gardening?"

Mæve shook her head.

"I suppose not, being the wife of a wealthy noble."

So that was the story Giselle was circulating.

Ardra's eyes were two deep pools of swirling onyx. The way she looked at Mæve with her curious smile, she appeared to sense Mæve's secret.

She returned to her gardening and Mæve followed her lead, helping to plant seeds.

They sowed until the faint glow of dawn appeared on the dark horizon. Mæve wiped her brow and Ardra leaned on her shovel, considering the little mounds of dirt that marked their night's work.

"Thank you, dear. Violets are best planted a few days after a full moon. I use them often in my healing. They have many magical abilities."

"You're magical?" Mæve asked, curious.

"I'm the village healer. Although I'm getting far too old these days. Can't help as many people as I used to," Ardra said. "You do realize you are one?"

"Pardon me?" Mæve asked.

"A healer, dear, you are one."

"What do you mean?" Mæve didn't dare mention her past in Callium, but she was curious how Ardra knew this without any tests.

But Ardra just laughed. "There is a language beyond words, if we can but remember how to listen. Yes, most healing is done working with plants. This is surface level healing. But some healers can go deeper and heal by walking between the veils of this reality. Each veil has its own rules. The Way Station, for example. That place where spirits wait before completing their journey into the spirit world. Here, healing can be done to help a person let go of some past matter so that they can cross fully into death. Sometimes a skilled healer with a great desire can heal mortal wounds in this place, bringing a person back to the waking world, but that is very difficult and requires a sacrifice to the river of the dead."

Mæve stared at Ardra, unsure of what to say, and the resulting smile on the old woman's face hinted that she had expected no less.

"I have heard of traveling the veils, but I did not realize it was possible to bring a person back from the dead," Mæve said.

Ardra laughed out loud. "No, no, that would be black magic. For that there is always a price, and it's never worth paying." A pause as Ardra set down her shovel and wiped her brow. "No, traveling the veils is something far more natural and yet difficult to do. I can teach you, if you like."

"I would," Mæve said, intentionally not mentioning that she had some training traveling the veils, not wanting to expose the truth about her and Betha's past.

Ardra nodded, a twinkle in her eye. "I knew there was something about you when I saw you riding in, child. Anyone on an Allanian horse must be special indeed. Those horses don't carry just anyone. Humph, very interesting." She gave a little cackle. "People no longer care for the old ways or remember mystical beasts."

Tráthóna was Allanian?

Ardra turned and walked back towards her own cabin. "Good night, little sparrow. See you tomorrow."

"Good night," Mæve responded. "Thank you!"

On her walk back to Giselle's cabin, Mæve's heart was lighter than before. She had met a teacher. Mæve had worried that without practice, her magic would wither and atrophy. She smiled, drawing her hands to her heart with joy and gratitude. As she did, her hand grazed her obsidian tree pendant.

How would she ever find her parents now, being so far away from the capital? Worry gnawed at her. Were they in danger now? The rebels Giselle had spoken of might know something. The rebellion was a good place to start. She would find her parents and bring them here to safety with her.

15

Q ueen Druscilla's heels clicked on the tiled floors. It was a brief walk along the corridor to her husband's chambers. She wished it were longer.

She passed the guards outside King Regauld's room without pause.

Inside, gray light streamed into the chambers and the putrid smell of the sick invaded her nostrils.

Just let him die.

She walked to his bedside. He was only seventy-three years old but he looked twenty years older, his skin tinged yellow. The doctors said it was something with his liver.

"Druscilla?" he croaked, a faint smile forming on his lips.

"Yes dear, I'm here," she said.

"I haven't seen you in so long. How have you been?"

"Running a kingdom is hard work. I've meant to come more. Our kingdom grows weaker by the day from the deterioration of our crop at Falls Hollow. Please my king, have mercy on our people, have mercy on me, your queen." She handed him a set of papers and a quill. "I'll call the priest to witness, as is our law. Sign to break the treaty of Falls Hollow. Sign to allow me to call forth our army. It's our only hope."

"For the last time, Druscilla, I will not." His voice rumbled in the empty room, surprisingly strong for someone so frail. "Creating yet another terrible war with our neighbors is not the answer. Leave them alone and they will leave us alone too."

Anger shot through her veins. Her sanguine smile dissolved for just a moment.

"Fine," she said, taking back the papers and quill. "Then at least allow me to administer your medicine."

The king smiled at this. He liked the idea of her taking care of him; it seemed to bring him comfort.

She walked to the medicine table on the right side of his bed and slipped out a small vile from her pocket. Blackroot was a clear liquid with no smell or taste. It was toxic and killed slowly. The queen had been sneaking it to the king for the past two years—first in his tea, now in his medicine.

"Here you go, my dear," she said, and kissed him on the forehead.

After he fell asleep, Druscilla walked back to her chambers.

Suji had warned her the poison would take a while, but surely the day must come soon.

Suji understood. He cared about what was best for Azantium. The best warrior in the kingdom, he had served well during the Lumani wars and became her personal guard when the Lumani started raiding the palace.

He was always there. Hidden in the shadows, watching her, protecting her.

Now inside her own chambers, the queen poured herself a glass of wine. Light spilled out from underneath her closed bedroom door. A smile danced on her lips and she poured a second glass. She let down her hair, the red waves flowing down her back.

She entered the bedroom, where Suji waited. He smiled at her as she handed him the wine.

"I thought you might like to relax after such a tense meeting." He stepped behind her, loosening the bodice of her dress and massaging her shoulders. Druscilla sank into the pleasure, and for a moment she could forget all that plagued her mind.

THE NEXT MORNING, Queen Druscilla steeled herself as she stood upon a raised dais just outside the capital walls, watching twenty thousand Lumani march out of the Black Forest and onto the Main Road. Migration Day.

The queen squinted against the early afternoon sun, searching... there. The new Lumani king. She recognized him by the Fallion Crown upon his head, three obsidian triangles that jutted down over his forehead. The new king sat upon an enormous black elk. The queen scoffed, her upper lip curled into a sneer. Their *false* king.

There was only one ruler in Azantium, and it was her. As soon as the kingdom rid itself of this pestilence, the better. The Lumani Wars had already dragged on for generations. Then the raids into the palace had begun.

Druscilla winced. She still remembered that night well. It was just over ten years ago, when the entire palace was in a state of terror. One night, she had awoken from a deep sleep to her sister's blood-curdling scream. Druscilla had grabbed the first thing her eyes fell on: her scepter. A ridiculous weapon, but she didn't stop to search for a better one.

Druscilla had sprinted down the hallway in her bare feet to her sister's rooms. Lucius was just a boy and still sleeping in the small room next to his mother's. Lucielle's scream must have woken the child, because when Druscilla burst in, Lucius was kneeling on the bed trying to shake his mother awake.

Guards searched the closets and under the bed, but the queen ignored them and pushed her way onto the bed, enveloping Lucius in her arms. Lucielle lay unmoving, her blue eyes staring at the ceiling. Blood splattered her sheets from the gaping wound at her throat.

Lucielle's death had finally spurred Druscilla's idiot husband into action—but not retaliation. Instead he had capitulated and signed that damned treaty.

A better king would have rid the earth of the Lumani for killing his wife's sister.

Seething, the queen now watched the Lumani approach the palace walls. She thought a little show of force was in order.

At her request, the queen's men had brought her the slave girl's parents a few days ago. When the couple first saw each other, they broke free of their guards and lunged forward to reunite. Surprised, Druscilla found herself moved by the scene for a moment, but then she waved for the guards to pull them apart.

The queen had intended for the parents' execution to be retribution for Lucius' murder, but why not capitalize on the occasion? Use it to send a message to the new Lumani king; a reminder of Azantium dominance.

The executioners brought the slaves out. The woman still had that empty look on her face.

Druscilla had expected supplication from the parents, but when she had told them what their daughter had done, the mother had just thrown her head back and laughed.

The queen had ordered the woman beaten by the guards while they forced her husband to watch. It seemed she had sustained some significant injuries: brain damage or perhaps... Druscilla had heard of the soul departing before the body. Now she just stared ahead, blank-faced, lips slack, eyes empty.

The queen nodded to the general at her side. It was time to begin.

The Lumani continued to march past the parapet where Druscilla stood, their black hair and the marks on their chest shining in the autumn sun.

The king approached and Druscilla stood tall. Their eyes met. His eyes bored into hers, unwavering, probing.

The queen held a dangerous smile on her lips.

The slave man's screams ripped through the peaceful afternoon. Druscilla's eyes remained on the Lumani king. The sound broke his gaze. He looked as if he meant to reach for his swords, and she smirked.

He looked back at her, disgusted. His mouth was a tight line, his eyes fierce. Druscilla met his gaze and waited until he looked away first.

The Lumani marched slowly past the gruesome scene. That cursed mother never did scream. She just sat there looking dumb the entire time. Pity she could not join her husband in feeling such relentless pain at the end of her life. Well, no matter. She would be dead soon enough.

16

Eod at night. Jaleh sighed, savoring the sound of the Kalim river lapping in the near distance and the stars peeping through the tree canopy. What a relief to have the distance between the Lumani and the capital, especially after the events of migration.

Jaleh wrapped her shawl tighter around her shoulders, sheltering herself from the crisp autumn air as she walked through Eod with her friend and fellow elder, Bala.

The sound of raised voices from a dwelling above pulled Jaleh out of her ruminations. King Armaiti's abode. Arguing with his new bride. Again. Couldn't they at least take their arguments inside?

"Maybe one of us should go up there and show the king how to be with a new bride," Jaleh suggested with a wry smile. Bala chuckled.

"I don't understand what the problem is. They are both young, they are good friends. What more do they want?" Bala said.

Jaleh shrugged with a grumble. The young king had proven to be a thorn in her side. Although he had handled the Azantium queen rather well during migration, he was often too headstrong. A king needed to be supple—to bend with the wind, not stand rigid and break under its pressure.

"Those two had better figure it out," Jaleh replied. "We need them united for the challenges we face."

"Hmmm, yes, migration was most unpleasant this year," Bala observed.

"And that my friend, is but the least of our worries."

"The least?"

"Look..." Jaleh stopped walking and channeled, calling forth threads of æther. She started a simple weave, creating one of the light orbs that lit up Eod each night. Bala watched as Jaleh wove and sure enough, the weaving fell apart before it was finished. The threads of æther simply disintegrated under Jaleh's fingertips.

Bala gasped. "What... What happened?"

"I'm not sure, but it's happening more often. I either lose the threads mid-weave or I can't channel them at all."

"I've heard complaints of this from the other clans," Bala said. "But this is the first I've heard of it affecting an elder."

Jaleh stopped walking and considered a nearby Chrysillium tree twinkling indigo blue in the surrounding night. Its hum sounded healthy, and she did not detect any discord from the tree.

"I don't know. I've felt no disturbance in the Chrysillium trees," Jaleh said.

She paused again. The gravity of this situation left a heaviness in her heart. "I'm not sure what the answer is, but I suspect it lies in the Mycellium Forest and I haven't a clue what to do about that."

"Yes, it's not like we can go in there," Bala said.

"Anyone who has tried either ends up dead or returns mad," Jaleh said. "It's the mist. As we speak, Kalouq works diligently in the Kråshain library to find answers."

The Lumani library lay hidden, tucked deep within the Obsidian Cliffs on Eod's northern border. They were looking for records from that time, three hundred years ago, when the wizards bound the Mycellium, anything that might help provide a hint about the magic the wizards had used and its ramifications upon Zama. Was there a way through the toxic mist that surrounded the Mycellium Forest?

Jaleh believed they needed to find out. She believed this issue was far more pressing than the political threat from the Azantium. Not just the Lumani, but all of Zama was at risk. There were no more Shalik. Those rare beings born from a union between a Lumani and an Allanian. Legend said it was the Shalik who had created the grove at Falls Hollow. They were the only beings who could create new Chrysillium trees and do the work of Uthera.

Without the Allanians, there never would be another Shalik. If the Chrysillium trees died, the Lumani magic would die with them. Jaleh was not about to let that happen.

EARLIER THAT NIGHT, on the banks of the River Kalim, Armaiti searched for equanimity.

He left the banks of the river and made his way back to his arbden at the center of Eod. Iraji. Their relationship was not doing well.

Armaiti climbed the many steps to his home. Iraji stood on the large wooden porch that surrounded their dwelling, looking out over the village.

She was beautiful, Iraji Jashira of the Air Clan. She had long, straight, black hair. Her blue Ki stretched across her chest and arms in swirls, like a cool spring breeze. Such was her magic; light and cerebral in nature.

Secured on a black leather belt around her hips were her throwing knives.

"Good evening," Armaiti said, but her jaw tightened and she said nothing. "Iraji..." But he didn't know what to say. There were so many important matters they needed to discuss, but he couldn't get past her animosity towards him.

"Iraji, I needed to move forward with our marriage. We needed to. The elders rejected our idea and the Air Clan stood ready to leave. And with our situation with the Azantiums worsening... I could wait no longer. I wish you could understand—"

"You didn't even talk to me about it! Nothing, just Armaiti has decided, and that is it. I thought you were my friend. I thought we were working on this together. 'Don't worry Iraji, we'll find a solution,'" she said, deepening her voice, mimicking him.

"I did what I needed to do for the people, for *our* people!"

"Funny thing that you did it right after Mæve abandoned you in the glade that night."

Hurt and disbelief fueled Armaiti's anger. "That had nothing to do with it."

"Well, I just think it's very convenient, Armaiti."

"I planned to talk to you that night, but then Mæve didn't show up, and we spent all night looking for her. It's just the way it worked out."

Iraji turned back to look out over Eod. Her bottom lip quivered, but her eyes stared more fiercely than before.

Armaiti walked up to her cautiously. Only when she turned to look up at him, tears in her eyes, did he lean forward and envelop her in a hug.

"We don't have to link. If people wonder, we'll just say one of us can't conceive."

"They'll send a healer."

"We'll figure it out. Go see Ariol. You'll feel better."

"I can't," Iraji said, her voice hitching. "My family has forbidden it. And what would people think if they should catch me with another man?"

He didn't know the answer to their problems, just that in these hard days before them, he wanted his friend back.

ARMAITI FELL into a troubled sleep that night. Mæve was there in his dreams and they ran together through Eod, laughing and playing. There was a child, their child. The little girl was beautiful, and Armaiti wept at the sight of her.

But as they played, a vortex appeared in the woods. It pulled Mæve and his daughter away from him. They called out and he screamed, reaching for them, but he was too late. The vortex swallowed them and disappeared.

Iraji shook him awake.

"Armaiti, Armaiti! You were screaming. Are you all right?"

"Yes, yes." He gulped for air and steadied himself. Drenched in sweat, his body shook with anxiety. "I'm sorry to have woken you. It was just a nightmare."

Iraji looked concerned, but she nodded and climbed back into her own bed. It was still a few hours until dawn.

Iraji's breathing lengthened, becoming more rhythmic as she fell asleep. Armaiti remained awake, staring at the ceiling, unable to shake his dream.

Eventually he threw back his covers, scarcely remembering to dress before he went out the door. Once on the ground, he sprinted with ease to Ayin. He slowed his gait upon approaching the ancient Chrysillium tree. She stood tall and he could hear the clink of her luminescent fruit in the still night.

Armaiti kneeled and rested a shaking hand upon Ayin's trunk. She sang to him, and it soothed his frayed nerves.

"Please share with me your wisdom. So much is unclear and I do not know the way," Armaiti whispered. He closed his eyes and waited. The vibrations within him joined those of Zama, and a great calm came over him. Deep from Zama's memory, his aunt smiled back at him. Armaiti's heart swelled. He had seen many of his ancestors through Ayin, but never his Aunt Mallon. From the way she looked upon him, he knew she was proud of him.

"Armaiti. The people do not realize how dark and lonely your path is. Only a true companion will ease your passage. You must be whole; only then can you complete your destiny. Zama chose you at your birth to bring the Lumani into a new age amongst our darkest hour. Your fierce heart will be your lantern in the dark. Change is our only protector."

"Wait," Armaiti said to the image of his aunt, desperate. His voice shook. "There was a child, a special child."

His aunt only smiled and faded back into Uthera, the great beyond.

"Wait!" But it was futile. The ancestors had spoken.

Change is our only protector. Armaiti did not return to his arbden. Instead he sat by the banks of the Kalim and watched the dawn.

17

Enraptured by the scent of The Kahrakusk Market at night—cardamom and cinnamon—Isaac breathed deeply as he made his way through the back-alley streets of Allam on the kingdom's northern coast. He stopped and considered the crumpled piece of parchment in his hand. He could scarcely make out the flowery writing in the prismatic light from the lanterns strung overhead.

8 Birj Street
green door, gold knocker

He looked up. This was the place.

He knocked once. Twice. As he reached for a third time, the door opened. A man of middle age, with rusty hair and midnight eyes answered.

"Can I help you?" The lines in his face spoke of hard times.

"Adrian sent me," Isaac replied and the creases around the man's eyes deepened. "I hear your spice trade is the best."

"Yes, of course, of course. Come in."

The man shut the door as Isaac crossed the threshold.

"Please take a seat," the man said, gesturing to some cushions upon the floor. He closed a nearby window sparing a quick glance outside. "You're a bit finely dressed for a resistance member. If you hadn't spoken the code word, I was not about to let you in."

"Hmmm, yes, hazard of my position, I fear," Isaac replied.

"Tea?" The man asked.

Isaac shook his head. "I won't be long. I'm here to ask about a woman."

"A woman?"

"Yes, a beautiful woman with lavender eyes and tattoos on her hands. She may have been seeking passage on a ship."

"I think I would have remembered such a woman."

"Nothing comes to mind? She would have been traveling with another woman with black hair and blue eyes."

The man shook his head. "I've seen no one like that."

"If you should, would you be so kind as to call on me. I am staying at The Stone Hollow Tavern."

The man nodded. "Is she in some kind of trouble?"

"You could say that." Isaac ran a hand through his dark curls. "What news of the rebellion?"

"The numbers are growing," the man said. "Weapons training is happening at all locations and there is talk that fighters may begin to gather at headquarters soon."

"Headquarters you say?"

The man nodded. Isaac stood and thanked him.

As he exited into the chilly star-studded night, Issac let out an exasperated sigh. It had been a month and no sign of Mæve. The woman stood out with her unusual looks. If she had passed through Allam, someone would have seen her by now. He had exhausted all his contacts. Where else could she have gone if not to the port cities for a ship?

A FEW WEEKS LATER, on the other side of the kingdom, Isaac threw on his jacket and top hat, wrapping his long scarlet scarf around his throat, preparing to leave yet again with no sign of Mæve. Winter was fast approaching. He could feel it in the air, and he hurried to the stables.

He had never liked Essendial and had been longing to get out of the town of religious zealots since he'd arrived the night before.

Now he untied his horse from the inn's stables and set off along Main Road, heading east. He passed the Church of Light on his way out of town. The large pristine building loomed ominously over the main road. The Azantium one-god wanted people to know his power.

Relieved to be free from the awful town, Isaac appreciated the beauty of the Azantium countryside before him: a spattering of farms, but mostly rolling fields that stretched to the horizon, bare now that the harvest was over. Winter was a quiet time in the kingdom. Everything slowed down as the earth slept.

Everything, that is, except Isaac. He had always used this time to get ahead while others relaxed. The idea of a respite had never occurred to him. But now, after some time away, Isaac knew that he could never go back to the work he had done before. His days as a merchant were over.

Over the years, as the royals' wealth increased from the labas bean, the peasants and slaves remained in poverty. With plenty of money flowing into the kingdom, only one small group was benefiting—the royals. The rest of the kingdom toiled. And the Lumani were no safer after Isaac's work bartering the treaty of Falls Hollow.

The rebellion was growing. Isaac would attend the next meeting and offer his full support to the cause. After the meeting, he would travel to Eod and meet with Armaiti to brief him on the rebellion and his fruitless search for Mæve.

Isaac focused on the road before him and spurred his horse along faster. The sun rose and then fell. Tendrils of the unknown reached for Isaac, taunting him, and an unease, unlike anything he'd felt before, settled into his bones.

Then he arrived at a crossroads.

To the north, was the city of Quan.

Isaac knew what lay between him and Quan. The Mycellium.

He stood still, barely breathing, as a late autumn gray breeze curled around him. The forest called to him, promising him the answers he sought about his powers.

Was he losing his mind? He shook his head. He didn't have time for any detours. Resolved, he turned his horse down the road heading east and took off, leaving a plume of dust behind them.

The sun was setting, the shadows growing long, as Isaac at last approached a sign. Just enough light remained to read it and confirm that he had arrived at his destination: *Welcome,* it said, *to the Town of Epoth.*

18

Mæve cupped the rounded mortar in her hand as she diligently ground clove and star anise with her pestle. Satisfied with her work, she set it aside and brushed away a stray hair which had escaped from the thick braid down her back. She took a moment to appreciate the setting sun's golden light streaming through the windows of her cottage as the sweet pungency of the spices filled her nose.

From the next room her patient coughed. She got back to work, pouring the ground spices into a small mesh bag filled with hyssop leaves and setting the mixture to steep.

It had been one month since Mæve had begun her training with Ardra. During that time, Ardra had been teaching her healing arts, primarily using plants, but once Ardra had learned of Mæve's knowledge in traveling the veils, she taught her how to use both her ability to journey between realms and herb medicine to heal a patient.

The tea was ready. Mæve carried it into the next room where Chalen waited.

"Here you are," Mæve said.

"Thank you." Chalen reached for the tea.

He had intimidated her when she had first met him, but as Mæve had gotten to know him better she'd discovered that Chalen was a warm and decent person.

"The place looks nice," he said, nodding in approval, and then wincing from a sip of tea. "Wow, that's potent."

"Drink all of it. And thank you for those iron pegs you brought me the other day; they were just what we needed to fix the roof. Giselle was pleased."

"It's nice to see someone in here again," Chalen said. "It's so far away from the town center, though. You don't feel isolated?"

"I rather like it, actually."

It was true. Mæve enjoyed her cozy cottage, tucked away on the edge of the wood. She could see Epoth from her front door, but Mæve preferred solitude right now.

"Betha says you plan to join us tomorrow for the Loth meeting," Chalen said.

He and Betha had been trying to involve her in the rebellion for the past month. Mæve finally agreed to join them. She wanted to find her parents and bring them to safety. She had learned the rebellion worked closely with slaves, especially slaves in the Palace of Light. A vigilante named the Red Fox was their contact, an informant who was also helping to involve the slaves in the rebellion. He may be Mæve's last hope for finding her parents.

"Yes, I'll be there," Mæve responded.

"Good, good. The resistance is growing; training is occurring here in Epoth as well as Quan and Lakos. Your skills with archery would be most helpful."

"I'd be happy to help."

Chalen gulped down the last of his tea. "I'm feeling better already."

"Here," Mæve said, handing Chalen a sachet of herbs. "Make the tea three times a day."

The sun had set by the time Chalen left. Mæve returned to her workroom, where she scrubbed her hands with salt and doused them with warm water. She grabbed her cloak, picked up the basket she used for gathering herbs, and headed out into the dusk.

The moon illuminated the abundance of vegetation along the woodland path: ferns, milkweed, thistle. Mæve hugged her wool cloak tighter around her and savored the scent of lavender as she stepped out onto the path that ran past her cottage and into the forest beyond. Ardra had warned Mæve not to stray too far, but she could still gather plants in the nearest fringes of the trees.

Tonight, Ardra had charged Mæve with picking rosehips, which were best gathered by starlight.

During one of their first training sessions, Ardra had explained the two methods of healing. First was nonmagical healing. They used this for ailments like colds, flesh wounds, and burns. Surface healing used herbs and tinctures.

Healing magic involved traveling through the veils. When Mæve finally told Ardra she was familiar with the veils from her training in Callium, her teacher was not surprised. She just smiled and continued on with the lesson.

During these moonlit herb-gathering expeditions, Mæve would often stop and practice.

Mæve set down her basket and sat on a rock by a small stream in the forest. She closed her eyes. The eyes deceived. She let herself sink deeper. She felt a wind upon her face. She was passing through the veils, but suddenly Mæve was falling, fast and out of control. She opened her eyes to darkness; reached out, but there was nothing, and then she landed with a dull thud upon a misty earthen floor.

The air was stagnant and thick. Where was she? It was not the spirit world, not the way station, and not the waking world. She was in a dark forest, surrounded by odd trees. They twisted and spiraled up to the sky. An alien place. It smelled of sweet grass, moss, and something old—the faint scent of decay lingered in the air.

A sound drew Mæve's attention. She turned around and stopped her scream only by slamming her fist against her mouth. An enormous black wolf with eyes of golden flame walked toward her along a barren riverbed. It turned its giant head and looked at Mæve. She froze, scarcely able to breathe. A god? It must be.

The god-like creature opened its mouth and howled. Mæve had

heard nothing like it before. The sound reverberated through the air, pulsing, and then the wolf's back split open, revealing a blue-black canopy of stars and nebulae. It looked like the universe itself, flowing from the creature and filling the empty riverbed. The surrounding flora and fauna illuminated and sparkled. The forest was coming to life again. The ground itself moved, vibrating with the energy coursing through it. Yet no sooner had it begun than the energy hit an invisible barrier just beyond where Mæve stood. The wolf let out a mournful cry, and the riverbed was once again dry.

Mæve stepped back from the scene, terrified and befuddled. That beautiful, arcane magic from the beast had been severed by an unseen force at the edge of the wood.

Mæve wanted to get out of there. She wanted to get out of there now. And there she was, back on the rock by the stream in the waking world. Her body shook. The faint taste of sulfur lingered in her mouth.

She stood and snatched up her basket, hurrying back down the woodland path. She wanted the safety of her cottage.

DESPITE A SLEEPLESS NIGHT, Mæve rose with the dawn and went out onto her front porch with a steaming cup of tea. The crisp fall morning greeted her with the scent of wood-smoke. It was a splendid morning for a ride. Once she finished her tea, she would take Tráthóna into the village.

She needed to prepare for the Loth meeting tonight. The Loth was a secret publication printed in Epoth that documented rebellion efforts across the kingdom. It was also used to communicate plans to disrupt trade routes and supply lines or share information about trainings. They wrote the Loth in code and each delivery included a separate key. So that if the publication ever fell into Azantium hands, it would not make sense without the key.

Betha and Giselle were hosting the meeting tonight.

She went back inside her cottage to fetch carrots, then fastened her boots and wrapped her cloak around her shoulders as she slipped out the door.

"Hey, girl," Mæve greeted Tráthóna. The horse nuzzled her. Her coat shimmered now. The knots brushed out of her mane and tail that now sparkled with threads of gold and silver. She was the most beautiful horse Mæve had ever seen. Escaping the Palace of Light seemed to have restored the mare back to her natural beauty and power. "I brought you your favorite treat."

Mæve held out a carrot to the horse, who gobbled it up. Their moonlit escapes into the forest seemed so long ago now. Mæve's heart pinged at the memory. She brushed it away with the shake of her head.

"How about a ride?" Mæve asked, as she scratched Tráthóna's nose.

In town, Mæve stopped by Ardra's home to drop off the rosehips. The old healer answered Mæve's knock with a wide smile.

"Mæve, you dear." She leaned in and kissed Mæve on the cheek. "Thank you, I'm far too old to be wandering the woods at night these days."

Her black eyes held Mæve's for a moment, searching. "Well, come in, come in. You're letting the chill in. I've got some violet liqueur to warm you."

Mæve sat with Ardra by the hearth's warmth.

"The seasons are shifting. Winter will be here soon. Strange happenings in the world these days." Ardra stared into the flames, entranced. "As if we stand on the cusp of something. Tell me, Little Sparrow, how was your time in the forest last night?"

"Something odd happened," Mæve said.

"Oh?"

"I was practicing traveling the veils. I did everything correct. The moon was full, and I spun a protective circle and yet, I found myself in a strange place. A place that I've never been before."

Ardra leaned forward. "Go on."

Mæve told her teacher of the enormous wolf god and his truncated magic.

"Shadowlair," Ardra whispered, contemplative. "How... unexpected."

"You know this god?" Mæve asked.

"Oh yes. A god from a time long ago, a time forgotten." Ardra drew long from her drink, her face animated and her cheeks flushed.

"He is one of the seven gods bound in the Mycellium Forest."

"The ones the wizards bound?" Mæve asked.

Ardra nodded. "For the royals. They used their learned magic."

Mæve frowned. "Learned magic? Like black magic?"

Ardra cackled. "No, although that does exist. Black magic is the perversion of natural magic. Learned magic is exactly what it sounds like: magic that relies on the use of books, seeing stones, and amplifiers. It is a different magic than the Mycellium Forest or the Lumani. When the Wizards of Arkas bound the Mycellium, neither the Lumani's natural magic nor the power of the gods could remove the seal."

"And this... Shadowlair?"

"Shadowlair is the most elusive of the gods. He keeps the magic flowing through Ulli, as a conduit that feeds the great Mycelial connection that forms a webbing throughout Zama. It is the very source of magic. If Shadowlair cannot touch it, if he cannot feed the mycelial network as he must, it will die. This explains so much. It means the magic of this land may be dying a slow death. I have felt this, though I've denied it."

"Magic dying... but the Lumani! They use magic like we use bread and water."

"I know. The Lumani will suffer the most if magic should die."

Ardra appeared deep in thought before she continued. "There once was Shalik. Special children born able to create new Chrysillium trees and thus new magic on Ulli. But the Shalik are no more."

"What happened to them?"

"Time passed, and those that were not killed by the Azantiums died of old age. The Shalik are only born of a union between a Lumani and an Allanian. Without the Allanians, there is no hope for new magic in Ulli."

Ardra appeared deep in thought. "I always wondered if the lost tribe made it."

"The lost tribe?" Mæve asked.

"A small faction of Allanians, trying to survive, planned to leave the shores of Ulli and find a new home."

"How do you know this, Ardra?"

"I was there!" The older woman's eyes twinkled.

"But that would make you..."

"That's right. Two hundred years old. I'm 223 to be exact."

"But how?"

"Our typical lifespan is three hundred years. I survived in hiding, and over the years blended in with the Azantium common folk."

Mæve shivered. Ardra was Allanian. Then she suddenly remembered the time.

"I'm sorry, Ardra, but I must leave. There's a meeting."

She kissed her teacher on the cheek and rushed out of the door.

19

By the light of flickering candles, the leaders of the rebellion gathered around Betha and Giselle's kitchen table. They discussed ideas and jotted down notes as they pored over the maps spread out in front of them.

They were not many: Chalen, their leader, oversaw rebel communications inside the capital using his extensive spy network. Gema, the town baker, and Giselle wrote the stories, and Mitch the butcher printed them on the presses. Then Jacyle, their distributor, delivered the copies to his connections in nearby towns who would spread them throughout the kingdom.

"We should get started. We have a lot to go over tonight," Chalen began, rubbing the bridge of his nose. He rummaged through some papers. "Our numbers in the border towns and villages have tripled in the past year. Interest is growing. Some of these factions, especially in Quan and Lakos, are getting large enough to risk drawing unwanted attention. I think we should pull them here to Epoth. They can set up tents in the field past Mæve's house."

"That will draw attention to Epoth. And what about the tax collectors?" Gema said.

"She's right," Giselle said. "The last thing we want is any attention turning towards Epoth. Our defenses are not nearly strong enough—"

"But if we draw together, we will collectively be stronger," Chalen said.

"But our anonymity is our greatest protection right now," Gema argued.

"What if," Mæve spoke up. "We had the newcomers stay in the woods just beyond the fields by my house?"

But Chalen shook his head. "Then we risk upsetting the Lumani. That's the last thing we want to do."

Mæve blanched. "The Lumani? But Idris is days from here..."

"The Lumani aren't in Idris, Mæve. They migrated to their fall home in Eod a month ago. Eod is just a few miles into the woods."

"Chalen," a man entered the room. Mæve didn't know his name, but she knew he'd been on watch that evening. "A man claiming to be the Red Fox has just arrived and is asking to speak to you."

Chalen's brows knit as he rose from his seat.

"I'll go with you," Mitch said, hefting a hand ax upon the table. "Make sure you got protection."

"Is it just one man?" Chalen asked.

The brewer nodded. "He looks wealthy. More like high-class scum than a soldier."

"I'll go alone," Chalen said, and he followed the brewer out the door.

The rebellion members exchanged worried glances.

Chalen soon returned, speaking over his shoulder to someone. Everyone at the table craned their necks, trying to see. Mæve gasped as the man behind Chalen came into the light. Isaac Houghton?

"I'll introduce you to the rest of our group," Chalen said. Isaac looked around the table, and his gaze stopped at Mæve. He looked just as surprised to see her.

"Oh," he said. "Well, there you are."

Mæve tilted her head in question. Chalen's eyes danced between them, and then he addressed the group.

"It's true, this is the Red Fox."

The rebellion members took turns getting up to shake Isaac's hand and introduce themselves and then Isaac and Chalen took a seat at the table.

"So you've left your position in the capital then?" asked Chalen.

Isaac glanced at Mæve before he responded.

"In a sense. I am now fully committed to the rebellion and to continuing my communications with our contacts in the capital. I did not give my resignation to the queen just yet. I've been working with my contact Lacian, a slave in the Palace of Light. He assures me the slaves are ready to revolt. They await only our word."

"Good," said Chalen.

"And the surrounding towns are preparing for the external attack," Jacyle added, his eyes fierce.

"Our hope is that this will create a diversion," Chalen said. "That the queen will send the royal army to meet ours. Then the slaves will revolt at the defenseless Palace of Light."

"Have you considered," Isaac added as he nonchalantly spun a coin over the tops of his slender fingers. "Engaging the Lumani in your plans?"

The room was silent. Isaac uncrossed his legs and leaned forward.

"I depart for Eod tomorrow to meet with the Lumani king. Your rebellion interests him."

Mæve snorted. "Armaiti would never meet with you, Isaac. Better if you send someone else."

"*King* Armaiti," Isaac said. "Requested the meeting personally."

Mæve's cheeks burned, but Chalen interrupted.

"Yes, I think the Lumani's support would be a significant advantage to us, but why would the Lumani king want to break the peace treaty?"

"The queen has been plotting an attack against the Lumani," Mæve said.

"For years," Isaac interjected.

"How do you know this?" Chalen asked.

"I was a royal servant to the queen in the Palace of Light. I snuck information from the palace to King Armaiti in secret. I fled with my best friend, Betha, after I killed the crown prince in self-defense."

There were some gasps at the table. Then Mitch burst out:

"Well, nice work, that!" He raised his mug of ale. "We can all drink to that."

"If we could access the woods, just to start, if the Lumani king could grant us this, our problem of where to house the rebellion soldiers will be solved," Chalen said. "And then, if the Lumani want to involve themselves in our cause, we would of course welcome this."

"I'll talk to Armaiti about it tomorrow," Isaac said.

The group agreed to break for the night, and Isaac made his way to Mæve.

"I've been looking for you."

"Why?"

He seemed almost sheepish as he looked down at his coat sleeves, adjusting them.

"I just needed to know, was the idea of marrying me so terrible you needed to murder the crown prince and run away to the other side of the kingdom?"

Mæve laughed unexpectedly, and his face split into that smile of his. She had missed him a little.

"Is that why?" she said.

"I'm glad you're safe." His eyes were warm, but then his face sobered as he said, "I need to talk to you. In private."

"Why don't you come to my place? We can talk there."

They said their goodbyes, and Isaac promised to update Chalen as soon as he returned from Eod. On the walk to Mæve's cottage, Isaac told her everything that had happened from the night he rode into Idris to this evening when he rode into Epoth.

As they arrived she hesitated just a moment and then said, "Armaiti, was he well?"

"He's riddled with worries and I wouldn't say he was pleased with his new marriage, but yes, he's doing well."

Mæve turned from the merchant and walked towards the kitchen. She thought she had a bottle of wine in there somewhere. She found it and two glasses, then turned back to Isaac and shrugged. "I thought maybe there was something more between us, but then he was gone and married and that's the last I heard."

She busied herself with opening the wine bottle.

"I'm sorry," Isaac said as he approached.

"Don't be."

"There's other news," Isaac said, taking the wine she offered him and setting it back down without a sip. "I think you should take a seat."

Mæve sat down, not taking her eyes off the merchant.

"Your parents.... The queen found them. I tried to get to them first, but I'm so sorry Mæve. Your parents are dead."

She leaned away from him as if slapped. "What?"

"The queen was in a rage after Lucius' death. She knew it was you, the tattoos, your eyes. I'm so sorry."

He put a hand on her arm, but it barely registered. If she hadn't killed Lucius, everything would have been fine. She would've escaped with Isaac and Betha. They would have found her parents and then joined the revolution. This was all wrong. All terribly wrong.

She couldn't breathe. She needed air. She slammed through her back door and fell to the ground, sobbing, gasping.

Behind her she heard the door open and close, then felt a warm hand upon her back.

"How... How did she kill them, Isaac?" she managed.

"Mæve, don't... don't do this to yourself—"

"How?"

A pause. "Public execution. I'm not sure of the exact method. I wasn't there."

Mæve sat up, trembling, and wiped her face.

"Were they together?"

Isaac pulled her in close. "Yes," he said, and Mæve wept on his shoulder.

Finally, she found the strength to sit back. He helped her up and back inside the cottage.

"It's late," Mæve said. "You're welcome to stay here if you like, and ride out to Eod in the morning."

"I'll do that. Thank you."

Mæve made a bed for Isaac in the living room by the fire and then, without bothering to change her clothes, she sank into her bed and fell into an exhausted, troubled asleep.

20

Warmth seeped back into Isaac's bones as he sat beside the Lumani king's arbden, waiting for a response. The fire illuminated the contours of Armaiti's face as he considered Isaac's request.

Isaac looked out over Eod. Little lights adorned the spiraling staircases winding up the arbdens. They hung suspended, dancing along the bridges that connected the massive trees. Eod was aglow in the evening, enchanting Isaac with its beauty.

"Jaleh will not be pleased," Armaiti said. "But I do not see the harm in having your army so close to Eod. Not if they stay off our land and cause no trouble. How is the rebellion progressing?"

"People are moving. It's a good plan. A solid plan. I can't know for sure, but I imagine we will be ready for an attack by late winter, maybe three to four months."

"The Lumani are running out of time," Armaiti said. "I fear an attack will happen soon. We may need to act before your resistance is ready. If so, it should not hinder your efforts. In fact, it may make them easier."

"Fewer of you will die if you can wait, Armaiti," Isaac pointed out.

"Many more may die if I do not act first," he said.

Isaac leaned forward. "Join us—"

"Isaac?" A voice in the near distance cut through their conversation. "Isaac Houghton?"

Isaac stood and turned to see the smiling face of Mohlin.

"Mohlin!" Isaac embraced him. "You made it."

Mohlin smiled. "It was you that night, wasn't it?"

Isaac lowered his eyes, suddenly reticent.

"I am alive today because of this man," Mohlin said to Armaiti.

Armaiti looked at Isaac, but Isaac could only think of Lilya. He knew he should tell Armaiti, but he couldn't form the words.

"Have you come back to live with us?" Mohlin asked.

"No, no," Isaac said. "Trying to keep a low profile, actually. But I'm glad you're safe, Mohlin."

Mohlin ran off with a wave. Isaac turned back to Armaiti.

"If you joined us," Isaac said. "And we combined the forces of the Lumani with the rebellion fighters, we could not only protect your people from an attack but we could have a chance of overthrowing the royals. A real chance."

Armaiti was silent, staring into the fire. "Change is our only protector."

He looked at Isaac. "Your words are wise. I support your rebellion, merchant. I will speak to Jaleh and the elders."

"I leave for the capital in a few days to tie up loose ends with my contacts there," said Isaac. "I will ride to Eod again on my return to Epoth and we can talk then."

"In the meantime, we will welcome the rebellion soldiers to camp in the woods by Eod."

"Good," Isaac said. "Thank you."

"And... any sign of Mæve in your travels?" The king's voice was hesitant, and he avoided Isaac's eyes, staring into the fire.

"Mæve is in Epoth."

"Epoth?"

"Yes."

"And she is well?"

A shot of jealousy coursed through Isaac.

"She is safe and involved in the rebellion. Grieving the murder of her parents by the queen, though. Publicly executed during migration."

Armaiti's face darkened. "Those were her parents?"

"You saw them?"

"I did."

Armaiti was quiet and then he said, "Tell her I asked of her. Tell her..." Armaiti hesitated.

"I will," Isaac said.

The two bid their farewells and agreed to meet again when Isaac returned from the capital. Isaac spurred his horse back to Epoth, back to Mæve's cottage near the woods.

AFTER ISAAC LEFT to return to Epoth, Armaiti continued to sit by the fire for a long time, thinking. Eventually he stood and put out the fire, then made his way home.

Iraji was there, getting ready to retire.

"I think we should try to talk to the elders again," began Armaiti.

Iraji looked at him, incredulous.

"We'll argue again for you to be my personal advisor. Your family will remain in their dwelling here on the inner rim, and I will grant you my blessing to marry Ariol. You're my best friend, Iraji. I don't want to lose you."

Iraji stepped forward and embraced him.

"You're a good person, Armaiti Avari," she said. "We'll make them listen to us."

"Change seems to be all around us," Armaiti said. "I fear if we do not embrace them, we will not survive."

"You're not just talking about you and I, are you?" she asked.

Armaiti met her eyes, then walked to the large windows that looked out over Eod. She was right. This was far bigger than them and their desires, and Jaleh needed to see that. Change was upon them.

21

It was late when Isaac arrived at Mæve's cabin on the edge of the wood. Candles flickered in the windows and the sweet smell of wood-smoke greeted him. As he entered the front door, his heartbeat quickened. Mæve was curled up in a chair by the fire.

"Isaac!" Mæve smiled, "You're back."

"Good evening," he said as he hung his coat and hat by the door. "You didn't need to stay up."

"I don't mind." She unfolded her legs, rising with a natural grace from her seat. "Tea?"

"Yes, thank you," Isaac said.

"How was your trip?"

"Eod is as breathtaking as I remember it. Armaiti asked about you."

Mæve averted her gaze, focusing on the tea.

"He's well?"

"As well as he can be, with the challenges that face him," Isaac said as he set his satchel by the kitchen table. "He's considering joining the rebellion. He gave the okay for our soldiers to camp in the woods by Eod as long as they don't venture onto Lumani land, but he has a battle ahead of him in dealing with the elders. I meet with him again once I return from the capital."

Mæve frowned. "I appreciate his willingness to let the army stay so close to Eod, but when we march on the capital I think the Lumani should stay behind."

Isaac laughed out loud. "Armaiti would never involve himself in a rebellion and then stay behind for the battle."

Mæve went silent and looked into her tea. "When will you leave for the capital?"

"Oh, so you don't want Armaiti in the capital, but I am free to go," Isaac said, smirking.

She tossed him a look. "I don't want you there either."

"Oh?" Isaac stepped closer to her, but she turned away from him.

"The Loth meeting is tomorrow night. I'll leave the following morning," Isaac said as he began unpacking.

"You look drawn," Mæve observed. "Are you okay?"

"Just old ghosts visiting me along my night ride," Isaac said.

"Do you want to talk about it?"

Isaac considered for a moment.

"The woman I told you about from my time living with the Lumani." He took a sip of his tea, trying to swallow down his swirling emotions.

"I was the one who tried to help her escape, but..." he paused again, and swallowed. "But it didn't work. She was killed."

Mæve's face was sympathetic.

"Isaac, that's horrible. I'm so sorry. There's nothing you could have done."

"Well, see, that's the thing," he said, squinting. "I was there. I hid in the woods and watched her die at the enforcers' hands."

Mæve placed a hand on his arm. "Isaac, you couldn't have saved her."

He nodded. Mæve gently pulled him into an embrace.

"She's Armaiti's cousin. He deserves to know what happened to her."

"Next time," Mæve said. "Maybe you can tell him next time."

Isaac nodded as he pulled back and straightened. "I've kept you up late enough tonight."

"You're a good man, Isaac." Mæve stifled a yawn as she got up and squeezed his shoulder.

A warmth bloomed in Isaac's chest and spread down his arms. "Good night."

Mæve went into her room and closed the door. Isaac grabbed his still-steaming cup of tea and went out onto the porch. Mesmerized by the beauty of the speckled night sky—he never saw stars like this in the capital—he set his mug down on the porch rail too close to the edge. The cup teetered, Isaac reached for it too late as it fell... and then it stopped mid-air, cup and liquid hovering above the ground.

"What the..." Isaac began, his skin prickling. He was doing this.

Then a scream cut through the night. The mug dropped to the porch and shattered. Mæve.

He ran to her bedroom, where she twisted and writhed under the covers.

Isaac gently wrapped his arms around her, whispering soothing words into her ear, and waited for her to wake.

Her violet eyes, terrified and confused, stared up at him.

"I'm so sorry," she said.

"Please, no need to apologize. I'll stay until you feel safe again."

"Thank you." She swiped away tears, then curled back up on her pillow. How he wanted to reach out and hold her, but he knew that would be inappropriate. Right now, she needed companionship. So he lay on top of the covers and simply held her hand.

THE NEXT DAY, Isaac and Mæve spent the afternoon chopping vegetables and fresh herbs for a stew. Isaac had never cooked anything before in his life. Mæve had learned from her father, which brought up bittersweet memories. Though she tried to hide her quivering chin, Isaac noticed. His attempts to make her laugh resulted in a sliced finger; not the result he had planned for, but it had the desired effect. Her attention diverted to his gushing thumb.

She guided him to the table and applied pressure with a rag.

"Keep the pressure on, I'm going to grab some ointment and bandages." Mæve hurried into the back room, but by the time she returned the bleeding had stopped.

"That's impossible." Mæve turned his thumb over, looking for the wound, but there was scarcely a nick now. "I thought I was going to have to give you stitches."

"Hmm," Isaac said with a shrug. "I've always been a quick healer. What's next?"

Mæve shook her head. "Um, I think that's it." But she didn't stop looking at him, questioning.

Later they settled onto the porch with wine. As they waited for the Loth members to arrive. Mæve's gaze settled somewhere in the woods behind Isaac. He turned to see what she was looking at.

"We have a watcher."

Isaac leaned forward, alarmed, but he saw nothing.

"Don't worry," Mæve said. "He's Lumani. I noticed him this morning."

Realization dawned on Isaac. "He sent someone to make sure you're okay."

Mæve's cheeks flushed, and she avoided Isaac's look.

"It's kind of sweet, isn't it?"

Mæve ignored him.

"People are arriving," she said, as a small group approached the cottage.

Isaac laughed out loud.

"*I* think it's kind of sweet."

They rose to greet their guests.

Inside, candles were lit, maps strewn about the kitchen table, and the provisions that Isaac and Mæve had spent the day preparing laid out on tables.

"I see you've returned from Eod," Chalen said. "What news from our Lumani friends?"

"King Armaiti has granted us his blessing to use the woods by Eod," reported Isaac.

"Great work, Isaac," Chalen said. "Gema, how quickly can you get the stories written?"

"They're ready," Gema replied. "I started them yesterday, in case the answer was yes."

"And we love you for it," Chalen said, a large smile warming his face. "Mitch, how long will it take to print them?"

"If I could get a hand or two, and we worked through the night, morning after tomorrow."

"That'll have to do," Chalen said.

"It's those machines, they take so long—" Mitch began, but Jacyle cut in.

"I'll ride fast as soon as they're ready," Jacyle placed a hand on Chalen's forearm, an unmistakable look of love in his eyes. Chalen held his hand back.

"I'm supposed to ride back to the capital tomorrow morning," Isaac said. "I can delay my trip a day and deliver the copies to Clatos. Then in the capital I'll touch base with the slaves at the Palace of Light and tell them to await word from us."

"And is it safe for you to do this? What about the queen?" Jacyle asked.

"I will need to pretend to return to my duties for a time so that she doesn't suspect anything."

"This is good," Chalen said. "At last, it's finally happening."

"All those lost during Bloody Harvest will be avenged," Jacyle said.

"For all the bloody injustices," Mitch added.

"Is there anything else we need to discuss tonight?" Chalen asked.

"I want to help," said Mæve, unexpectedly. Chalen turned to look at her.

Isaac wasn't surprised. Still, he felt a brief pang of protectiveness. He really didn't want Mæve involved. She was a healer, she had no place on the battlefield. But then he remembered Lucius' ruined body on the floor of the lord's office. Maybe there were some things about Mæve he didn't know yet.

The meeting adjourned and Isaac found himself alone with Mæve again. They cleaned up after their guests, both pleased but exhausted from the day.

"That was quite a meeting tonight," Isaac said.

"It was," Mæve paused for a moment to look at him. "Do I need to worry about you?"

Isaac laughed. "Always worry about me."

"I'm serious. I don't want you to return to the capital. It's..."

"Dangerous, I know. I'll be careful. I'm good at staying out of trouble." He winked at her.

Mæve rolled her eyes, but the corners of her mouth ticked up a bit. "Just be careful, Isaac. I'll miss you while you're away."

Again, that warmth spread throughout his body.

"I'll be back before you know it."

Mæve smiled and squeezed his hand as she walked past him.

"I'm off to bed. Good night Isaac."

"Good night, Mæve."

But sleep eluded Isaac that night.

FOR THE NEXT few days Isaac, Mæve, and the other members of the Loth worked around the clock on printing copies and binding them together for delivery. By the following evening everything was ready.

"We did it." Mitch wiped his brow. "Let's celebrate."

They built a bonfire in the center of town and laughed and drank and danced around it.

Mæve and Isaac stood together, giggling into their ales.

"Can you imagine if we had gotten married? You would be accompanying me to court gatherings as my wife..." but he couldn't finish. They were laughing too hard.

"Those jealous court bitches would have cut me." Mæve laughed even harder, thinking of the absurdity of Valentina with an actual knife in her hand.

This thought practically brought Isaac to his knees, and he took a seat on a log by the fire. Mæve joined him. They subsided into silence, staring into the flames.

After a moment Mæve sighed.

"You okay?" he asked.

"Just sleepy," she said. "And you have an early ride tomorrow. Maybe we should go back."

He nodded and took her hand. They said goodnight to their friends and rode back to her cottage.

She'd go see Ardra tomorrow for some training. That would help set her mind back on course. And then maybe have dinner with Betha and Giselle. With some peace of mind, she sank into a restful sleep.

22

It occurred to Armaiti, watching Jaleh glower at him, that her stare could likely make an angry boar reconsider before it charged.

He and Iraji stood waiting before the council elders: Jaleh and Alman, Queba and Shal, Bala and Rechon.

"To be sure I understand correctly," Jaleh said. "You are not only allowing a foreign army to amass right outside our borders, but still clinging to this absurd notion of separating from your queen?"

"This union is not fooling anyone," Armaiti said. "People know something is wrong. It is better if we break it and allow Iraji to be my advisor."

Armaiti looked at Iraji, whose eyes shone a fierce gold.

"Jaleh, let me serve my king," Iraji said. "I cannot in this role you have assigned to us."

"The last thing we need is the Air Clan leaving over this," said Jaleh.

"I will talk to Simal. He will understand." Iraji bit her lip.

A pause as the head of the elders considered them. "If you can get him to accept this, then I will grant it."

"I'll go get him," Iraji said, and with a squeeze of Armaiti's arm she ran off to fetch the Air Clan leader.

They returned shortly. Simal bowed to the elders, but his smile did not reach his eyes as he looked at Armaiti.

"For what reason am I pulled from my family meal?"

"I want to be advisor to the king and we need your blessing," Iraji said.

Simal looked dumbstruck. "I believe that is what the queen already does, Iraji."

"Not queen. Just an advisor."

"What is the meaning of this?" Simal snapped, his attention now turned to Jaleh, but Iraji answered him.

"You know how Ariol and I have felt for each other, ever since we were kids. I cannot be forced to be with a man I do not love, but what I can be is a powerful advisor. Someone who represents the Air Clan on the right-hand side of our king."

"There is no way to get closer to a man than his bed, Iraji," Simal fired back.

Armaiti's anger flared. He would not strike Simal, but how he wanted to at that moment. He stepped forward, shielding Iraji from any more disparaging comments.

"Her family will not lose their status. She will be my closest political advisor."

"And what will happen when you remarry? The Air Clan will be pushed, once again, to the outskirts."

"I have no plans to remarry," Armaiti said.

"A king without a queen?" Simal scoffed. "That is absurd."

"Why not?" Armaiti remained calm. "With Iraji as advisor, I need no one else."

"Simal," Iraji said. "Please, don't make me do this any longer. As an advisor, the needs of the Air Clan will be better met. Please, I beg of you, let me be done with this farce of a marriage."

Sympathy graced Simal's face for his childhood friend, but it slipped away again as he looked back to Armaiti.

"Fine," he said with a sneer. "But if you marry again, King Armaiti, I want your word it will not be of your own clan."

It was an easy promise. "You have my word."

"Then it will be done," Jaleh said solemnly. "Never before has this happened. I hope you are right, King Armaiti. For all our sake."

23

The chapel was still and empty. The folds of Druscilla's black dress splayed out around her as she knelt on the dais of the massive white room. Before her, a brilliant sun shone. The symbol of the Lord of Light.

"May the light bless us in your splendor," she said, drawing her hands to her heart.

A soft snow fell outside the large arched windows. Finally, Druscilla was at peace. Queen regent no longer.

She had taken control not because she wanted it, but because she knew she must. Still, she remembered the way the king's feet had twitched as she smothered him. The way his weak hand had clawed uselessly at her arm.

Wealth would flood back into the kingdom upon the blood of the Lumani. She was a pure woman, forced to do dark things in these evil times. The Church of Light forbid murder, and she prayed for forgiveness. But a greater sin would have been doing nothing while her people fell into ruin.

Druscilla bowed her head. As she straightened, a shadow joined her side. Sují.

"Is it done?" His voice was barely a whisper.

She nodded, and he leaned in to kiss her, but Druscilla leaned back. He cocked his head at her.

"The door to the chapel is locked, with a guard outside. I told him the queen requested some time alone to mourn her king."

"Aren't you brilliant," Druscilla replied, but he was already kissing her deeply, sliding the wide collar of her black mourning dress off her shoulders. He took her there upon the chapel dais, the golden sun of the Lord of Light blazing above them.

IT HAD BEEN a busy couple of weeks in the capital and Isaac was grateful for the warm food and wholesome company before him now. He finished his bowl of stew and before he could put down his spoon, Berit had already whisked his bowl away to the kitchen to refill it for him.

Anders chuckled as Isaac called after her, "Berit, I'm perfectly capable of fetching my own stew."

"Not in my house," Berit said, placing a fresh bowl in front of him. "You're too thin. Eat up."

Anders chuckled again, which brought out giggles from the two children at the table, Helene and Erik. Isaac ruffled Erik's hair, and the boy smiled up at him.

"All right, off to bed with you two," Anders said to the children.

"And no scaring your sister, Erik," Berit called as the children scampered away. The boy let out a malicious chuckle and Berit turned to Isaac with a twinkle in her eye. "Little hellion, that one."

"What is this talk about leaving the capital, Isaac?" Anders' face was somber.

"War is coming. I know it's not a pleasant thought, but it won't be safe for you here," Isaac said.

"Joining the rebellion in Epoth seems unsafe too," Anders said.

"It is," Isaac agreed. "Riskier to stay, though. When the fighting begins do you really think the royals will care about you and your family?"

"Isaac, you know we love you," Berit said. "But we have responsibilities, and mouths to feed."

"Bring your family. I'm leaving at the end of the week and I want you all to come with me."

Berit looked at her husband.

"Let us think on it," Anders said. "Can we give you an answer in a few days?"

"That would be just fine," Isaac said.

"You be careful, snooping around the palace, Isaac," Berit said. "I don't want to see your pretty head on the stone of virtue."

"The stone of virtue?" Isaac asked.

"It's a dais the queen had erected just outside the capital walls for public executions," said Anders. "Her new favorite has been disemboweling, quartering, and then beheading on the stone of virtue."

"You need to be careful," Berit said.

"I will. I should go. Busy day tomorrow at the palace."

Isaac and Anders stood, and he shook Anders' hand, thanking him for a wonderful meal, and headed out into the starry, snowy night for the long ride back to his home in the hills.

THE NEXT MORNING, a knock interrupted Isaac's morning routine. It was Lord Stefor, the eldest son of Baron Cato, a wealthy landowner.

"Sir," Isaac said, with a brief genuflect.

"Oh, knock it off, Isaac," the baron's son swatted at him as he entered.

"You never know who might be watching," Isaac said as he closed his front door. "Brandy?"

"At this hour?" Stefor smiled. "Absolutely. Beautiful home you have here, Isaac."

"Oh, I'm sure it pales compared to your father's."

Stefor scoffed and took the brandy Isaac handed him with a thank you.

"Come, let's talk on the veranda," Isaac said, guiding the young lord outside. They took a seat and exchanged a few more pleasantries before Isaac began. "Is everything in place?"

Stefor's eyes widened, and he swallowed a sip of brandy. "Yes. I've even been spending more time at high society gatherings."

Isaac grinned at Stefor's clear distaste. The young lord despised high society. He had joined the rebellion after Bloody Harvest, when his love—a farmhand on his father's estate—was killed. Stefor had not been allowed to mourn him properly, as a relationship between classes was frowned upon.

"There have been no whispers," Stefor continued, "Nothing to show they have knowledge of what we've been planning."

"Let's hope it stays that way for just a little longer."

"Yes, well, with the king dead, most of the royals are now preoccupied with the new social hierarchy. They haven't even burned him yet and—"

"The king is dead?" An icy chill gripped Isaac's heart. "How? When?"

"Died in his sleep, two days ago."

"Zama's breath." Isaac stood abruptly.

"Whose breath?" Stefor asked.

"I have to go," Isaac said. This put a wrench in his plans. He still had work to do, people to connect with, but there was no more time. It would be a two day ride to Eod. "Keep in contact with the slaves while I'm gone. I will return. It won't be long and when I do..."

"We'll be ready," Stefor said.

———

Isaac spurred his mount at a reckless speed through the southern forest. How much time did they have? The queen would sign the order, officially declaring war. They would pass this to the chief of arms. Then there was calling in the army. Maybe the Lumani had a few weeks, if they were really lucky it might take a full month. It wasn't enough time.

Isaac had stopped by Berit's house on his way out of town with two horses from his stables. He told her that the king was dead; the war was starting. She and Anders said they would set out for Epoth that night.

By the second day of hard riding both Isaac and his horse were exhausted. His horse maneuvered more slowly around boulders and felled trees. The forest grew thicker, the trees taller. Then the arbdens appeared.

Three Lumani patrols appeared in the road ahead of Isaac. He dismounted from his still moving horse, hands up in the air, but too late—one of them had already shot a bolt of fire at him.

There was no time to think. Isaac was vaguely aware of the youth's comrades yelling at him, saying that was a guest of the king, but his attention was only on the flames.

Isaac did not wish to be burned alive.

The fire dart suddenly jerked left and zipped past him, singeing his jacket and hitting a sapling that burst into flame.

For a moment, no one spoke. Isaac gaped at the little tree.

"How did you do that?" one of them asked.

Isaac shook his head. "I don't know. But I must speak with your king."

They led him to the center of Eod, where Armaiti greeted him with a smile. "Let's walk, shall we?"

"Armaiti, the news I carry is grave."

The smile faded. "What is it?"

"King Regauld has been dead for four days now. I have just ridden from the capital as fast as my horse could carry me to bring you the news."

Armaiti's gray skin seemed to pale a few shades. "The time is upon us then."

He met Isaac's gaze. "The Lumani will join the rebellion, but first I would like to attend one of these meetings."

"Give me a chance to return and gather everyone. Two days?"

"Two days will suit."

"Will your queen join you?" Isaac knew that the king and queen made political decisions together.

"I no longer have a queen," Armaiti said.

"What happened to Iraji? Is she okay?"

"Iraji is fine. She is no longer my wife, but my political advisor and yes, I would like for her to join me."

"She is most welcome. You serve your people well, King Armaiti," Isaac said. Then he took off for Epoth.

24

Mæve was cleaning up after her last patient when she heard a knock at her door. It was Isaac, looking drawn, upset, and cold. His eyes softened upon seeing her and she ushered him inside.

He seemed to relax a bit once he was by the fire, but his eyes remained shadowed.

"Are you all right?" she softly asked.

"It was a long, cold ride. But I'm here."

"I'll put on some tea and get you a blanket." Mæve busied herself at the stove. Isaac was quiet. After a moment she sat beside him and handed him a cup of tea. For a moment she caught his scent of cloves, cedar, and cinnamon.

"It's good to see you," she said, but Isaac seemed not to hear her.

"The king is dead."

Mæve froze.

"What?"

"I visited Armaiti in Eod before coming here. He wants to join the rebellion. I need to talk to Chalen and schedule an emergency meeting."

Isaac stood, but Mæve stopped him with the gentle press of her hand.

"You've just ridden almost the entire length of the kingdom in the freezing cold. I'll go talk to Chalen. You need to get some sleep. Come on."

She helped him up and to her bed.

As he lay down, Mæve gave his hand a squeeze and turned to leave the room. But he did not let go. Confused, she turned back to look at him. His tired eyes smoldered, and Mæve considered the silent proposal. Her home felt complete with Isaac here. She would be lying if she denied her desire for him at that moment.

She pulled her hand away. Isaac lowered his eyes.

She kissed his forehead, then closed the door to let him sleep.

WHEN ISAAC WOKE the fire had long since faded to embers. There was a faint pulse of light spilling through the crack under the door. The mouth-watering aroma of whatever Mæve was cooking for dinner lured him out of bed and into the living room.

She sipped wine as she cooked.

"I'm making some soup."

"Marvelous," Isaac said. He had eaten very little on his return journey and was famished.

"I talked to Chalen. He's supportive of meeting tomorrow."

"Good. And how are you feeling about it?"

A pause and then Mæve answered, "This is the best way to protect the Lumani. They need us and we need them."

She paused. "Armaiti will be there."

"You don't have to go to the meeting."

"I can't miss it, Isaac."

He almost told her about Armaiti's separation from his wife. Almost.

"I have very much missed my quiet village life here in Epoth." But what he really meant to say was that he missed her. The comfort of his life here... being with her.

He settled into the warm meal she had prepared. By the time they finished, he was exhausted again.

"I guess you'll have to sleep in my room while Berit stays with us." Two red patches formed on Mæve's cheeks.

Isaac couldn't resist. He wiggled his eyebrows and smiled with mischief. Mæve laughed as she swatted at him playfully.

"There's also the barn," she said, laughing.

THE NEXT MORNING, a light snow fell. It was the first time Mæve had seen snow, and she caught a flake on her tongue as she and Isaac walked back to her home. She smiled, a bit abashed Isaac had been watching her.

"It's beautiful," she said, her cheeks burning. Isaac's smile deepened as they walked up the stairs of her front porch, their arms full of goods gathered from town to prepare for their guests. His red scarf stood out against the bleak backdrop of winter. The snow-laden trees and sugared ground carried the scent of more snow to come in the gray afternoon.

Once inside, Mæve shrugged out of her cloak. Her obsidian tree necklace slipped out of her sweater.

"That's beautiful," Isaac remarked. "It looks like a Chrysillium tree."

"It was my mother's." She tucked the necklace back into her sweater as tears formed in her eyes. "Shall we start on the bread?"

Mæve and Isaac spent the afternoon cooking and laughing. They spared no more thoughts on distant loves or impending war. With the cooking complete, they went outside into the chilly winter afternoon. Mæve grabbed a broom and swept the fresh snow from the walkway when she felt something cold and wet pelt her arm. Startled, she looked and found Isaac's smirking face as he knelt to gather another snowball.

"Isaac!" But another ball hit her before she could say more.

Laughing, she knelt to form her own little fluffy weapon, which caught Isaac on the side of the head with a satisfying smack.

Mæve walked up to Isaac, still laughing, as she brushed the snow from his curly hair. His sandalwood eyes caught hers. She was so close to him, but she didn't move away. His hand found the small of her back and drew her nearer. His face was very close to hers now. Mæve's heart pounded. The smell of cinnamon and cloves—oh, how she wanted to melt into his warmth and surrender...

But she hesitated and Isaac loosened his hold on her.

"What is it?" he whispered.

"I can't. I'm so sorry, I just can't."

Isaac nodded, and with an understanding yet sorrowful smile, he released her.

———

THE SNOWSTORM PICKED up as Mæve and Isaac walked over to the resistance meeting, an icy wind swirling around them. They headed for the woods, where forty or so tents of varying sizes were clustered under the trees. The meeting was in the largest one.

"Removing the royals will create a power vacuum," Chalen was saying as they entered. Jacyle appeared deep in thought. "It's something we need to discuss tonight. The last thing we want is a new, perhaps even worse, threat to the kingdom after we overthrow the royals."

Chalen turned his attention to the sizable crowd now assembled. Giselle and Betha were there, and Gema, Mitch, and a few others from Epoth. The rest were strangers. Mostly farmers and poor folk from other towns and villages. No Armaiti.

"Gather round, everyone!" he announced. "Isaac has informed me that King Regauld is dead. The Lumani king will join us tonight to discuss this news."

Excited murmurs coursed through the room and this would have been the perfect moment for Armaiti to walk in, but he still hadn't arrived. Isaac spoke up instead, updating them on his progress with the slaves. He mentioned how he had met with Lacian, the leader of the slave revolt and a slave himself in the Palace of Light. Isaac explained how Lacian had told him the palace slaves were ready and waiting for the final word. Then they established a series of passwords in the event it was not Isaac notifying Lacian.

When Isaac was finished, Chalen talked about coordinating attacks with the soldiers they had gathered.

But Mæve couldn't focus. Armaiti was still not there.

Isaac approached. "We need to talk," he whispered.

She nodded and followed him to the tent's narrow vestibule.

"I'm worried."

"Me too," Mæve said.

"I'll ride to Eod after the meeting," Isaac said. "And make sure everything is okay."

"The storm, Isaac," Mæve said.

"My horse can manage."

"Maybe." But Mæve was doubtful. "If you must go, go now before the storm gets worse. Shall I ride with you?"

"No need," Isaac said. "Better if you stay here. I'll return with haste."

"Be safe," and she embraced him. He lingered just a moment before he pulled away and walked into the white of the snowstorm.

25

Anchored fire orbs lit the inside of Jaleh's healing abode. Kalouq sat across from her, three large books laid on the table in front of him. They were from the Kråshain library, the place that housed the Lumani's record of their histories and the history of Ulli, tucked deep within the Obsidian Cliffs.

"If we look at the accounts of Marius Vellum, he believed the seal was not merely meant to be a barrier from the magical creatures getting out of the forest. It was more like a tomb, a place for the magic of Ulli to die," Kalouq was explaining. He stifled a yawn; it was quite late.

"Can it be destroyed?" asked Jaleh.

"It's not clear," Kalouq said. "But from our records it appeared in the early days of the seal, the Lumani attempted to destroy it." Jaleh had no recollection of this. If there had been an effort, it had not been talked about. "It was a team of Earth Clan mages who journeyed to the Mycellium to study the stone and came back with these findings."

Jaleh sat back, considering these words, when the floor of her dwelling rumbled.

A sound ripped through the night, and Jaleh yelled, covering her ears. The thunderous roar sounded as if the heavens had crashed into the earth. Kalouq looked just as shaken. Jaleh ran to the window. A blue flash, then another concussive sound. On the ground people ran, children screamed.

"What in the gods," Jaleh said. She grabbed her staff and ran down the many steps of her arbden, Kalouq panting and following closely on her heels.

The center of Eod was a mess of confusion amongst the screams and hurried fleeing of her people. Another blast ripped through the night, followed by more screams and the unmistakable crack of a shattering tree trunk and branches snapping.

Armaiti stepped outside into chaos.

People screaming, and flashes of blue light. He flew down the stairs as fast as his legs would carry him. Around him, people fled their homes.

"Run to the river!" Armaiti called out. "Away from the center!"

He turned in a circle. Azantium soldiers were closing in, clinking about in their silly metal suits. They had labaton, those weren't the source of the enormous explosions. They must be the weapons Isaac had warned him about.

Another blast and flash of blue light. One of the giant arbdens along the second rim of Eod made a terrible cracking sound. There were families in the dwellings on that tree. He could hear their screams as the tree fell. There was nothing he could do.

He turned and ran towards the outer rims of Eod, searching out the explosions. Two Azantium soldiers crossed his path by the third rim. Armaiti cut them both down with a snarl and two slices of his large curved blades. Two more soldiers crested a hill, carrying labaton.

Armaiti ran from them, then circled around to attack from behind. Labaton was useless at close range.

Armaiti continued on. He needed to find the source of the big blasts. Another concussive sound ripped through the night, and he saw it.

He stopped running and gaped at the monstrosity in the near distance. It was large and made of dense black metal, with a circular gaping mouth.

Armaiti watched as two soldiers hoisted a large sphere into the contraption. As they turned, he ran forward and called forth the threads of water around him, channeling them into his swords before striking the earth. The threads of water coursed through his swords into the ground, which erupted under their feet.

Armaiti gave out a battle cry; he reached the first soldier and, with one hack of his curved blade, hacked off his head. The other soldier was in range; Armaiti raised his blade, but something bit into his side and sent him catapulting to the ground.

He cried out in pain. It burned and seared. His side was on fire and then darkness.

TAP. Tap. Tap. The sound of Mæve's foot thudding against the ground sent her upright and back to pacing again.

"Here Mæve, sit with us and have some wine."

"Something's wrong, Betha," Mæve said. "I'll give it another half hour, and if Isaac has not returned, I'm riding out."

"Mæve, there's a storm, and it's very late and-" Betha said.

"I'm going. I'll be fine."

The door to Mæve's cabin swung open. In walked Isaac, accompanied by a gust of wind and a flurry of snow. His face was ashen, and when he spoke his voice was barely audible.

"The Lumani were attacked."

"What?" Mæve whispered.

"It's... bad. Many are dead. And, um... they injured Armaiti. Gravely, I was told. The elders don't think he'll last the night. I'm so sorry." Isaac lowered his eyes.

No. Mæve could not accept this.

"Then we must leave," she said, reaching for her cloak.

"My horse cannot make the journey again," Isaac said. "Not in this weather-"

"Take mine," Giselle offered.

The woodland path was a ribbon of moonlight cast upon the iridescent snow as Mæve and Isaac rode for Eod. The storm had slowed, but the wind still bellowed through the night air. Mæve covered her face with her scarf to keep out the biting cold.

Wait for me at the way station. Mæve sent the desperate thought into the æther.

The way station was the place where spirits waited before fully crossing over to death. Some spirits had a brief stay, and some lingered for eternity. If Armaiti had already crossed, she could not follow.

As they neared Eod, Isaac looked back at her and shouted, "Keep your hood up! Stay close!"

An arrow whizzed by Mæve's head, just missing her.

"Isaac!" she gasped. Isaac's horse reared, then he threw up his hands.

"It is me, Isaac," he shouted into the trees. "I have brought a healer for the king!"

A tall woman stepped onto the path and squinted at Isaac, then held up her hand, motioning for the archers to cease.

"Iraji," Isaac said. "You must bring us to Armaiti at once."

Iraji considered Mæve for a moment, her face unreadable. "Jaleh says he is crossing."

"There may still be time," Mæve said.

"Leave your horses," Iraji instructed.

They followed her into Eod. Some of the trees had fallen, the little homes upon them shattered and ruined. The smell of smoke and something else... death... hung upon the air.

Iraji led them up a staircase to a humble dwelling and opened the door.

The faint scent of sage and myrrh permeated the room. Armaiti lay on a bed of furs, pale, his energy gone. Two older Lumani women were also in the room. One sat at Armaiti's bedside, holding his hand. The other stood by the foot of the bed, rummaging through herbs.

Mæve pushed back her hood.

"My name is Mæve. I'm a healer, and I'm here to help."

"Mæve?" the woman holding Armaiti's hand said. "Armaiti told me about you. I am his mother, Humana. Can you save him?"

"I will do what I can."

Mæve crossed to Armaiti's bedside and caressed his pallid face.

"Come back to us," she whispered. She lowered her eyelids and spun a protective circle around herself and Armaiti, then travelled to the veils that lay hidden just behind this reality. She lifted one and stepped through.

She was still faintly aware of her presence in the waking world, as a small part of her remained there as a beacon to draw her and Armaiti back.

The light in the other realm was different. A putrid grayish-green, like the sky before a thunderstorm. The air was thick and left a film upon her skin. Walking would get her nowhere here. Words would fall dead at her feet. Only intentions mattered—only a person's desire produced results.

There was the sound of rushing water. She turned and saw a river. Armaiti stood upon the bank, his back to her. He appeared to be ready to dive. Armaiti's spirit was strong, and he knew what he needed to do. He did not realize it was possible to return to the waking world.

She tried to yell his name. But there was no sound. Of course. The language of humans held no meaning here. Mæve set her full intent upon touching his shoulder. At first, there was nothing, but she did not break her focus.

Suddenly, she was there by his side, her hand upon his shoulder. It was nauseating to travel like that, but Armaiti turned and looked at her.

She took his hand and began to walk away, but Armaiti did not budge.

No! He must want to live. She thought seeing her would be

enough. She reached up and caressed his face. He looked back at her and touched her arm, sending a course of electricity through her center. There was love there in his eyes. Then why would he not follow?

She took him by the elbow, but again he stopped and looked out at the water.

Confused, she realized it was the river that was holding him. He had been ready, and the river wanted its flesh. She would need to make a sacrifice.

Her bracelet. The one Armaiti had delivered to her with his raven. The thought of parting with it saddened her, but she remembered how much joy receiving the gift from him had brought her.

She removed the bracelet and tossed it into the river.

Armaiti looked at her and smiled. She drew him in close and held him as they fell through the veils.

A searing pain burned Armaiti's lungs. He gasped for breath and his back arched, trying to make space to fill his sluggish lungs. He took a couple of deep breaths before his breathing normalized and the pain subsided.

As his vision cleared, he saw Mæve on the floor by the side of the bed, unconscious. Someone was calling her name... Isaac?

"Mæve?" he asked, sitting up and reaching for her. His mother stopped him. Isaac and Iraji lifted Mæve's unconscious body, laying her at the foot of the bed.

"Just rest, my son," his mother said. Dried tears stained her face.

"She's unconscious, but she'll live," Jaleh said, her face screwed into discontent. "Tell me, where is she from?" Her interest surprised them all.

"Callium," answered Armaiti. "Far to the North, across the North Sea."

Jaleh blanched. "She wears the Ullium. Impossible..."

"The Ullium?" Humana asked.

"Tree pendants the Lumani gave to the last twelve Allanians as they fled these shores; to remind them of home. We crafted them of obsidian mined from our very own cliffs. I am curious to know how she came to possess such a relic. And even more curious..." Jaleh turned a furious eye to the king, "how you know her story, Armaiti."

"My son is tired and in need of rest," Humana hissed. "Stand down, Jaleh." She turned to her son. "Come, let me bring you back to our arbden."

Armaiti cautiously lowered himself from Jaleh's healing table. His side burned; there were bandages around his waist. He undid them and examined his side. There no longer was a wound, but his muscles still ached.

"I will stay here with Mæve."

Part III
Eod

Two lovers
spiraled the night sky
an entwined helix
infinite they loved

Until the day Shadowlair
called down the stars
and Zama was born
of the sun and moon

A sacrifice
their helix split
one lover planted in the west
the other planted in the east
Ayin of the fall
Oyela of the spring

They rooted into the earth
and reached for each other
under the ground
the mycelia was born

The moon of Ayin in Eod
is Oyela's sun in Idris
only on the equinoxes Equilan and Equilĭum
do the lovers reunite.[1]

---

1. *Source: Origins of Zama*
   Year: unknown
   Current location of text: *Kråshain library on the outer rim of Eod*

26

Mæve willed open her heavy eyes. Her head throbbed. Wincing, she drew her hand to her brow. She lay upon soft brown furs, an unusual scent of oakmoss, orange blossom, and myrrh in the air.

From where she lay, she could see shelves of jars and a counter with small piles of herbs on it. Then she remembered. Eod. Armaiti.

She rose slowly upon an elbow.

"You're awake," said a familiar voice. Mæve paused, unsure if this was real. There had been so many dreams...

But the faint taste of sulfur on her tongue—a remnant from travelling the veils—was real. This was no dream.

Armaiti. He sat beside her, the kishaye on his forehead shining silver in the firelight and his long black hair framing his angular face. He appeared drawn, whether from his injuries or the grief of the attack, she couldn't tell. She reached out for his cheek.

"Armaiti," Mæve whispered.

"I saw you," he said. His voice wavered. "You came for me."

His fingertips upon her hand sent a current up her arm.

The door to the room clanged open and Mæve jumped. Just as quickly, Armaiti released her hand. Jaleh entered, her eyes on Mæve.

"You're awake."

Mæve sat up. "I'm so sorry for the attack on your people. Isaac said it was devastating. I'd like to help however I can."

Jaleh considered her. "We can use your help in the healing tent." She paused, and then, "If you are feeling well enough, of course."

She turned to Armaiti and snapped, "And if you're done holding hands with the healer, there is work to be done."

"Yes, of course." Armaiti looked at Mæve. Gods, he was beautiful. Her breath caught for a moment. "How are you feeling?"

"Better," she replied. "I'm sure there is much work and I'm eager to begin."

Armaiti helped Mæve to the ground, holding her for just a moment as she found her feet again. Mæve tried not to look at him.

"The war council needs to convene, King Armaiti." Jaleh's voice crackled between them.

Armaiti paused. "How significant is the damage?"

"The people need their king," she said. Armaiti nodded and turned to go. Mæve and Jaleh followed him out.

They made their way to the central fire pit. The smell of death lingered in the air, combined with the faint odor of smoke from discharged weapons. The cries of the injured surrounded them.

The makeshift healing station looked overwhelmed. Next to it, several uninjured Lumani piled bodies into a wagon.

Mæve reached for Armaiti's hand as they continued through the village, witnessing the devastation. She would not let him face this alone.

Mæve spotted Isaac crouched amongst a gathering of Lumani children. He was speaking animated Lumani to their wide eyes, a story perhaps.

The merchant saw them approach and smiled widely, but faltered when he saw their entwined hands.

His eyes darted back up immediately. "You are both up and well. Nothing could make me happier."

"You made some friends," Mæve said, smiling.

Isaac stood. "They're orphans. Every one of them."

Mæve's heart sank. There were at least twenty children.

"There are those in Epoth who could help, Armaiti," Mæve said.

"Bring them," Jaleh said. "And if that army is still willing..." Her voice trailed off. The fierce leader appeared to blink back her tears. "Well, change is upon us, as you would say."

Armaiti addressed Isaac. "Would they still join us?"

"I know they would."

"Isaac, can you ride to Epoth? Talk to Chalen. Bring back as many as you can," Mæve said.

Isaac nodded. "I'll go immediately."

"Ride carefully," Mæve said. Their eyes met. All that was there remained still. No time for words. No time to dwell in confusion.

Isaac turned and left. Mæve hurried to the healing station.

She began to help the healers there, and as she worked a slow fury grew within her. So many injured—too many of them children.

Mæve turned to a young girl with a badly mangled leg. She swallowed at the sight of the injury and crouched down.

"What's your name?"

"Maela," the girl whispered.

"I'm going to work on your leg, okay Maela?"

Mæve got to work cleaning the wound, then wrapped it and splinted the girl's leg. By the time she finished, Maela looked ready to fall asleep. She wondered where the girl's parents were, and if they were alive. She wondered who would put the girl to bed that night.

She was torn; she wanted to care for Maela, but she needed to continue working in the tent. Then she caught sight of the woman who had sat by Armaiti's side during the healing—his mother, Humana.

"I'll be right back," Mæve said.

The little girl nodded and Mæve stepped out of the healing area. "Humana!"

Armaiti's mother stopped and turned.

"Are you okay? Is Armaiti okay?"

"He's with Jaleh about to address the war council. But I need help. There's a little girl, she's injured and lost her parents. She needs someone to care for her and change her bandages. I'd do it myself, but I'm going to be here awhile and it's no place for a child."

Humana's face softened, and she touched Mæve's arm. "You have a strong heart. Bring her to me, I will care for her."

Mæve sent the girl off with Humana and returned to her work.

As the night wore on, she found herself often frustrated. There were so many wounds that just would not heal, and people in excruciating pain. She couldn't figure it out. It was unlike anything she had seen before.

A man with a gaping wound in his side screamed and writhed before her. Bala, one of the Lumani elders, explained that the man was stable yesterday. Then his condition worsened in the night and nothing would ease his suffering. Now the man's pain was at a maddening level.

She tried her best, but she was at a loss. The man died writhing in pain until the end.

Mæve sat, and could do nothing but stare for a moment while inside she relived the moment again and again.

"It wasn't your fault," Bala said. "We have seen it before. It's the Labaton. There is a poison inside the little ball of fire. If you get it out quick enough a person can live. But if the poison gets inside, it can fester and once it gets into the blood, there is very little you can do."

Many had already died in a similar manner from the slow, painful effects of labaton's poison, but this was the first time Mæve had seen it. Her hands shook, her stomach churned painfully. She needed a moment. She walked a short distance into the woods. Put her face in her hands and cried.

She needed to get back. There were so many others who still needed help, who could still be saved. She would get through this. She stood, readied herself, and walked back to the healing station.

THE COUNCIL GATHERED around a large fire in the center of Eod. It brought warmth to the deep chill of the winter night.

Armaiti stepped forward to address the gathered members.

"I have already requested help from the village of Epoth. They will join us to help heal our wounded and bury our dead."

Simal glowered at Armaiti.

"Who says we need help from outsiders?" he asked. "We can take care of our own. It was outsiders who caused this atrocity."

Armaiti looked at Simal. "These people are different. They are forming a rebellion to fight the royals. They are not our enemies."

"We are the best warriors in all of Ulli! We do not need help from foreigners," Simal said.

"Yes, we do, Simal," Armaiti said. "Azantium weapons continue to advance beyond what we can defend against. They have a new weapon now, even worse than labaton and capable of causing mass casualties. I watched it fell an arbden. We do, very much, need help."

Jaleh interjected, "We are here to discuss joining our forces with this rebellion. I believe it is the only way we will survive this new threat."

Simal's lips curled in anger. Armaiti broke in before the other man could speak.

"We cannot win this battle alone. Change is upon us. If we are not ready for it, we will not survive."

A hum rose amongst the people. Most seemed pleased. Simal and a couple of men from his clan stormed off. Armaiti let them go.

As the moon rose, Isaac Houghton returned with a small crew from Epoth and introduced them to Armaiti. Chalen stepped forward.

"We are heartbroken to learn what has happened here. In the meantime, resistance fighters continue to gather in Epoth."

"The Lumani are still interested in joining your rebellion," Armaiti said.

"Good," Chalen said. "We are stronger together."

"Many of our dwellings are now empty after so many deaths. You are welcome to bring your army into Eod."

"I think that is a wise idea," Chalen said. "We will be better protected together."

"Yes, I agree." Armaiti considered the others in the group. "And thank you for those who came to heal. We appreciate your generosity in this time of need."

"Well, of course," an old woman with twinkling eyes said. "The Lumani are stewards of this land. It is our pleasure to help."

She added something in a language he did not recognize.

From somewhere behind him, a voice responded in the same language. Jaleh. She stepped forward into the firelight and nodded to the healer.

"You're Allanian. I thought your kind were no more."

"I am the last," the woman smiled. "Or I was."

"The girl," Jaleh said. "She wears the Ullium."

"Yes, I noticed."

Jaleh cackled. "Leave it to the Azantiums to be stupid enough to bring an Allanian back here."

"She is returned home," said the healer.

The hairs on Armaiti's arms rose.

"Please, can you show our visitors to their dwellings," he said to one of the Earth Clan Lumani.

As the healer followed the man into the center of the village, Armaiti watched her go and considered what he had just learned.

27

M æve squinted in the early morning light. She forced herself out of bed, despite working until late the previous night.

She tiptoed around Giselle and Betha, careful not to wake them as she got ready.

The healing station looked only slightly better today. They had crafted tables for the injured, but with the tables full, many sat on the ground or lay on woven blankets. An awning made from wooden posts, animal bones, and woven hides hung overhead.

Mæve worked through the day mostly with nonmagical healing using herbs and tinctures. She did have to travel the veils a couple times. Once to induce sleep in the veil of dreams and once to provide a deeper healing at the way station.

Traveling the veils exhausted her and as the sun set, the hollow feeling in Mæve's stomach reminded her she had not eaten all day and yet so much work remained. Brushing a strand of hair from her face, she looked up to see Armaiti just outside the healing station, watching her.

Mæve salted and rinsed her hands, then said goodbye to the Lumani women she had worked alongside and joined Armaiti outside.

"Please, take a break," he said gently. "I can see how weary you are." He held out an arm to her, which she accepted by wrapping her arm in his.

"I brought you something to eat," he said, handing her what appeared to be leafy vegetables wrapped around dried meat.

"Did you make this?" Mæve asked. She had learned Lumani men did most of the cooking. Armaiti nodded, and she smiled. "Thank you."

"I thought I would show you around Eod tonight, if you like."

"I would," Mæve mumbled through a mouthful of food.

Around Eod, Lumani men and women were busy rebuilding, clearing fallen trees and damaged homes.

People went about their evening activities both overhead, along the tree bridges, and upon the ground. Some looked at their king and the strange woman on his arm with interest, but Armaiti simply nodded and said hello. He had explained to her about his separation from Iraji. That she was in love with someone else and was now his advisor. But there was still one thing Mæve didn't understand.

"Armaiti, can I ask you something?" Mæve said.

"Yes, anything."

"Why didn't you say goodbye? Or send word before you left and married?"

Armaiti paused. "I thought you had intentionally missed our meeting that night. I had sent Iraji to check on you, to make sure you were okay."

"I would never do that. I would have told you," Mæve said.

"I knew that," Armaiti said. "I thought for certain you were in danger, and that was the only reason I would risk sending a Lumani onto the palace grounds."

"I was beaten that night."

Armaiti's face softened. "I'm so sorry."

"It isn't your fault. We're together now."

Armaiti untangled his arm from hers, grasping her hand. He smiled at her and it sent her back to the forest glade.

"Come with me?" he said.

She nodded. They took off running into the night. As the evening darkened, patches of moss came to life, glowing blues and purples and greens through the snow. Mæve followed Armaiti's lead, mesmerized by what she saw.

They slowed at a clearing where the gentle sound of a river lapping upon the shore greeted them, and then she saw it: the blue hue of a Chrysillium tree.

"Do you remember Oyela?" he asked.

"Of course, how could I forget?"

"This is Oyela's mate, Ayin."

"The two lovers in the stars, separated when drawn to earth."

Just being in the tree's presence was soothing to her frayed nerves. She turned to Armaiti, but something brushed her shoulder and she started. The Chrysillium tree had lowered one of its branches. Armaiti laughed.

"Ayin likes you," he said.

Mæve reached up to the receding branches, the hard crystalline beans gracing her fingertips. They felt cool as they sparkled in the night.

Mæve turned back to face Armaiti, and he reached for her. His eyes remained locked upon hers as his arm encircled her waist, pulling her closer to him.

"I don't want to deny what I feel for you anymore," Armaiti said.

"Then don't."

"It will not be easy."

Mæve drew him closer to her.

"I don't care."

He pressed her against one of the trees surrounding Ayin. Her heart raced, and she pulled him to her. His lips found hers in a collision of desire and longing, a rapturous plunge into all that had been denied for so long.

Mæve gasped. Her desire was blinding, consuming, as she ran her fingers through his long dark hair. His lips found the most sensitive part of her neck and her body erupted with pleasure. She pulled him closer, her nails digging into his muscular arm. She leaned in to kiss him again, but he stopped and pulled away, though she could tell with great effort.

"What is it?" she asked.

He brushed a strand of hair from her face and she kissed his fingertips. He placed his palm over the tree necklace on her chest, then his hand traveled her down arm in a final lingering caress that ended with his fingers twining through hers.

"Join me," he asked. "By the river?"

She nodded and followed his lead.

"Do you know your people's history?" he asked.

It was not at all what she expected.

"Not much. My father taught me to navigate by the stars, something he said our ancestors used to do."

"The stars? Did he work on a ship?"

Mæve shook her head. "We had no ships for sailing in Callium. Boats for fishing, yes, but nothing large enough to cover great distances."

"But still, your people held onto the tradition of navigating by the stars. As if perhaps one day they planned to return."

Mæve stopped walking, confused.

"Return?" she asked.

"You're Allanian. Your people fled these lands hundreds of years ago when the Azantiums threatened to annihilate you."

"What?" Mæve asked, incredulous.

"Jaleh recognized your pendant, a gift from my ancestors to yours."

Mæve touched her necklace, speechless. That was impossible. Could it be true? She remembered the way the earth spoke to her when she first left Jaleh's abode. She remembered Ezio, that frightful wizard from the night in the Palace of Light so long ago. His chilling words suddenly made sense: *Foolish woman has let her doom in through the front door.*

Armaiti said, "Be with me. Be my wife. Ayin told me and I know it in my heart, I don't want to be without you anymore. I knew as soon as I saw you in the haze of my death. I knew it the first time I laid eyes upon you in the glade, though I did not understand."

Mæve's heart filled with joy.

"Yes."

His lips grazed hers, slow and sweet.

"We must speak to the elders and ask their permission."

"What do you think they'll say?"

Armaiti shook his head. "Either way, I know in my heart this is right. Nothing will change my mind."

Mæve joined his side, reaching for his hand. "We'll do it together."

28

"So I hear you somehow redirected a fire dart from one of our best channelers," Armaiti said.

"Oh, you heard about that." Isaac gave a nervous chuckle.

"An unusual talent, although I am grateful you are still alive, merchant."

Armaiti had sought Isaac out to thank him for gathering the folks from Epoth. They now sat at a small fire sharing strong Lumani tea.

Isaac winced as he sipped the bitter drink. "I don't know how I'm doing it. It's not the first time it's happened. I can move things by thinking about them. Sometimes I can even sense what people are thinking."

"What are you frightened of?" Armaiti asked.

"Frightened of?" Isaac chuckled. "I'm frightened I might be losing my mind. They kill people in Thalis for this kind of thing."

Armaiti paused a moment before speaking. "Well, you're not in your country anymore. And you aren't imagining anything."

"The Azantium overlord in Thalis killed my uncle for allegedly having similar powers."

Armaiti sat back, raised an eyebrow. Then with a sudden movement, he picked up a rock and chucked it at Isaac's head.

The rock froze, hovering right before Isaac's eyes. Curses, the man had impeccable aim.

"So you see," Armaiti said with a half smile, "You're definitely not imagining it."

"What is it?"

"I don't know," Armaiti said. "I've not witnessed magic like that before. If your uncle had it, maybe it's something from your homeland. You will fear yourself until you understand yourself."

"I want to find answers, but I don't know where to begin. I think... I think maybe there are answers in the Mycellium."

"You can't get past the seal. People have tried entering the Mycellium and gone mad," Armaiti said.

"The Mycellium?" said a dry voice.

"Eavesdropping on our conversation, Jaleh?" Armaiti asked.

"Enough of it, yes," Jaleh responded, unabashed. "I've been studying how to destroy the seal."

"Destroy it? But won't that unleash the old gods and creatures back into the world?" Isaac asked.

Jaleh snickered. "Only the Azantiums should worry."

Isaac glanced at Armaiti with a slight shrug.

"But why destroy it?" Isaac asked.

"The magic of Ulli is souring," Jaleh replied.

"Souring?"

"Yes, think of it like still water. At first, the water would be fine, but if you left it contained and did not stir the water for a long time, it would still look like water, feel like water, but if you were to drink it, you would know the water had gone bad. I believe the same may be happening with our magic.

"Locked inside the Mycellium Forest, Shadowlair, the great wolf god who calls the cosmos down upon his back, cannot circulate the energy sources of Ulli. Shålan cannot regulate the æther. Magic here is stagnating without the gods."

"What about Xä? Do you think he can still regulate the mycelia underground?" Armaiti asked.

"Xä?" Isaac was unfamiliar with the old gods of Ulli.

"Long before the wizards from Arkas came to Ulli, long before the Azantiums, Uthera—the power of the cosmos, the great unknown, the creator of all things even Zama—banished the demon war god, Xä," Jaleh said. "The legend went that Uthera had forbidden Xä from seeing his love, Shålan, goddess and ruler of the Mycellium because the two possessed too much power, power that rivalled Uthera. So from his exile underground, Xä regulated the great network of mycelia while Shålan did the same for the æther above ground.

"I need to get a look at the seal to confirm some suspicions, but I cannot leave during war preparations." Jaleh looked at Isaac with more than a hint of suggestion in her eyes.

"There's no use for you here now," Armaiti continued. "And we won't be leaving to battle for at least another couple weeks."

"I could make it back in that time," Isaac said.

"You are looking for a stone disc," Jaleh began. "Outside the main entrance to the forest, marked by an obsidian arch. Look for any clues that might help us understand how to destroy it."

Isaac nodded.

"Good," said Jaleh. "I look forward to learning what you find, merchant. Oh, and don't touch the mist."

"Any developments after our talk about the Azantium's new weapon?" Armaiti asked.

"Your information after seeing the weapon up close has been helpful," Jaleh said. "We are working on a few ideas using æther and air magic, but we have come up with nothing that could be useful in destroying the weapon yet."

He nodded and Jaleh walked away. Armaiti rose from his seat as well.

"Armaiti," Isaac began. "There's something I've been meaning to tell you, if you have a moment more."

"Of course. What is it?"

"I have wanted to tell you, but with the king's death and then the attack... well, it's Lilya."

Armaiti sat back down abruptly.

"I tried to help her escape the Chrysillium Field and... she didn't make it. I'm so, so sorry."

"What happened?"

"She was killed."

Armaiti's face hardened, his fists clenched. "The sooner we rid Ulli of this Azantium abomination, the better."

"I cared deeply for your cousin, King Armaiti."

Unexpectedly, Armaiti embraced Isaac. Then he stepped back, squeezed Isaac's arm, and left to join the council meeting.

Isaac went back to his dwelling and began to pack for his journey to the Mycellium Forest. A knock at the door interrupted him.

It was Mæve. Isaac straightened. It had been so long since he had seen her; such an abrupt change from their time living together in Epoth.

"Hi Isaac. I hope I'm not bothering you."

"I've missed you." He embraced her.

Mæve stepped back and said, "I need to talk to you."

His smile wavered. "Of course. Are you okay?"

"I am," Mæve said. "Isaac, I..." She stopped, looking physically pained.

"It's okay," he said, stepping in closer and caressing her arm. "Whatever it is, you can tell me."

"Armaiti and I are approaching the council tonight."

"Oh?" Isaac's smile disintegrated with a slow unease. "Together?"

"Yes," Mæve said. "To ask permission to marry."

"That's rather sudden."

"We think Jaleh and the elders will approve." Mæve said gently.

Isaac tried to breathe, to focus on what was being said and not the rising hurt he felt.

"You shouldn't have pulled me into this," he said, and regretted it. Her face twisted in surprise. He pushed forward anyway. "You used me to get over your feelings for him and to get past the pain of your parents' death and as soon as you have the chance to be with him again you're discarding me."

The tears in her eyes shut him up. "I'm so sorry you feel that way, but that is not what I am doing, Isaac."

He stuffed the last item for his journey into his satchel and cinched the top.

"I have to go," he said.

"Where are you going?" she asked.

"Running an assignment for Jaleh," Isaac said. He flashed her his best smile. "I wish you and Armaiti all the best."

And he walked out the door.

WHEN ARMAITI and Mæve arrived at the meeting house, the elders were already there. Armaiti stood before them, the full weight of his decision upon his shoulders.

His mother tossed him an encouraging smile, and Iraji nodded. Mæve squeezed his hand.

Iraji joined them. "I will translate for you, Mæve."

Mæve nodded and thanked her.

"King Armaiti," Jaleh said. "Tell me, what matter do you bring before us today?"

"I am here to request your permission to marry—"

"Marry?" Jaleh looked at him as if perhaps she hadn't heard him quite right. "We are at war! We do not have time for a marriage ceremony. Is that what you have called this meeting for?"

A slight pause as Iraji finished her translation, and Armaiti considered his next words.

"We will shorten the ceremony," he said. "I think it could bring people hope at a time like this."

"People will not understand why you gave up an Air Clan bride for a foreigner. It would be just the thing to send the Air Clan over the edge," Jaleh said.

"We are in love." Mæve spoke before Jaleh could continue. "We did not plan for this and we both tried to run from it. Yet fate drew us back together even away from death itself."

"I can see that, child," Jaleh snapped. "Anyone with eyes can see the love you two share. But we must be smart and be prudent right now. I'm sorry I cannot support your union. Let us win this war against our enemies, return to Eod, and we can discuss the matter again."

Armaiti was about to speak, but Jaleh rose and said, "That is all."

The other elders followed her out of the room.

29

The cool, fresh air stung Isaac's cheeks as he rode east. Time away from Eod was a welcomed reprieve and as the Mycellium drew near, his excitement grew. Finally, he would stand at the threshold of the mystical forest he had been so drawn to.

An unexpected sound drew him from his ruminations. Was that a voice? Isaac slowed his horse to a trot and looked around. The fields surrounding him were empty.

"Halt! In the name of the queen," a voice shouted from the road behind him.

Isaac's horse bolted off the road, towards the nearby forest. What in Zama? Why were their soldiers this far east?

Without slowing, he steered his horse into the forest. To ride this fast amongst the trees was dangerous, but getting caught was far worse. Isaac ducked under a low branch just in time. The pounding of hooves grew louder behind him. He risked a quick glance over his left shoulder. They were close. As Isaac turned his head, there was a sickening crack and then darkness.

GUARDS LINED the stone curtain wall outside Queen Druscilla's window. After declaring war the queen had pulled in conscripts from the countryside, increasing the palace guards thrice-fold, lining the curtain walls at every hour of every day. She ordered guards to be placed outside the doors of every royal chamber in the palace.

With the capital on lockdown, frightened whispers spread throughout the kingdom, rumors that they were at war again with their fiercest enemy.

After the attack upon Eod, the queen was confident this battle would not be as bloody or as lengthy as the Lumani Wars. No, the Azantiums had far superior weapons now. The Lumani had suffered great losses. At last the Lumani had paid for the murder of her sister and they would continue to bear her wrath.

A knock sounded on her door, interrupting her thoughts.

Chief of arms Maximus Alius, stood before her, his stone-chiseled face unreadable.

"Your Highness," he said as he straightened. "We caught the merchant, Isaac Houghton."

She didn't hold back the smile that spread across her face. "That's wonderful news. Great work Chief Alius. I'm interested to see what answers the merchant will provide us with."

It had been disconcerting when they had learned the wealthy merchant had left the capital without a word. A little looking into the situation had shown that the merchant's accounts had been drained and his servants let go.

"How would you like to proceed, Your Highness?"

"Send Algar," she replied. The thought of their most ruthless integrator working the truth out of the pampered merchant made her quiver with anticipation. What secrets was Isaac holding?

30

A nauseating pain radiated from the right side of Isaac's head. One of his eyes wouldn't open. He tried to reach up to touch his wounded face, but found he could not move his arm. Terror washed over him. Was he paralyzed? No; someone had restrained him.

He was on a wooden table in a dim room. There were no windows, and deep shadows flickered in the candlelight. Two muffled voices wafted in from the other side of the large wooden door. Isaac strained to listen.

"You may not have a choice in the matter," one of them was saying. "The queen is mobilizing everyone she can. Well, everyone that isn't in Idris, anyway."

Fuck, Isaac thought. *They are in Idris. Why, you bastards? Tell me why?*

"Rumor says one month and then we ride back to Eod. Finish what we started. Fuck your pretty young wife good and hard. You won't be seeing her for a while."

A snicker, and then the jingle of chainmail.

"Sir!" both men called in unison.

"Is he in here?" asked a harsh voice.

"Yes, sir," the first voice responded.

Isaac recoiled. That harsh voice was coming for him.

The man who entered the room was enormous, his inky hair and beard laced with silver. His eyes were a steely blue. A cruel smile played on his lips.

"Merchant!" he bellowed. The sudden noise hurt Isaac's ears, and he winced. "What a pleasure. To have such a high-class, privileged shit in my graces—and the queen is mighty pissed at you."

He dropped his bulk onto a stool by Isaac's side, then leaned in close. He reeked of onions.

"Looks like you messed yourself up good, without any help from me." The man poked one of his sausage-like fingers at Isaac's damaged eye. Isaac yelled out as excruciating pain radiated through his body.

"Please," Isaac panted. "I am the High Merchant of Azantium. I have done nothing but serve my queen."

"Ha! She disagrees with you, merchant." The man picked up a large cudgel and held it up so Isaac could see it with his good eye.

"Wh-what do you want from me?" Isaac asked.

"Why are you slinking around in the eastern realm, hm?" asked the man. He looked at Isaac's hand, then at his cudgel. "No answer. Nothing to say?"

Brutality was a trademark of Azantium interrogators. Isaac swallowed his dread. He would die on this table. But terrible as his end would be, he would never tell them about the resistance.

He took a deep breath. It would be his last without pain. "I have nothing."

The man's eyes sparkled. It was the answer he was hoping for. "Indeed," he replied, raising the cudgel.

31

M æve looked for Isaac as she crossed the center of Eod. It had been just over two weeks. He was probably running a little late, but she couldn't help but worry.

Instead, Mæve found Armaiti and Iraji training. Mæve could not see the threads of water Armaiti pulled from the æther to channel, but as he swung his massive curved blades in an arc the air rippled. Iraji appeared to catch that ripple and redirect it into a straw target that exploded a moment later.

Armaiti smiled. "Good."

As Mæve approached, Armaiti turned to her. "Care to train?" he asked her.

He had been teaching her how to use the sword. Mæve was proficient with her bow and shinal, but had never trained with a longer blade and Armaiti had wanted her to be prepared for the battle ahead.

He unsheathed his swords, handed her one, and adjusted her hands on the hilt, his arms momentarily around her. She could not focus with Armaiti so close.

Thankfully Ariol, Iraji's husband, interrupted as he rushed up behind Iraji, and kissed her cheek. Mæve marvelled at the change in the Lumani woman. Her hard features softened and her face brightened as she looked at her love.

"Did you tell them?" Ariol said.

"Love," Iraji said as she swatted at him. "We are trying to train."

"Tell us what?" Armaiti asked.

"We are with child," Iraji said, her cheeks blushing as she clasped her husband's hand.

"That's wonderful!" Armaiti exclaimed.

"Yes, we are overjoyed," Ariol said, beaming.

"I'm so happy for you," Mæve said. She wanted to ignore her jealousy over the news and be happy for their friends; it was what she and Armaiti wanted for themselves.

Her archery students arrived, and Mæve excused herself. Armaiti grabbed her hand.

"Meet me tonight," he said.

Mæve blushed and nodded.

Mæve joined the students and began by showing them how to draw a bow. Drawing the bow was most difficult. Few had mastered it after weeks of training. Mæve instructed those who had mastered their draw on how to use their breath to steady the bow and hit their target. For many of the resistance fighters from Epoth, learning to fight with weapons was new.

Armaiti and Ariol left while Iraji and Mæve trained with the resistance fighters well into the afternoon.

Exhausted as the group broke for the day, Mæve wiped a thin film of sweat off her forehead.

Iraji approached her. "They are getting better," Iraji said, smiling. "They will get there. Their hearts are strong."

"Yes," Mæve agreed. "They have come a very long way thanks to the Lumani."

"But of course," Iraji said. "We are all one, now. Our battle is the same."

Iraji's thoughts pleased Mæve, but Iraji's clan didn't share her sentiments. The Air Clan kept a distance from Mæve and the resistance. She didn't understand what had caused the problem, only that this went beyond just having foreigners in Eod.

"Where is Isaac? I have not seen him for a time."

Mæve's smile evaporated.

"I don't know. I thought he would have returned by now. I'm a little worried."

"Hm, I'm sure he'll be back soon." Iraji gave her arm a reassuring squeeze and said, "I'll see you later tonight."

As Armaiti walked away to prepare for the war council meeting, Jaleh approached.

"It's ready," she said.

Armaiti followed the elder to a nearby clearing. Armaiti nodded at the two Air Clan mages waiting there.

"Watch," Jaleh said as she opened her hand. Inside was a small orb, only slightly bigger than a bird's eye. It was clear and inside swirled a phosphorescent blue-white light.

He was about to ask what it was, but before he could form the words, Jaleh hurled it into a target ahead of where they stood.

A flash of white light and a large blast ripped through the clearing and Armaiti's ears rang.

"We call it æthersphere," Jaleh said. "I channeled a small ball of æther and then the Air Clan mages channel lightning inside the ball. Then we tighten the æther and air inside the ball so that when it impacts, it explodes."

A smile stretched across Armaiti's face. "It's perfect."

"Yes, if you throw it inside the mouth of the weapon, it should destroy it," Jaleh said. "The difficulty will be getting close enough to it. They seem to have them well guarded in battle, as you experienced during your last encounter with the weapon. This delicate weaving takes much time to create. We cannot make many before you leave, but it should be enough if you are careful."

Armaiti nodded, picking up one of the little balls of æthersphere. If they could destroy the weapon early on, there may be hope.

32

The flames of the bonfire reached for the stars and illuminated the center of Eod, where all five clans gathered. Mingling amongst them were the Azantium resistance fighters. Change was indeed upon the Lumani, and witnessing this pleased Armaiti. Ayin had told him that this moment would come.

Tonight they rallied for war. Armaiti and Chalen planned to march their armies, to draw the Azantium army out of the capital.

Armaiti looked out over his people. They weren't warriors, but they had become the fiercest the world had known in order to survive. How many more Lumani would die in this battle?

Mæve and Chalen joined Armaiti's side. He drew strength from his friends as he addressed the people before him.

"The time is upon us now to abandon thoughts of peace with this enemy. Azantium greed has overrun their better senses and they must be stopped. We will ride into battle together against them. We will withstand their hatred, their greed, their weapons. We are still here!

"Azantium terror draws to an end!"

Swept up in the intensity, the people, Lumani and the others alike, cheered and made battle cries. With their common purpose, this bond, they were a formidable force. As their voices echoed through the night, the very forest vibrated with the force of their will, the passion of their resolve.

Caught up in the moment's fervor, Armaiti reached for Mæve's hand and threaded his fingers in hers. She looked at him, a bit surprised but not without welcome.

"Change is upon us. There is no greater time than now," Armaiti said to the crowd as he looked at her.

A voice cut through the night.

"And what change do you speak of, *King Armaiti*?" Simal emphasized Armaiti's name with disdain. "The erosion of our ways? The permission to... consort... with foreigners?"

Armaiti let go of Mæve's hand and advanced upon the Air Clan leader, vaguely aware that Mæve stayed by him.

"Do you suggest we abandon our accordance with the resistance fighters? Those who have left their livelihoods behind, risked their very lives, to stand by us, to help us in our time of need. Or do you foolishly refer to the woman I love?"

Simal laughed. "All of it. All of this... this abomination! What about the attack upon our people? I am talking about the five thousand Lumani dead, the orphaned children, the families ripped apart! I am talking about the atrocities we are being made to suffer for your ideal of change and your infatuation with a foreigner."

Silence fell. Armaiti paused. Anger coursed through him. He took a moment to still himself. It was a time of war. He would take no more strife from Simal. This ended tonight.

"My personal affairs are not of your concern, Simal. We are at war and should band together, not create discord amongst the people for personal gain."

Armaiti unsheathed his swords. Beside him, Mæve reached for her shinal.

"So you have a choice. Submit, or we end this tonight. I will not allow our people to be divided any longer for the sake of your insatiable ego."

Simal snarled and pulled his spear from behind his back.

"Stop!" Iraji interjected. "Simal, enough! You do our clan shame, talking to our king this way."

Simal scoffed. "This from the woman he cast aside like garbage. I think we should question your judgement on many things, Iraji Jashira."

Armaiti advanced towards Simal, fuming. He wanted Simal's blood. How dare Simal speak this way to the people he cared about?

"No!" Iraji yelled, putting a hand up towards Armaiti. "Simal, you do not speak for the Air Clan. I call for new leadership. Armaiti is a just ruler and our only way out of this is through our combined efforts with the resistance fighters. You are behaving like a fool!"

"Fine," Simal said, his eyes burning, his lips twisted in hatred for Armaiti. "We will fight in your war. We will fight beside strangers. But when this is over we demand the clan leaders examine his ability to lead and take a vote on whether we should remove Armaiti from power."

Jaleh stepped forward. "Let us do it now." All heads turned to the elder. "Malia, leader of the Water Clan, what say you?"

A tall woman stood. "I support my king." Her eyes filled with disgust for Simal.

Jaleh nodded. "And what say you, Relan of the Earth Clan?"

"I support my king."

The leader of the Fire Clan replied the same.

Jaleh nodded, eyes down. A moment's pause. Then her eyes rose to meet Simal's and the Air Clan leader took a step back. "And I, leader of Æther Clan, in my two hundred and fifty years on Ulli, I have not witnessed a king more competent than the one before us now. King Armaiti is our leader. Now sit down and be quiet, Simal."

Jaleh spat on the ground, then returned to her seat with the other elders.

Simal sat down, glaring at Armaiti.

Armaiti turned back to the group.

"Most of you will ride to face the Azantium army. I will march our army down the main road, hoping to draw the army out of and away from the palace. Meanwhile, Mæve and Iraji will lead a smaller group of our best warriors into the palace to assassinate the queen and give word to the slaves that it is time to revolt."

Armaiti paused. He hated to be separated from Mæve, but he knew his place was with his people and leading the larger battle. Mæve was the only one who knew the palace layout, and Iraji was the best guard he could afford her.

"Mæve used to be a royal servant to the queen," Armaiti continued. "She is the one who killed the crown prince and she will help us win this battle."

"The battle is three-fold," Jaleh interrupted. "Kalouq and I will ride to the Mycellium and attempt to break the seal the Wizards of Arkas created. We will free the old gods and heal the magic of Zama."

"King Armaiti!" a voice called out. "King Armaiti!"

"Mohlin," Armaiti said. "What is it?"

"Come quick," he said, breathless. "It's Isaac."

HE WAS on a litter just outside the village center.

"Isaac!" Mæve gasped. Her handsome friend was so deformed it shocked her. He had a large gash down his face and one eye was completely swollen shut. Part of his cheek was missing, exposing the tendons and muscle in a festering wound. His left hand had been crushed beyond recognition.

A tall, withered Lumani man—little more than a skeleton—stood nearby. Mæve spun on him.

"What happened?"

"The inquisitors," he said. "We got him out of there, but Lashal... he did not make it."

A pause. Mæve stared at Isaac.

"Bring Jaleh," Armaiti said, and Iraji ran off.

In Jaleh's workroom, Mæve and Jaleh treated the infection setting into the cuts on Isaac's face and gave him tinctures to manage his fever and pain. He was in awful shape and had been this way for too long.

They worked through the night. Chalen retired and Armaiti slept nearby. Eventually, even Jaleh got up.

"We've done all we can tonight. I'm heading to bed."

Mæve thanked her and said goodnight. Armaiti stayed, and so did the man who had saved Isaac.

"What is your name?" Mæve asked.

"Randir," the man responded.

Mæve moved one of Isaac's curls from his forehead.

"What was he doing in the capital?" Mæve said to herself, but the man answered.

"I don't know, ma'am. I worried when I learned they had captured him. The slaves have started to run away—we've been hearing rumors of war and unrest. Lashal and I decided to try for it, and we happened across him in an interrogation room on our way out."

"They tortured him," Mæve said, tears falling freely now.

"I tried to get to him as soon as I could," Randir said. "But it took time to arrange our escape. And then—" he began to weep, "—then Lashal was shot as we fled."

Chalen reached out and put a hand on the man's shoulder.

"What you and Lashal did was very brave," Chalen said. "You saved a man's life because of it."

Mæve closed her eyes, holding her friend's good hand.

"You should rest," Chalen said to her. "I'll keep the night watch tonight. I'll wake Jaleh at the first sign of trouble."

"No, I don't want to leave him," Mæve said.

"You will be more present for him tomorrow, if you rest tonight," Armaiti said.

She knew he was right.

He walked her towards the center of Eod, but when she turned towards her own dwelling he put out a hand to stop her, a question on his lips.

"Would you... like to stay the night with me?" he asked.

Her heart jumped at the question, her eyes searching.

"With the Air Clan so riled up, you might be safer with me."

Mæve smiled. "Thank you." But her heart beat so loud she was sure he must hear it.

Armaiti's abode was beautiful. The main room had a fireplace at one end and a bed at the other. Benches made of fine leather and well-worked wood stood by the fire. There were large windows along one wall. She could see the outline of treetops amongst the orbs outside.

Mæve was suddenly uncomfortable. She cared for Armaiti, true, with all her heart, but she was exhausted. Their nighttime escapes had become more passionate as of late and now being alone in his home together... did he expect anything from her?

As if he had read her mind, Armaiti said, "We're just here to rest. We can go back to your place if that is more comfortable."

"I don't want to wake Giselle and Betha."

"Okay. We can stay here then. Nothing can happen between us," Armaiti said. "So there is no need to worry."

Now Mæve was confused, and she stared at Armaiti blank faced.

"The Lumani cannot link until we are married. It is our magic. When we link, it forms a lifelong bond. I know Azantiums do not take things so seriously, but we do."

"Oh," Mæve said. "I'm glad you told me that."

Armaiti fetched one of his tunics and she thanked him for it. She went into an adjacent room to change. When she came out, he was in bed gazing at the stars. It's true she was exhausted, emotionally spent, and really just needed to sleep, but seeing him lying there looking so beautiful without a shirt on was almost more than she could bear.

He looked at her, and she felt the heat rise in her cheeks. Armaiti smiled as she climbed into his bed and lay close to him. He wrapped his arms around her, and she thought she had never been in a more blissful place. Just as she nodded off she murmured "Thank you."

She didn't know how he responded. She was already asleep.

33

The pain was excruciating. Isaac couldn't breathe. He couldn't see.

"It's okay, Isaac. You're okay," said a familiar voice. It sounded like Chalen. Where was he?

"Burns," he rasped out.

Another voice. An older woman's voice. "Here. You just need a little of this. Now swallow." Jaleh?

He tried to open his eyes, but only one worked. More pain.

"It's okay," Chalen said. "You've been through an awful lot, my friend."

Isaac's vision focused and he saw Chalen smiling down at him.

"Aw, there you are. I'm glad to see you, although Mæve is going to have my hide that she wasn't here when you woke."

"Mæve?"

"Yes, she sat with you most of last night until Armaiti and I forced her to get some rest."

"What happened?"

"We were hoping you might tell us."

Then it came back to Isaac. The inquisitor's repulsive breath. The twisted excitement on his face every time he pulled out a new tool to use on Isaac's writhing body.

Isaac closed his eye. "Curses," he whispered.

Chalen lay a firm hand on Isaac's shoulder and then another voice spoke in the next room. A familiar voice.

"How is he?"

"He's awake," Chalen said.

"What?" Mæve sounded surprised. "That's astounding. Isaac?"

He smelled her scent first: lavender and sage. With an effort, he reopened his one good eye.

"There you are," Mæve said.

A WEEK PASSED. Isaac continued to heal at a miraculous pace. Mæve remembered the time he had sliced his finger while cooking, and how quickly the cut had vanished.

Isaac said he hadn't broken under the torture, and had told the inquisitor nothing about the resistance.

Now, a week later, he was up, walking around, eating, drinking, even cracking jokes from time to time. His left eye was still swollen shut; Mæve suspected he would need to wear an eye patch for the rest of his life. The large gash on the left side of his head wasn't looking as puffy and had scabbed, but it was still bad. A light cloth covered the wound on his cheek—a scar he would bear on his handsome face for the rest of his life.

They were preparing to leave for battle tomorrow. Butterflies danced in Mæve's stomach at the thought. She would ride to the capital with a small group of Lumani assassins who had run night raids into the Palace of Light during the last war. There, they would assassinate the queen and send word to Isaac's contact, Lacian, for the palace slaves to revolt.

Assassinate the queen. Mæve remembered Druscilla's shadow guard and shivered. She was grateful for the company of the more experienced Lumani assassins joining their group and made a mental note to warn them of the queen's protector.

Isaac and Ardra would join Jaleh and Kalouq on their journey to the Mycellium Forest. Mæve thought it was too soon for Isaac to be traveling, but Jaleh had said she had a suspicion Isaac would be helpful.

But it was Armaiti she would worry about the most when he rode out at the head of their army to face the Azantiums; the Azantiums who had greater numbers and terrible weapons. She wanted to beg him to stay with her, but she knew his place was with his people, and she would never put herself between him and his duty.

A bonfire was lit in the center of Eod, where people danced and celebrated, arms flailing, laughing, moving around the fire, Lumani and Azantium rebels alike. Mæve's eyes fell on Armaiti. He was looking straight into the fire, face somber as he listened to Chalen, who stood beside him talking. His eyes found hers and Mæve's heart stopped for a moment.

Armaiti motioned to Chalen, then rose from his seat. He did not take his eyes off her as he approached and lay his forehead upon hers, his hand at the small of her back, gentle but firm. Their hands found each other, and they moved together, away from the fire.

It was their last night together. They didn't need to speak any words. One look was enough to know they were thinking the same thing.

They made their way to Armaiti's arbden. No sooner had they entered than his hands found her waist, pulling her closer to him. Like magnets, the weight of his lips found hers. Those aureate eyes consumed her, his desire mirroring her own. She pressed herself into him, pulling him closer, their kiss deepening.

And she paused.

"Armaiti..."

Breathless, he gently brushed aside a strand of her hair. She wanted to melt back into those kisses. He rested his forehead upon hers, lightly grazing her lips with his.

"I want to be with you," Armaiti said. "Now. I don't need elders or the Air Clan to decide who I can love, who I can spend my life with. I want it to be you."

Tears filled her eyes. Oh, how she wanted this.

She caressed his square jaw. Her lips grazed his again.

"And I want it to be you," she said.

Laughter and tears as they held each other. Her kisses traveled across his neck to his ear; her hand caressed the ki on his chest. She felt a faint electric pulse as his body trembled. She lowered her lips to his ki, softly kissing the luminescent silver markings as tingles danced upon her lips. Armaiti's head was back, overtaken by pleasure, his mouth open.

Mæve reached for his mouth again, running her tongue over the points of his teeth. Armaiti lifted her and carried her to the bed.

THE NEXT MORNING, Mæve and Armaiti walked to the meeting place where everyone was gathering to depart Eod.

Armaiti drew her close and she nuzzled his ear. She whispered, "We are linked now, my love, my mate. If one of us should die, something of the other will live on."

He cupped her face in his hands. "You stay alive. When this is over, we will be wed and we will live out the rest of our lives together in peace."

She laughed, tears streaming down her face. "I want children," she said. "Lots of them."

He laughed and kissed away her tears. "Me too."

She reached up for him, and he leaned down into their kiss. It was deep and full of the passion they had experienced last night.

She mounted Tráthóna and rode over to where Iraji, Ariol, and the other members of her contingency waited.

34

Mæve's group departed Eod. She was silent as they rode, until they stopped mid-morning to stretch and water the horses. As she watched the others move around, Mæve found herself trying not to cry. Iraji approached.

"Mæve? Are you... did you..."

"Yes," Mæve said.

"I'm sorry. It's difficult to leave your love behind."

It was. Mæve felt the linking between her and Armaiti even now as the distance between them grew.

"But Armaiti will be okay."

Mæve took a deep breath and nodded.

"Tell me what you know of this personal guard for the queen." Iraji said.

Sují. Yes, getting past the guards was just the beginning. There was still the matter of Druscilla's bodyguard.

"He keeps to the shadows," Mæve said. Just recalling her odd encounter with the man made her shiver. "He doesn't make a sound. It's like he's invisible. I never knew if he was there in the room with us, even when I was looking for him."

"Sounds like black magic," Iraji said.

"The queen said he was an assassin during the Lumani Wars."

"Sují Allam?" asked Quial, one of the Water Clan assassins. "He was a butcher during those days. He killed more of the Water Clan than all the other guards combined."

"I remember him too," Si contributed, her red kishaye glinting in the sunlight. "The Fire Clan had him at the top of our hit list, but he's like smoke. I saw him once. Actually saw his face. I don't think he's Azantium."

"Whoever he is," Iraji said. "All men bleed."

ARMAITI HALTED atop a hill and looked back over the army he led as they marched down the main road. Worry plagued him.

It's not that they weren't a formidable force. They were. During their final war council gathering, Chalen placed their numbers, Lumani and rebel, at seven thousand fighters. But Chalen's spies had reported there were currently about eight thousand soldiers in the Azantium army, not to mention the deadly advantage they held with their weapons.

Chalen rode up beside him. "Do you think we still hold the element of surprise?"

"Let's hope so," Armaiti replied.

Surprise would be their only advantage against the superior force. It was but a desperate hope, but it was all they had.

The sun rose, and they marched. It was a half-day to Essendial. Attacking innocents unsettled Armaiti and he had given strict orders that children, elderly, and other vulnerable people were not to be attacked. Essendial was the royals's most fervent supporters. Armaiti and Chalen believed that once the queen learned it was under attack, she would send the full power of her army.

They had gone over formations; they had gone over contingency plans. Armaiti and Chalen had made sure their four generals were aware of the plans. They were as ready as they could be. Now they marched to the unsuspecting town of Essendial and hoped to draw the attention of a much stronger and bigger enemy.

———————

Isaac and his group arrived at the Mycellium as the sun reached its highest point in the sky. Isaac's wounds itched and the achy effects of a low-grade fever were setting in, but his exhilaration at finally reaching the gate superseded his discomfort. He dismounted his horse and stood before the giant obsidian arch, glinting in the sunlight.

A sea of mist stretched beyond the arched gateway, with only the tips of trees poking out.

"The mist is a toxic barrier," Jaleh said. "People have tried venturing into it. Most were never seen again, and those that did return were insane. Whatever you do, do not touch it."

"The stone," Ardra said. She was indicating a small stone disk with intricate writing around it that sat before the arch.

"The writing is Lumani," Kalouq said. As he spoke, his excitement grew. "This must be from the original Lumani who came to examine the Mycellium three hundred years ago."

"What does it say?" Isaac asked.

"It's old Lumani, I cannot read it," Kalouq said.

"Let me see," Jaleh snapped, squinting at the stone. "Not of Ulli... Not of Zama..."

"Isn't that the symbol for stone?" Kalouq said pointing.

"I am trying to concentrate," Jaleh snapped. "The sun is cursed bright and half the letters have worn away with time."

A pause, then Jaleh continued to read out loud.

"Not of Ulli, not of Zama. Ash and bone brings twisted stone..." Jaleh fumbled.

"Magic not of Zama?" Kalouq looked ready to leap out of his skin.

Jaleh looked at Ardra. "Magic of a foreign land."

All eyes turned to Isaac.

35

"Now wait a minute," Isaac said. "Let's not jump to any conclusions—"

"You can control things with your mind, can you not?" Jaleh asked. "And your magic is not of this land, not of Ulli..."

"Is it learned magic, though?" Kalouq interjected.

"That remains to be seen," Jaleh said. "But it's the best option we have, unless anyone else has suggestions."

Silence.

"Go on then," said Jaleh. "Break the seal."

"How?"

"I don't know, merchant," Jaleh said exasperated. "Your magic is foreign to us. Figure it out."

Isaac approached the stone and considered it. It was about the size of a carriage wheel, propped up at an angle on an earth embankment. He laid his hand on the cool surface and felt a low vibration. Not an ordinary stone.

Isaac remembered the little figurine at Berit's house, the tea mug at Mæve's cabin, the rock Armaiti had so lovingly chucked at his head. The magic within him was real. And now his friends needed him to believe in himself, in his magic, and break this seal.

He focused. His vision softened, and in his mind he reached out to the solid stone before him. He could sense the particles that made the stone what it was. He thought of destruction and the awesome force of breaking. He longed to split those little particles apart and scatter them to the wind. He felt the particles begin to dance, wildly. He kept going. Kept pushing. Yet the stone resisted him. It wanted to stay together.

Isaac strained, sweat rolling down his forehead. He needed to remember something lost and ancient, from Thalis, buried in the desert sands during the long years under Azantium subjugation. Something stirred within him and he yelled out. The pulsing desire inside him snapped and the rock particles flew apart.

Isaac crashed to the earth and all went dark.

THE AZANTIUM ARMY found them as the sun reached its apex on the second day. Essendial had been a massacre. The villagers had not been prepared. It would seem the element of surprise was in their favor.

They set fire to the Church of Light in the center of Essendial. It was Chalen's idea. He had thought that would get the capital's attention. It had.

Armaiti's scouts raced back to him with their report: Eight thousand Azantium soldiers, full armor. They counted about a thousand of those soldiers carrying labaton and they were rolling two of the new large weapons.

He thanked the scouts and called forth a small group of five Lumani stealth warriors who had been ready for this mission. They each took a handful of æthersphères. They had carefully transported the little explosive balls from Eod in a padded basket. With the information from the scouts, the stealth warriors took off. Their mission was to destroy the weapons before they reached the battlefield.

The main road rumbled under the footfalls of the approaching army. Armaiti looked out over his people, arrested with sudden doubt. They had been training hard for this, true, but they were not ready. None of the resistance fighters were seasoned soldiers. And although the Lumani were raised as warriors, their numbers were so few.

He steered his massive black elk to the front line. There was nothing else he could do.

An Azantium horn sounded. They were close. Armaiti turned towards his army.

"Pick up your weapons. Channel your fear, all your hatred for the injustices done upon you, and be merciless. Today we reclaim Ulli!"

Armaiti let out a fierce roar. The Lumani and resistance fighters echoed it.

"Archers!" Chalen called out.

A swoosh of arrows flew over their heads from their archers positioned on the hill behind them. The first round had little effect on the armored soldiers. They continued to march.

Two more rounds of arrows and then the noise Armaiti had expected, but dreaded all the same: the blast of the weapon. An explosion carved through the middle of his army. Blood plumed and body parts flew in the afternoon air.

Chaos. People running, screaming, trying to get away from the gore and the horror of the blast. "Hold your positions!" Chalen called out.

Another blue flash. Armaiti looked out over the field. He only saw one. Perhaps the stealth warriors had been successful in destroying the other. Were they now on their way to destroy the second one? He could not spot them amongst the throngs of Azantium soldiers.

Armaiti nodded at Chalen.

"Charge!" Chalen yelled. They needed to force the battle into close quarters—if their troops were interspersed with Azantium troops, then they could not fire the weapon without also destroying their own soldiers.

But as they surged forward, the Azantiums changed formation, drawing forth their labaton fighters. It was then Armaiti saw his stealth fighters. Their heads upon the tips of spears being thrust into the air.

A blast ripped through the right flank of Armaiti's army. He would need to take out the other weapon himself. He carefully gathered the last handful of ætherspheres, hard and cool in his palm, and placed them in a leather satchel at his belt. They would be secure there but he would need to be careful and he needed to be quick.

The weapon was across the battlefield from where he stood, chaos all around him as the Lumani fell. He began fighting his way towards it.

And then a familiar face caught his eye: Betha, eyes wide with fear. Jacyle had fallen and appeared to be dead or maybe just unconscious. Betha had him by the arm and was crying in her futile attempt to drag his limp body away from the fighting around her.

Armaiti channeled water into his swords and cut his way through the surrounding soldiers, desperate to reach her. He was almost there when a sword cut deep into her throat.

"No!" Armaiti screamed. He cut down the soldier and raced to her side, but Betha was already on her knees, fumbling at her throat as blood spilled out over her hands. She slumped sideways and the light faded from her eyes. She was gone.

Armaiti screamed with fury and turned to cut down two soldiers as they rushed him.

Another blast.

Armaiti flew through the air and crashed to the ground. Something warm covered him and his ears rang. He needed to make it to the other side of the field and destroy that weapon. But he could not move.

A RED MOON crested the horizon as Mæve waited with the others. An ill omen. They watched it rise from the glade in the woods where Mæve and Armaiti used to meet. When night fell, they would begin.

Darkness crept over them and they made their way down the

path until the palace came into view. Mæve looked at Iraji, and Iraji nodded at Jana and Quial. The two Water Clan Lumani ran to the curtain wall. Their gray skin and dark clothing made it impossible to see them at night.

The rest of them watched from the forest cover as Jana and Quial scaled the large semicircular wall of the slave quarters. The dangerous part would be when they reached the top and walked across the slave chamber walls to the curtain wall. Then they would risk being seen by both the slaves and the guards.

But this was the best place to enter the palace. Once they killed the guards, they would go immediately to the slave chambers and rally the slaves.

Then their cohort would find the queen.

Jana and Quial were almost at the curtain wall when a soldier spotted them.

"Halt!" he yelled, drawing his labaton. He was far outside the range of Mæve's arrows. But Quial leapt from the wall, his blade already out, and slit the soldier's throat. But other guards were already advancing towards them.

What happened next was a rush of fluid motion from the two Lumani, blades flashing as they cut down the remaining soldiers with ease. Mæve suddenly understood why the Lumani raids had inspired enough fear from the royals to necessitate the treaty. Quail and Jana had just killed five guards in a matter of seconds.

They motioned towards Mæve and her crew hiding in the woods.

They ran towards the entrance to the stables. As they entered, Mæve was arrested by the familiar smell.

She shook off the sudden onslaught of memory and raced into the stairway that led up to the slave quarters. They needed to be quick and careful. Mæve and Iraji would continue on to find Lacian, while Ariol and the two Fire Clan assassins would join Jana and Quial on the curtain wall and make their way across the rooftops to the queen's chambers.

Isaac had instructed her on how to find Lacian and the passwords she would need. Mæve counted the doors: second floor, third door on the left. She peered in, looking for the man Isaac had described to her: dark brown skin, bright green eyes, and tuft of grey at his hairline. She spotted him, awake and staring at her. He gestured her inside.

"You look lost," the man whispered in a thick accent.

"I carry a message from a friend," she replied.

"It is safe to deliver such a message. We are all supporters here."

"The rebellion is here. The Red Fox says to wait for our word. It will happen tonight." The code. Mæve had almost forgotten. "May your blade be swift and justice swifter."

A smile stretched across Lacian's face.

"I will prepare our people and we will await your next word." A pause. "Tonight we taste freedom."

He had delivered the second half of the code.

Mæve nodded at the man, and she and Iraji slipped out, ready to join their comrades on the curtain wall.

But as they rounded a corner they came face-to-face with Ms. Eda. The head of house seemed just as surprised to see them. She opened her mouth, but Iraji's blade sliced open the woman's throat and all that came out was a sickening gurgling sound before she fell to the ground in a silent heap.

Lacian appeared in the doorway and whispered, "Nice work. We will take care of this. You go."

Mæve and Iraji wasted no time. They sprinted the length of the hallway back to the stairway.

Once reunited with the rest of their group, Mæve and Iraji crouched down low to avoid being seen by other guards. Mæve needed a moment to orient herself. If the slave quarters were there, the queen's chambers were slightly to the north, just to the left of where they stood.

Si leapt onto the curtain wall. She drew her long knives and ran to meet the guards. One guard aimed a labaton at her.

Mæve stopped running and drew her bow. She nocked an arrow and took aim. The mossy scent of Callium filled her nose. Her mother's loving smile. She let an arrow fly.

The guard fell. Humana crested over the curtain wall next, landing in a roll fall before drawing her swords. Mæve rushed to catch up.

The guards ran in the other direction. They were making too much noise.

Mæve took aim again and shot another guard, then another. The last guard made it inside. Curses.

They followed the soldier inside the palace. Mæve caught up just in time to see Ruli throw two fire darts that engulfed the soldier in flame. But more guards waited for them inside the palace and a loud noise rang out in the night.

"No!" Si called out.

One guard at the far end of the hall had shot Ruli. Labaton. He fell to the ground, and the guards raced towards the intruders.

Before the soldier could readjust his aim, Ariol's axe split his head open.

The guards were close now. Mæve drew her shinal. She took a sweeping arc at a soldier, then maneuvered herself to his oblique and sliced up high, nicking the large artery in his neck. He yelled and fell to his knees.

A blast ripped through the hallway. Jana, the Water Clan assassin, writhed on the ground and then went still. A ripple of foul air brushed past Mæve, and Iraji's scream ripped through the hallway. Mæve turned frantically. Iraji was on the ground, kneeling next to Ariol, whose eyes stared straight ahead. A small blade protruded from one of them.

Mæve reached for her friend and stopped. An icy chill ran down her spine. She turned. Suji stood before her, his dark-rimmed eyes peeking over the black cloth covering his nose and mouth.

36

Armaiti had recovered from the blast, but his lungs ached. Blue smoke clouded the air and blood covered almost every inch of his body. The sun was about to set. It had been hours. It was impossible to tell how many had died with the smoke of the weapon engulfing the field.

Armaiti got up and noticed his pouch that had held the æther-spheres was empty. They must have rolled out when he fell. He was lucky to still be alive.

He searched for the ætherspheres amongst the body parts that peppered the ground, and he spotted Giselle sobbing, her chest heaving. Dirt, soot, and blood covered her.

Armaiti sheathed his swords and reached for her hand. His touch seemed to ground her. Her eyes met his, her breathing slowed, and she closed her eyes for a moment. Another blue flash ripped through the afternoon air. The ground shook, and then that terrible concussive sound again. The Azantium soldiers had retreated to the perimeter of the battlefield and shot their weapons at the Lumani and resistance fighters in the center.

Armaiti and Giselle ran from the flying dirt and blood, the never-ending screams.

Someone approached through the foggy haze and Armaiti slowed. It was Simal. His face twisted in rage as he approached Armaiti.

"You did this," Simal said. "You are to blame for this atrocity!"

He lunged at Armaiti, his knife drawn.

"The blood of our people is on your hands," he yelled.

Armaiti parried the knife attack and struck Simal at the base of his neck. The warrior stumbled but turned towards Armaiti with a fluid, graceful thrust of his knife.

Armaiti turned sideways, but the knife grazed his arm, opening the skin there. Armaiti still had Simal's arm. He swept the Air Clan leader's back leg and they struck the ground.

Armaiti kicked Simal's head away, but Simal blocked his leg. His knife arm was pinned under Armaiti's other leg, but he reached up for Armaiti's neck, grabbing it and squeezing. The pain that engulfed Armaiti was excruciating, his leg slackened and Simal freed his knife. He lunged forward, but something struck the side of his head, sending him stumbling off Armaiti.

Armaiti sat up, gasping, his neck still burning. Giselle approached Simal and planted one of her axes into his throat. Simal's legs twitched and then stopped.

Armaiti looked at her in surprise. "Thank you."

"Uh-huh. Now what?"

"We need to find that weapon," Armaiti said.

"Okay," Giselle said. "Let's go."

Isaac marveled at the shattered seal before him. The toxic green mist around the Mycellium dissipated and before them stood the forest, dark and old. The trees, impossible to see when shrouded in the mist, were visible now. Thick black trunks as wide as a cottage and taller than the Lumani arbdens.

The dark forest sprang to life. Plants unfurled and bloomed

sparkling radiant fruits of buds, flowers, and little crystals. It was as if the forest could breathe again.

Jaleh, Ardra, and Kalouq joined Isaac's side and they entered the forest, stepping tentatively. A low-lying natural mist blanketed the earth. Isaac wasn't sure where they were going or what they were looking for.

The tree canopy was so tall and so dense, it blocked out most of the light. As Isaac's eyes adjusted to the darkness, he saw them. Creatures creeping low to the ground, sharp teeth bared.

"Glyphium," Jaleh whispered, and stopped moving. "Guardians of the forest."

Isaac tensed. They were the creatures of nightmares, flowing in and out of the mists.

The largest of the pack leapt up on a large rock in front of their group. Its smooth black fur glistened and its tall horns stretched up to the heavens. It lowered down onto its front paws.

"We've been waiting for you," a melodic male voice said.

Isaac and his companions turned to see a humanoid creature behind them. Tall, with shimmering blue skin, he had large half-moon horns that curved inward and cloven feet. His eyes were large and completely white, angled sharply back towards his long pointed ears.

The being smiled, exposing a row of needle-like teeth.

"You have broken the curse."

A roar cut through the forest and the earth shook. Isaac gasped and Kalouq let out a little yell. But Ardra and Jaleh smiled.

"Shadowlair rejoices." The creature said. "I am Eco. Shålan requests your audience."

"The queen goddess?" Jaleh asked.

"She longs to meet the mind wizard," Eco replied.

The winds picked up and a terrible screech ripped through the air as something swooped down and landed on the ground before them. Something big.

Kalouq screamed again. Isaac gaped at the creature before them. It was an enormous harpy-like bird, large black wings furled. Blood stained its cruel hook of a beak. It moved closer, pointed talons clicking on twigs and stone.

"A falstorm," Ardra said, breathless. "Do not look into its eyes."

Isaac glimpsed its eyes before he looked away. Human eyes.

Ardra reached into her pouch and spread what looked like salt around them, whispering words Isaac did not recognize.

"There is no need to fear," Eco said with a bemused smile. "The falstorm is here to deliver you to Shålan. He has strict orders not to eat you. You are our welcomed guests."

Eco gave a bow, then faded into the mists and left them alone with the bird.

The falstorm clicked closer. Kalouq appeared dazed by the creature. As if in a trance, he stepped towards it.

"Don't look at its eyes!" Jaleh shouted at him as she smacked Kalouq upside the head. This broke his gaze.

Isaac focused on the center of the bird creature's forehead. It cocked its head at him. There was a tether, visceral and unexpected, between them.

"Please, you must take us to Shålan," Isaac said.

The falstorm screeched, then bent its massive body low to the ground.

"Let's go," Isaac said and he led the way toward the bird. It was large enough to carry the four of them. They settled onto its back and the falstorm stood up.

"Oh, for the love of Zama," Kalouq said in a panicked voice.

Isaac grabbed a handful of feathers, exhilaration racing through him as the falstorm jumped into flight.

"Oh my." Jaleh looked green, but Isaac loved this. Butterflies danced through his stomach and he sat up. Misty air rushed past his face. The ground below them looked foreign and miniature. He whooped and laughed. He even caught Ardra smiling, though she kept her full body plastered to the bird.

Almost as soon as their journey began, it ended. The falstorm landed, the impact knocking Kalouq from its back as the other three scrambled off.

"You can talk to it?" Kalouq asked Isaac, as he got to his feet and brushed himself off. "You're not afraid?"

"No," Isaac chortled. "When you must converse with the manner of scum I have endured during my time as a High Merchant, talking with a monstrous oversized bird creature is no big deal."

"Hush," Jaleh said. She was looking in awe at something behind them. Isaac and Kalouq turned.

Like the bright of the sun upon fallen snow, a luminescent being stood before them. Her eyes were the ethereal light blue of crystalline sky.

"Breakers of the seal, saviors of the Mycellium, I am Shålan."

"It is an honor and privilege to meet you, Your Grace," Jaleh said with a deep bow. The others did the same.

"A Lumani healer, a Lumani scholar, an Allanian healer, and a mind wizard of Thalis. I sense the work of Uthera and the winds of destiny have drawn you all together."

A mind wizard. Eco had called Isaac that too. Is that what he was?

"It is," Shålan said, looking at him.

Curses, was she one too?

Shålan smiled. "The mind wizards of Thalis are powerful mystics, practically destroyed by the Azantium domination of your country. I am glad to see the old ways are awakening in you, merchant."

"I... don't know what I'm doing or how to use it. I was hoping there might be answers here."

Shålan nodded. "There are answers for you, but not here. You must travel back to your homeland of Thalis. Find a teacher. There are still a few in hiding, if you look. They can be found in the desert hills, far from Azantium eyes."

The answers were in Thalis. The thought had never occurred to him. He had spent his entire life trying to stay away from the wretched place.

"We need your help," Jaleh said to Shålan. "Desperate times have fallen on the Lumani and we face annihilation at the hands of the Azantium. They have used the Chrysillium trees to make weapons."

Shålan smiled an eerie smile. Her eyes darkened.

"They take land that does not belong to them and create death out of magic. They destroyed the Allanians and now turn their destructive eye towards the Lumani. They have nearly killed the gift of Zama, the magic that courses through Ulli. We almost destroyed them once."

Shålan turned her attention back to Jaleh.

"You have the power of the gods at your service, healer."

Sují stood before Mæve. She tightened her grip on her shinal as he began to move, gently, like dancing. His shoulders swayed, his waist flowing back and forth, the rhythmic movement drawing Mæve in. Then, with a harsh whipping motion, something flew out from Sují's hands and bit Mæve behind her left ear. She cried out.

Sují's hips snapped again. Mæve realized he was using a cord with a small blade on the end. It wrapped around his body as he flowed and danced, but his eyes were deadly serious and they remained on Mæve.

She tried to get a feel for his timing, but it was difficult to measure. She swiped with her shinal, but she knew it was too soon. He stepped out of the way with ease and whipped out the cord again. This time it wrapped around Mæve's neck, where it cinched and tightened as she struggled. The pressure built and she panicked, dropping her shinal and clawing at her throat.

A yell. Mæve thought she saw Sují drop to his knees, but her vision was fading, she was sinking to the ground.

Air came burning back into her lungs. She gasped. The pain in her throat was unbearable. Iraji smiled down at her, one of her knives in hand. She turned and blocked a kick from Sují, then drove her knife into his opposite thigh. He howled in pain. Iraji drew another knife, but he blocked her arm, sending it flying. He followed up with a punch to her jaw, whipping her head to the right as she crumbled to the ground.

Mæve's vision was still blurry, but she let out a yell and swiped once at Suji and he fell back, unbalanced from the knife still in his thigh. Mæve took a quick look around. Iraji still lay unconscious. Humana, Quail, and Si were fighting the royal guards a short distance away. It was just her and Suji.

Mæve scrambled to her feet and swiped down low, opening his leg with the sharp blade of her shinal, then pivoted to swipe high, but he elbowed her forearm out of the way and followed it up with a punch to her head. She hit the ground again.

Suji's head snapped back, a small hilt sticking out of his cheek. Iraji followed it with a blast of air from her open hands that knocked the assassin to the ground. She kept the air blasting against the assassin as she moved towards him. He couldn't move, though he struggled uselessly. Mæve seized the opportunity, rising to her feet and swiped, with all the power and speed she could muster, at Suji's throat.

It nearly took off his head.

Iraji released the air and they both sank to the ground, continuing to catch their breath.

"Are you okay?" Iraji asked.

Mæve nodded, then hugged her friend. Iraji embraced her in return.

"Let's finish this."

They left their dead behind and made their way into Queen Druscilla's chambers. Her guards all slain, her shadow assassin destroyed, the queen cowered alone in a corner.

"You!" the queen shouted at Mæve. "How could you betray your queen like this?"

"You!" Mæve said, her throat still burning from Suji's cord. "You are not my queen—"

"I did you a favor, pulling you from the pitiful existence in the woods. You should be grateful."

"You killed my parents," Mæve cried.

The queen laughed cruelly. "Retribution, my dear. It doesn't matter. Even as we speak our army marches upon the Lumani armed with enough labaton and labaldis to wipe them from existence. No matter what happens to me tonight, the sun has set on the Lumani forever."

Mæve drew the sword Armaiti had given her. It was long, with a curved blade. A single rune was engraved on the blade. The Lumani symbol for heart.

"Know that as you die tonight, the slaves will revolt and destroy your bloodline. They will demolish the Palace of Light from the inside out. Your reign of terror is at an end."

Mæve thrust the sword into the queen's heart. Druscilla gasped.

The queen fell to the floor, one hand lifted and grasping for a moment before she died. Mæve turned to Quial and Si. "Find Lacian."

They nodded and left.

"We need to get to the battlefield as soon as possible," Humana said.

"If we keep to the main road, we should find them," Mæve replied.

They both looked over at Iraji, who had returned to the hallway and sat weeping over Ariol.

"I cannot leave him," she said. "I must return him to Zama."

Mæve and Humana helped Iraji lift her husband and carry him outside. They heard the rumblings of the revolt as they made haste to the stables and out beyond the walls—screams, breaking glass, yells.

Once outside, they laid Ariol's body down on the grass.

"Do what you must," Mæve said to Iraji. "But Humana and I must leave to join the battle."

"I will return him to the earth," Iraji said. Mæve embraced her.

"I wish I could stay and help you."

"Go. Fight by the side of your love, our king. I will join you once Ariol is with Zama."

Mæve nodded, and with Humana by her side they rode off into the night.

37

The blood moon, large and ominous, cast an eerie red hue over the battlefield below. Mæve and Humana looked down from the top of a ridge to where hundreds of Azantium soldiers surrounded the Lumani and resistance fighters. There were so many dead.

A blue flash coursed through the night. There was an explosion of earth and blood.

Mæve saw Armaiti racing towards the eastern perimeter, Giselle by his side.

He was alive.

Mæve took off, Tráthóna's hooves thundering into the earth as they raced towards the field.

A group of Azantium soldiers spotted Armaiti and Giselle. One of them took aim with his labaton.

Mæve willed Tráthóna on faster. She would not lose him. She would get there first.

As she approached the soldiers she leapt from Tráthóna's back, her shinal drawn. She swiped her shinal in a powerful arc at the closest soldier, splitting his face, then pivoted outward and away from the next man, slicing the tendons behind his knee. He fell and she slit his throat.

"Armaiti!" Mæve called out. "Armaiti!"

He turned and smiled. Mæve ran to him. She was almost there when a blue flash of light blinded her and she fell back. The ground erupted. Armaiti soared into the air, landing unmoving on the ground before her.

No. Mæve got to her feet. Gods, no.

"Armaiti?" He was covered in blood, eyes closed, his long dark hair splayed out wildly around him. "No, no."

"Armaiti!" Mæve called out, and she scooped him into her arms. "Armaiti."

A weak lift in his chest. Did she imagine it? She placed her ear to his nose. He was breathing.

And a screech split through the night. What in the gods was that?

She looked up to see an enormous bird blot out the blood moon. A man appeared to sit on the creature's back.

"Mæve?" It was Giselle, running towards her. "Gods, is he...?"

"No, he's still breathing," she said through her tears. "He's just unconscious."

"Look!" Giselle said pointing. In front of them, glowing blue eyes appeared through the haze of the smoke, then a set of long, spiraling horns. The glyphium.

Mæve placed Armaiti on the ground and stood over him. Giselle raised her axes.

Two more snarling glypium emerged from the haze.

Mæve yelled, conjuring her bravery, but the glyphium ran past her and attacked two Azantium soldiers who were advancing from behind.

Mæve's chest heaved at the sound of tearing flesh. Once the horrified screeches of the humans ceased, the glyphium ran off into the blue haze.

Mæve looked at Giselle, who looked as astonished as Mæve felt.

Armaiti stirred and his eyes fluttered open.

Mæve knelt and caressed his face, "Armaiti."

He looked at her and smiled.

"I must be dead," he said. "Have you come to fetch me again?"

Mæve laughed. "No, my love, though I would bring you back every time."

He sat up, weaving an arm around her waist, and drew her close.

"Are you all right?" he asked, and she nodded. A blinding light streaked across the battlefield, the ground shaking. Mæve stood and assisted Armaiti to his feet.

"Look out," Giselle called out.

Rough and sudden, Armaiti pulled Mæve in close to him, away from the swinging sword of another Azantium soldier. Armaiti decapitated the man with one powerful hack of his blade. But Mæve noticed how her love's arm hung after the swing. She didn't think Armaiti had much fight left in him.

Another soldier approached from behind. Mæve drew her shinal, dodged a clumsy swing and sliced at his neck. The soldier dropped to his knees, gagging as he bled out.

More Azantium soldiers appeared. There had to be at least ten of them, two with labaton. Armaiti looked ready to collapse again and Giselle didn't look any better. Mæve was ready to charge when a gust of wind and a loud whooshing interrupted her.

The giant bird swooped down and landed with a rumbling thud between them and the soldiers.

"A falstorm!" Armaiti said. He grabbed Mæve. "They were successful at the Mycellium. They must have been. The gods are with us!"

The falstorm screeched and advanced on the soldiers, who appeared to be in a trance. They didn't move, not even as the bird began to feast upon them.

A man slipped off the creature's back. He looked up and smiled. A beautiful smile.

"Isaac!" Mæve ran to her friend and they embraced. Armaiti joined her side and clasped arms with the merchant.

"I'm not going to ask how you managed to catch a ride with a falstorm," Armaiti said, laughing.

"A story for another time, perhaps," Isaac said.

In the near distance, a commotion broke out. They peered through the smoke. Soldiers hacked desperately at the legs of an enormous wolf. Shadowlair. But the god seemed unbothered by the swords, slowly making his way through the field, crushing or eating the remaining Azantium soldiers. Around his paws, glyphium slunk in and out of the blue haze of the battlefield, dragging soldiers into the mists where only their pain-filled screams could be heard. Across the field, a large black serpent erupted up through the earth and swallowed a handful of Azantium soldiers whole before diving back into the dirt.

Mæve gasped. "What was that?"

"Xä, the demon god of war," Armaiti said. "We should take cover."

The four of them ran to a nearby tree and crouched down low as they watched the carnage. Xä rose again and this time shot flames from his open mouth, incinerating a quarter of the battlefield.

Then, there was a stillness. An ethereal being, shimmering with white iridescence, made her way to the battlefield atop an elegant white beast.

Xä sprang up from the ground, earth flying around him, and transformed into a creature—part man, part beast—with hooves, large fur legs, and twisted horns upon his forehead. His eyes glowed red as he approached the white figure.

"Shålan and Xä," Armaiti whispered. "It is said Uthera cursed them because together they were more powerful than the cosmos themselves. Too much power in one place. So Uthera confined Xä to the underworld and Shålan to rule above ground in the Mycellium Forest."

They watched as the two gods kissed before Xä sank back into the underworld.

Once he was gone, a momentary sadness graced the goddess' face. Then with a gentle blow of her lips, the smoke of the battlefield dissipated.

Thousands lay dead. Nearly all of the Azantium soldiers, and three-quarters of the rebel army. It was over. There were battle cries from the remaining Lumani and cheers from the resistance fighters.

Mæve, Armaiti, Isaac, and Giselle approached Shålan.

"And so ends you," said the goddess with a voice like glass. She touched the earth and an electric energy ignited the Mycellium deep under the ground. The energy incinerated the dead Azantiums. The Lumani and resistance fighters would be buried. "You are but smoke and ash."

Shadowlair roared.

"We shall breathe life into Zama once more," Shålan said. Then she turned her oceanic eyes, chilling and deep as the sea itself, on Mæve and Armaiti. "There is new hope. The lovers are reborn." A deep, knowing smile from the goddess. *"Da Shallan, Da Shallak. La Forigé."*

Shålan faded into the æther. Shadowlair walked slow and purposefully back towards the great Mycellium Forest, followed closely by the glyphium, the enormous falstorm circling above.

Ulli was free and the mycelia would flow once more with the magic of Zama.

Mæve kissed her love with a fervent passion. Finally, they could be together in peace.

She turned to Isaac, who smiled—one of the few genuine smiles Mæve had seen upon the merchant's lips. Mæve and Armaiti embraced Isaac and Giselle, pulling them in close.

They were family, they were together, and they were free.

Upon return to Eod, the Lumani and resistance fighters lamented their dead for seven nights after the battle. They lit candles and placed them upon the River Kalim. Mæve and Giselle lit one together for Betha. Silence fell over Eod as they mourned. Little more than twelve thousand Lumani remained. It would take them a long time to rebuild, and to heal from the great losses they had suffered.

Isaac approached Mæve one night as she sat alone by the banks of the Kalim. She had seen little of her friend since returning to Eod. He looked out over the river and the burning candles floating on its surface.

"I need to leave for a time," he said.

"Leave? What do you mean?" Mæve asked.

"I have some things I need to figure out back home in Thalis."

"Thalis?" Mæve said. "I thought you hated it there."

"Yes." Isaac said. "But where I am going, the Azantium had little control, and there are few people."

"I don't understand," Mæve said.

"I know," Isaac said. "And I'm sorry. I'll return. And when I do, I'd like to continue living here with you and Armaiti and the Lumani."

"Of course, Isaac," Mæve said as she embraced him. "You're family."

He nodded, smiled, and caressed her cheek. "I wish you all the happiness in the world. I'm glad you finally get to be with him."

Mæve's eyes welled with tears. "Thank you, Isaac. Your blessing means the world to me."

They embraced again and then Isaac walked off into the night, a single satchel slung over his shoulder and his top hat on his head.

At the end of their week of sorrow, the silence ceased and was followed by a vibrant celebration of life. Large bonfires were lit day and night. People danced and feasted and loved.

Jaleh approached Mæve and Armaiti one night as they laughed by the fire.

"It is time," she said, clasping both their hands.

A LIGHT SNOW fell the next morning. Spring flirted just beyond the late winter chill as Mæve and Armaiti approached the elders. Armaiti wore the Fallion Crown.

Jaleh smiled upon them, the other five elders by her side. Iraji, Humana, and Giselle were there too. They gathered under the soft twinkling branches of Ayin.

"Mæve of Epoth," Jaleh began. "Daughter of the lost tribe, you have saved this man's life, loved him, and stood by him, a man of the Lumani, our beloved king. Do you now claim him as your mate for as long as Zama gives us life?"

"I do," Mæve replied.

"King Armaiti, child of Zama, you have risked your stature, loved this woman and stood by her, a woman of Zama and friend of the Lumani. Do you now claim her as your mate for as long as Zama gives us life?"

"I do," Armaiti replied.

"Then let us begin," Jaleh said. "May the earth welcome you on this new journey together."

Jaleh pulled forth a jar containing an earthen substance. She smudged a small amount on each of their foreheads.

"Ayin, one of two eternal lovers, connects us to the divine. From her wisdom, we draw forth the elements to join these two souls. From the earth may you bring forth your own life, a life together, a life that creates new life. May it be fecund and long lasting."

Then she pulled forth two obsidian blades. She gave one to each of them. "Place these blades in the fire," she instructed. Mæve and Armaiti obeyed. With the blades still hot, Armaiti nicked Mæve's chest by her heart, just enough to draw blood. Then she did the same to him.

Jaleh said, "From the fire comes life."

Mæve watched as Armaiti brought the blade to his mouth and licked her blood from it. His eyes stayed on her as he did this. It was an intimate gesture. Mæve followed his lead and did the same, the blood tasting metallic and slightly sweet in her mouth.

"Forged together through this fire, now breathe life into your union."

Armaiti's lips touched Mæve's, his hand resting on the nape of her neck. He breathed into her mouth, barely a whisper of breath. It was thrilling and her nerves caught flame as she pressed into him. As they parted, his smile hid none of his love and desire for her.

"One life, one breath, one water, one fire," and Jaleh wound a leather strap around Mæve's left hand and Armaiti's right hand. Once their hands were bound, she said, "Armaiti and Mæve, you are one under Uthera, under the stars and the moon."

Armaiti bent down to kiss her again, their hands still bound. Once they separated, Jaleh undid the bind and the two of them embraced.

38

A year passed. The Lumani migrated back to their spring equinoctial home. Golden light streamed through the trees of Idris as Mæve and Armaiti ran through the forest, laughing and playing with their infant daughter, who was strapped to Mæve's chest. The little girl cooed, delighted. Elijwa had inherited her father's gray skin and the brilliant silver Ki markings of the Water Clan, but she bore her mother's stunning lavender eyes.

They paused to catch their breath under the welcoming branches of Oyela.

Mæve touched Elijwa's face and kissed her little forehead. Hard to believe their baby was three months old already. Looking up, Mæve met Armaiti's loving eyes. A smile lit up his face as he stretched out his arms. Mæve laughed as she passed Elijwa to her husband.

Idris would bear its scars, as would they all, but they had worked hard over the past year, and now Idris flourished once again.

Mæve smiled at her husband and took his hand. A large part of why the Lumani were doing so well after such devastating loss was because of her husband's leadership. He had allowed them time to grieve, mended old rifts, and engaged everyone in the rebuilding efforts. They were proud of what they had accomplished and this was healing, too.

Mæve, Armaiti, and Elijwa were to join a gathering in Idris' village center that night. It was to be a night of celebration for Equilïum, the spring equinox, and a successful migration. The equinox was the only time during the year when Ayin and Oyela reconnected through the mycelial connection underground. As a result, there was a surge of energy through the mycelia that travelled through the ground, up the Chrysillium trees, and into the æther.

The energy made the Chrysillium trees glow and dance. The peace and equanimity their subtle vibrations created were felt by all.

As they approached the center of Idris, Iraji and her son Panez greeted them. Panez was seven months old and Elijwa cooed at seeing her favorite playmate.

Chalen waved from a distance. He had been around little these days. He spent his time in the capital, forming a system of governance after the dissolution of the Azantium kingdom. Armaiti often joined him, lending a hand when his own duties allowed him to. The Lumani had an interest in what would replace the Azantium monarchy and who was to lead.

The struggles and pressure of this task showed on Chalen's face; the lines had grown deeper and his hair was now speckled with gray. Still, he seemed to be enjoying his reprieve from the capital.

Giselle ran up to Mæve and kissed both her cheeks. Then she turned to Armaiti and kissed Elijwa's head. Armaiti handed the baby to Giselle who showered the baby with kisses.

Giselle had grown close to Mæve and Elijwa after Betha's death. The many nights that Armaiti was away in the capital, Giselle would often stay with Mæve and help with the baby.

Giselle and many other of the resistance fighters remained with the Lumani after the battle. Displaced from their homes, Eod and Idris had become a new way of life for these people, and Armaiti and Jaleh had welcomed them.

"Any word from Isaac?" Chalen asked Mæve.

Mæve shook her head. Just over a year had passed, and she had heard nothing from her dear friend. She kept expecting to see him saunter into Idris, flashing his infectious smile and saying something clever, but there had been nothing. She understood. Isaac had endured a lot, and it seemed he had things he had to figure out back in his homeland.

Berit and her family had made it to Epoth and remained in Mæve's cabin. Turns out Berit was just the leader Epoth needed after Chalen left for the capital. Mæve visited her often and her husband was still an amazing cook.

Jaleh was the last to approach their family. Her gnarled hand reached for Armaiti's as she said, "A new way is forming. You've done well, King Armaiti."

"There are still some that grumble," Armaiti replied. It was true, and Mæve took this more seriously than her husband. After Simal's death, Iraji was named the Air Clan leader. This made a few of Simal's most loyal followers angry. Armaiti continued to talk with them and believed they would eventually come around, but Mæve wasn't so sure. She worried about their continued lack of support for her husband's leadership.

"There are always those that will grumble," Jaleh said.

Elijwa squealed with delight. Mæve kissed her tiny nose as she melted into the arms of her forest king, her beautiful Armaiti. Ultimately, life was peaceful and prosperous. The world wasn't perfect, but they were together and they had Elijwa, and from there, anything was possible.

EPILOGUE

E zio clicked his long pointed nails on the white marble altar. The vidnoctere stood barren and muted before him. The message that it had sent him faded now.

The Shalik was born. How interesting.

There had been no Shalik in over two hundred years. Until now.

Ezio remembered the enslaved Allanian woman with the purple eyes. Enslaving an Allanian; that fool of a queen. She had got what she deserved.

The thought of the power of a Shalik, the promise of it, made Ezio salivate. With a flourish of his long gray robes, he left the altar and made his way to his writing desk. He sat, took a piece of parchment, and grabbed his quill. He would send word to Zial. The wizard wrote them in silver-laced moon ink and placed them in a dark blue satchel with silver stars etched upon it. It was an amplifier that would enable Ezio to cross into the world of dreams. Tonight he would sleep with the pouch under his pillow and deliver the message.

Yes, Zial would be perfect for this task. Time was... odd in the realm of dreams. Best to reach out to him now, in preparation.

In the meantime, while he waited for Zial, Ezio would watch the child through his vidnoctere. He would watch her grow so that when Zial was ready, they would act. Ezio would understand the magic of the Shalik. He would harness that power. And through it, he would take control of Ulli once again.

I HOPE YOU ENJOYED THIS NOVEL
PLEASE CONSIDER LEAVING A REVIEW

Reviews are how authors gain recognition. This is especially important to new authors like myself. I hope you will take just a moment to leave a review on Amazon and Goodreads. Thank you so much for considering it!

If you would like to continue to follow my work, here are ways to connect with me:

www.lakenhoneycutt.com

linktr.ee/lakenhoneycutt3

ACKNOWLEDGMENTS

It truly does take a village, and I'd like to thank the amazing, supportive, people who made up my village and helped make this book possible.

First, my readers! I was fortunate to find a dedicated team of alpha readers. They read this book in its messy inception and gave feedback that helped me cut through the muck of my mind to the true essence of this story. H. Ferry, Charlotte Taylor, Spyder Collins, Brandy, Eva Alton I appreciate you all so much and the encouragement you provided me to keep going!

I have so much gratitude for my dedicated beta readers: E.P. Stavs, Tiffany, Hayley Reese Chow, Kayla Wieland, H. Ferry, Charlotte Taylor, Brandy, Akernis, and A.L. Bentley, the feedback you provided, as well as your support for this writer was such a big part of what made this story. Thank you!

I also want to thank my editor. I was blessed by the many talents of George Rosett. She was the perfect editor for this tale and also for me as a new writer. From her developmental edits to the line edits, she cared for this story and helped me understand more of my craft. Thank you, George!

And many thanks to Mark Duffin, who created the incredible

Chrysillium tree artwork in this book. Your vision is nothing short of pure magic.

I'd like to thank my parents, who helped make this book possible through their support.

I am grateful for my son, Marcus, who lights up each of my days and gives me the inspiration to keep going, even during the difficult times. I love you.

And to you the Writing Community, all the gratitude and love for you. I will forever appreciate all of you and what you gave to this project.

Laken

ABOUT THE AUTHOR

Laken Honeycutt is a fantasy author weaving stories from the sanctuary of her forest home in New England. Enamored by the stars and with a deep connection to nature, Laken's work often includes celestial wonders and the natural magic of forests. She is also an avid reader who enjoys hiking, surfing, biking, trail running, and kayaking.

facebook.com/laken.honeycutt.1

twitter.com/MycelialWriter

instagram.com/mycelialwriter